TRICKY

TRICKY

Josh Stallings

Copyright © 2021 by Josh Stallings
Cover and jacket design by 2Faced Design

ISBN 978-1-951709-19-5
eISBN: 978-1-951709-44-0
Library of Congress Control Number: available upon request

First trade paperback edition January 2021 by Agora Books
an imprint of Polis Books, LLC
44 Brookview Lane
Aberdeen, NJ 07747
www.PolisBooks.com

For my son Dylan, one of the best men I know. I am always proud to be his father, even though I had little to do with who he is. He seemed to step from the womb wise, loving, and funny as hell.

And for Erika, who raised our two amazing sons, and never let either be defined by a label.

"Oh, I get it, you're going the tricky way."

-Dylan Stallings

Chapter 1

Los Angeles in summer is an inferno that will bake your brain, dull your judgment, and turn the gentlest Angelino into a killer. Saying, "At least it's a dry heat," to a guy trapped in a '96 F150 with busted air could get you shot. Not that Detective Niels Madsen was the killing kind, in fact one of the reasons he'd chosen Homicide was that the violence tended to be past-tense. But with hot air blowing through the windows and sweat running down his back, all kinds of heinous acts became possible.

Instead of going on a murder spree, Madsen decided it was time to embrace the heat. He cranked up Johnny Cash's "Ring of Fire" and sang along, full voice, not caring how ridiculous he looked. Two verses in, he started to smile. Life seemed survivable.

And then he saw it.

A police cruiser was parked diagonal to a bus stop with its light-bar flashing—both doors open, an officer aimed his pistol at a man in the bus shell. An instantly recognizable tableau forecasting bad things to come.

Do not stop. Madsen told himself. *It's fifteen minutes before your shift. Uniforms have it handled.* He might have bought his own bullshit and kept driving, but he recognized the officer. Russo, a rookie with a crew cut, chevron mustache, yellow lensed shooting-glasses, and pants tucked into eight-hole tactical boots. The look was more militia geek than police officer. Madsen had overheard Russo in the breakroom bragging to fellow officers, "Swear to Christ I could shoot the eye out of a Chihuahua at forty feet, if I needed to." No one had asked why the fuck anyone would need to shoot the eye out of a lapdog.

Pulling to the curb, Madsen slapped the steeringwheel. He was less than two miles from his air-conditioned office. He clicked his emergency flashers on, pulled on his white straw Stetson and dropped from the truck. He ran low to keep the patrol car between himself and whoever was at the bus stop.

Officer Hill, a five-year veteran on the force, hunkered down next to the front fender. His square head was covered in buzz-cut straw-colored hair. Mirrored Oakleys hid his intentions.

"Detective Madsen, coming up behind you." Madsen spoke loud but calm, not wanting to startle the officers, but needing to make them aware of his approach. "What we got?"

"Some banger had an extra helping of crazy puffs this morning." Office Hill grinned, "No worry it's N.H.I."

No Humans Involved. Old school LAPD bullshit that should have died out with Gates. Madsen squelched his anger. He snuck a look over the car's hood. Officer Russo stood legs apart, two-handed grip on his 9mm, aiming center mass at a man some twenty-plus feet away who was crouched over the bus stop bench.

"Put the goddamn gun down." Russo's voice was tight with tension. "Do it now."

Madsen kept an eye on Officer Russo while speaking to Hill. "He still on probation?"

Hill cocked his head, trying to gauge if a trap lay in the question, but said nothing.

"Whatever. Let's say he is and you're his supervisor." Madsen continued.

"I'm his FTO. He has two months left on the leash. We got a

problem?"

"I don't, nope." Madsen slipped on a smooth smile. "You called it in?"

"SWAT is en route."

"*SWAT?*"

"We have an armed suspect with a hostage. SWAT's the right call." Hill sounded almost sure of himself.

"Perfect. No way this can go wrong."

"You got a better plan, Detective?"

"Not yet." Madsen started to stand.

"The suspect has a gun."

"So does everyone else." Madsen moved around the patrol car exposing his head and shoulders as he stepped forward.

The man in the bus shelter was mid-forties, Latino. A bristle of short hair did nothing to hide the network of scars that laced his skull. Blue prison tats ran up his arms. "LA" written in Old English marked his neck. All his street bad-assery was juxtaposed by a He-Man cartoon t-shirt and Lakers sweatpants. He hunched protectively over what looked like a body on the bench. In his hand, the man loosely held a revolver, its barrel bouncing haplessly around.

"You see this uniform? This badge?" Russo plucked at his badge for emphasis. "Do you know what it means?"

The suspect said nothing. He didn't look angry or scared, he looked confused.

"Drop the gun or I will be forced to shoot." Russo's eyes narrowed, twitching in the corner of the left one. He was starting to lose it. "You're not giving me any choice."

"Take a breath, Officer Russo." Madsen stood up and away from the protection of the patrol car.

Russo flicked a look over. "I got this, Detective."

"I see that." Madsen stepped into the open. He looked at the suspect and gave a slight nod, international street gesture for respect.

9

The man didn't return the nod.

"¿Habla español?" Madsen said. The man squinted, screwing up his face, showing no sign of comprehension. "Vy govorite po-russki?" Madsen tried, then "Você fala português?" And "Sprechen sie Deutsch?" Nothing. In a weak approximation of American standard sign, Madsen bought his left fist down onto his right palm. He wiggled both thumbs. He knew he was either asking if the man needed help, or if he wanted to dance. Doubling down he kept wiggling his thumbs in bigger and wilder gestures.

A shadow of a smile passed over the man's face. He shrugged his shoulders broadly, almost touching his ears. Raising his shoulders had the unintended consequence of lifting the revolver in his hand.

"Drop that gun, now." Russo's fear sailed to eleven. "*Now.*" Slipping his finger onto the trigger, he readied himself to take the shot.

Madsen shifted focus from the suspect to the rookie. Madsen was a tall man with near freakishly long legs. He closed the distance between himself and Russo in one long sideways step. "Son, I got this."

"Hell you do." Russo kept his finger on the trigger.

Madsen gently placed his hand on top of Russo's pistol. "Take it down a notch or two." He calmly pushed the pistol down until it was aimed at the ground.

"What are you doing?" Russo hissed through locked teeth.

"Me and this fellow just need to chat."

"Goddamn it, Detective, he failed to obey my direct order to drop that weapon."

"I heard you. Just not sure he did. I need a minute."

"He's a shooter, I can feel it."

"Well, if he shoots me, then, officer Russo, you have my permission to shoot him."

"This ain't right Detective. Goes wrong, it's on you."

"Yes it is." With a nod and a wink, Madsen raised empty hands, palms facing forward and stepped toward the bus stop shell. The man's face contorted into an exaggerated squint. He watched Madsen's every movement.

God? If this guy's a shooter, could you make him a lousy one?

Madsen kept his face neutral and open. "Hey, Bud, you Ok?" He walked slowly forward. "My name's Detective Madsen, what's yours?"

The man blinked rapidly, shaking his head.

A response? A tick? Stress reaction? All three? Hard to tell.

"If you understand me, give me a nod...or a word...or wiggle your pinky." Madsen strolled casually on. He shrunk the gap between him and the man to fifteen feet. "No need to waste my breath if you aren't understanding me, right?"

The man nodded his head a fraction of an inch, his body loosening by tiny increments.

"There you go, that's a start." Two steps closer.

The man's face tensed. His hand tightened on the revolver.

"Whoa, Bud, ease up." Madsen stopped moving. "We're just two guys talking. Well, okay, I'm talking and you're listening." The man didn't soften. "Please. You ratchet this deal up, it's going to end badly."

"Th-th-the other m-m-man wants to shoot me, right?" His voice was eight miles of gravel and broken glass. Scars on his throat spoke of damaged vocal cords. "R-r-r-right?" The question wasn't rhetorical.

Madsen looked over his shoulder. Russo had his pistol back up. "Yeah, looks that way." He took a step to the left, placing his body between the rookie and the suspect.

"Whaa, whaa, what are you d-d-d-doin'?"

Madsen stopped, rocking back on his heels. "I won't hurt you." He let out a breath, calmly inhaled. "We do this right, we all get home safe. What do you say Bud? You wanna get home?"

The man looked down at the bloody body on the bench. He closed his eyes, then popped them open. "I want to see June. I need to go home."

"Good. Smart choice." Madsen started walking forward again.

11

"Want to give me that gun?"

The man looked down at his hand, vaguely surprised to see the gun. He shook his head muttering "No, no, no…" Pulling his hand up he pointed the revolver at Madsen's chest. "I have to protect David."

"I don't have a shot." Russo yelled.

No shit. Madsen kept slowly walking forward. "You think you might take your finger off the trigger?"

"W-w-won't work then. Need to pull the trigger to make it work."

"True. But if you shoot me, they will kill you."

The man looked past Madsen.

Russo moved left, reacquiring his target.

The man's finger tightened on the trigger. The hammer started to rise.

"Bud, please." Madsen froze. "Truth is, truth is, I didn't have any breakfast this morning. I like Shredded Wheat. Hem, my grandpa, I live with him, he's real old, he likes to put rhubarb and sugar on his Shredded Wheat."

"Rhubarb?" the man scrunched up his nose.

"Don't know where he got that from. He was born in Texas. You?" Niels inched forward.

"This is my home town."

"Eagle Rock?"

The man looked confused. "No. LA I'm from LA"

"Me, too."

"I don't think so." The man pointed the revolver from Madsen's Stetson, past his western-cut suit to his Lucchese boots. "You're a cowboy?"

"I have a horse."

"So you're a horse-boy."

"You say so."

"Why does a police dress like that?"

"To piss my bosses off, I guess."

12

"That's not a good word." The man's gun jerked as he spoke.

"Can you, maybe not point that at me."

"No, I…I have to…David needs me to keep him safe."

"Is that Dave?" Madsen nodded to the body. He was ten feet and closing.

"David."

"David, right, sorry." The dead man had flat facial features, with a small nose and an upward slant to the eyes, all physical signs of Down syndrome. He looked peaceful. Take away the two bullet wounds in his chest and the blood pooled under the bench, he could be enjoying a nap on a hot summer day.

"He's broken, right?"

"Looks that way."

"Can they fix him? Please." The man's eyes were filling with tears.

"Too late for that."

"They can."

"Not this time, Bud." Madsen jumped the last few feet, grabbing the man's gun hand. The guy was strong, he struggled to keep hold of the revolver. Madsen swung his free hand, connecting knuckle to jaw. The man let out a low grunt and stumbled. When he didn't release the gun, Madsen hit him again, harder. The man relinquished the revolver, stumbled back, tripped and fell. Madsen tossed the gun, sending it skidding across the pavement. He dove on the man, rolling him quickly onto his belly. Snagging his wrists, he cuffed him.

"Ow, that h-h-hurts me." Blood was running from the man's mouth, over his chin, dripping onto He-Man. "You're not a good man."

"No?"

"No, you are a tricker. Not a good man."

"Yeah, well you're not alone in that opinion. I need to search you. Is there anything sharp in your pockets?"

"No."

"No, you don't have anything sharp, or no, you don't want me to

13

search you?"

The man looked confused. "I don't know."

Madsen moved his hands over the man's body. "Stop squirming."

"I can't."

Madsen went through the man's pockets. Finding a wallet, he took it out.

"That's not yours." The man stated.

"You'll get it back." Madsen found a library card. "Francisco Gutierrez?"

"That's not my name."

"Is this your library card?"

"Yes."

"Are screwing with me?"

"Maybe." He started to smile. "My name is Cisco. They only call me Francisco when I mess up."

"Looks like you messed up big time, Bud." Madsen took a pause to give what came next weight. "Cisco, this is important, why did you shoot David?"

Cisco went deer in the headlights. "I didn't. No. I-I-I...did I?"

"You don't know?" Madsen laced his voice with compassion. Cisco slowly shook his head, clearly unsure.

Officer Hill moved in, pistol extended, ready to shoot.

Madsen looked up. "Really?"

Hill holstered his pistol. "He okay?"

"He's fine, peachy." Madsen stood up dusting off the knees of his trousers. "Get him out of the sun. And make sure you tell SWAT they're not needed."

"Right. On it." Hill started speaking into his shoulder mic.

Russo's face was red from trying to contain his aggression as he fronted Madsen. "That was crazy unprofessional bullshit right there."

"Son, I just saved you from an unpaid early retirement."

"I'm not your son, Detective."

"And aren't we both glad about that."

"Department policy, when confronting an armed suspect," Russo flicked his eyes back and forth like he was reading text he had memorized, "is to—"

"Department policy? You're not in the academy, and this, here, is not a test."

"Fair warning. I'm gonna write this like I saw it. Lone hero bullshit gets people killed." The last part sounded mechanically unemotional, like a bad PSA voiceover.

Madsen turned away, it was that or take the rookie's head off at the neck. "Officer Hill, did you call in a SMART team?"

Hill looked up from Cisco. "Why, wait…what?"

"Systemwide Mental Assessment Response Team?" Madsen spoke deliberately, as if to a recalcitrant child.

"I know who they are, but…"

"You rolled up on a man in mental distress, a man I might add with a less than stellar intellect, who is armed—yes—but protecting his friend, who has Down syndrome. Complicated as all this is, you decided SWAT was a better call than the SMART team?" He turned to Russo making sure he got the depth of this fuck-up.

"He had a gun." Russo's brashness was slipping into petulance.

"He did."

"Threatened me."

"Really? With all your half year of experience you knew he was intending to use it on you? What do you think the citizen's board would do if you had shot him, gun or not? The press? White cop shoots a childish brown man who's posing no clear threat? Son, they'd name the riot after you."

Russo leaned against the car letting out a long dry breath. Hill was about to speak when Madsen cut him off, "Why was your rookie in the line of fire while you were behind the vehicle? Fuck it, don't answer that."

Sirens wailed, coming on fast.

"Deciding time is up. You two gonna throw me under the bus?"

"No, sir." Hill spoke without hesitation. "And neither is Officer Russo."

"Whatever you say." Russo suddenly found his shoes fascinating.

"Good." Niels spoke fast. "The suspect had a gun, but he kept it pointed at the ground. He wasn't a threat. He was growing agitated. While Officer Russo covered me, I moved in to talk him down. I never struck Mr. Gutierrez, that's important." Cisco looked up hearing his name. "He stumbled and fell. That how you saw it?"

"Word for word." Hill said.

"Then it's the facts." A cloud of confusion crossed Cisco's face. He gave Madsen the hardest look he could muster, which wasn't hard at all. Madsen gave him a wink and moved to the street to meet the oncoming black and whites.

"Detective?" Russo kept his voice down, not looking at Madsen, as if he thought they were conspirators in a spy movie.

"Something else, son?"

"How did you know? How'd you know he wouldn't shoot you?"

"I didn't. But I was pretty sure you'd turn his lights out if he tried."

"Hell, yes. Glad I didn't have to, sir." Russo beamed, happy the natural order of the blue brotherhood was restored.

Chapter 2

Half a block down from the crime scene Cisco sat on the back of a paramedic van. He held a cold pack to the left side of his face. The handcuffs had been moved to the front. He was being examined by a young Latina. Except for the paramedic's uniform she could have stepped from a Frida Kahlo painting. Long braids down her back tied in a loose knot. Un-plucked eyebrows over dark eyes accented with smoky eyeshadow. Ruby red lips. If she cared that she wasn't anyone's idea of a paramedic, she didn't show it. Officer Hill sat a few feet away in his car, door open, feet on the pavement, keeping watch over Cisco while filling out a field report.

Cisco stared at a ruby red fingernail hovering in front of his face. When it moved left his head moved with it. "Just your eyes, Cisco. Your eyes." The paramedic said.

"My head keeps turning."

"You want me to help?"

"Yes, um, thank you."

She gently placed her hand on the top of his head, holding it still while she moved her finger. "Bueno, Cisco."

He grinned broadly without guile. It was a smile that she couldn't help but reciprocate.

"W-w-what's your name? It's fair. You know mine."

"True. Ok, my friends call me Marta."

Cisco mulled this over. "What should I call you?"

"Marta."

"Marta. Marta. Marta. Marta." He was feeling it new each time. "Marta. Marta."

"That's right. I'm Marta, and you need to let me finish examining you." She raised her finger, studying his pupils as they tracked the movement. "Good. Now down."

Cisco jerked back, pulling his head away. Marta snapped around to see what caused his reaction.

Madsen stepped off the curb, his expression forming into his best approximation of concern. "How's Mr. Gutierrez doing?"

"D-d-don't trust him. He's tricky."

"Detective Madsen?" Marta rested a reassuring hand on Cisco's shoulder. "He's one of the good ones."

"Nope." Cisco shook his head.

Madsen smiled at Cisco. "Is Marta taking good care of you?"

"Only her friends call her Marta." Cisco was defiant.

"Correctomundo." Madsen turned to Marta. "How's your abuela doing?"

"Doctor prescribed bedrest." Marta's eyebrows danced. "You can guess how well that's going."

"She still controlling the entire block?"

"From a La-Z-Boy on the porch. The kids think she's a bruja." Marta wiggled her fingers in front of her eyes like rays at Cisco. "Mess with her street and she'll give you el mal de ojo."

"No." Cisco's eyes popped wide. "Not for real, right?"

"For real." Madsen leaned in. "She's scary."

"You're lying. He's lying, right, Marta?"

"Sure Cisco, it's okay. She's not a bruja."

"See." Cisco pointed at Madsen. "I told you he was tricky." Marta looked skeptical, so Cisco ramped it up. "He is, really. He hurt me.

18

See?" He pulled the cool pack from his face revealing a cut lip that was growing fat, and a blooming mouse under his eye.

Marta's smile fell and she went professionally cool. "Did Detective Madsen do this to you, Cisco?"

"Y-y-yes. He is not a nice man."

"Detective?" Marta searched Madsen's face.

"Not quite how it happened. He tripped. I reached for the gun in his hand, he fell back."

"Gun?" Marta grew up in East LA She knew armed suspects rarely survived interactions with the police. "You disarmed him?"

"Seemed like a good idea at the time."

"He hit me. Tricky is lying."

"You had a gun, Cisco?" Marta said.

"Yes…but see, David…I…."

"It's okay, Cisco," Marta gently touched his face. "You're a lucky guy. You'll be fine."

Madsen looked off, his attention taken by the arrival of an unmarked sedan. A man in his early thirties stepped out. He had a new Suit Broker polyester number, white shirt and uninspired tie. *Fresh meat.*

"He's dehydrated." Marta brought Madsen's attention back to Cisco. "What flavor of Gatorade you like?"

"Blue. I like blue." Cisco flicked nervous glances at Madsen.

"Me too, red's okay, but blue is best." Marta handed a sports drink to Cisco, then looked at Madsen. "I'll get his fluids up, do a couple more checks, but I'm relatively sure he's fine."

"Thank you." Madsen gave her an almost imperceptible bow and headed toward the growing group of uniformed officers. Cisco guzzled from the bottle, a small amount of blue liquid escaping his mouth.

At the center of the uniformed officers was Sergeant Booker. Dark-skinned with white hair fringing his bald head. He had the stiff posture and demeanor of a military dictator. Calling up several men by name, he ordered them to secure the crime scene, others he deployed to direct traffic.

"Sarge, do we start a house-to-house?" One officer asked.

"Not necessary. No overtime on this one. Open and shut. Man A shot man B, with that revolver over there."

"Nothing's open or shut." The newly-minted detective countermanded Booker without hesitation. "We're going to need to check any stores around, see what they saw."

"And who the hell are you?" Booker asked.

"Darius Kazim." He held up his gold shield. "And this is my crime scene. Do we have a problem, Sergeant?"

"No, Detective." Booker made compliance sound more like 'fuck off.'

"I also want any security cam footage you can find."

"You heard the man. Move." The officers dispersed, giving Kazim dirty enough looks for him to know he was unwelcome.

"That went well." Madsen startled Kazim. "They teach you those interpersonal skills at IA sleepaway camp?"

"You're Detective Madsen." Kazim looked Madsen over. "I thought when they called you a cowboy, it was metaphoric."

"A bit of both probably. Do you mind taking my statement indoors?"

"Statement?"

"Come on, homicide's not even on the scene yet. Suspect is with the paramedics. I know a place makes a mean iced coffee, waddaya say?" Madsen walked away as if Kazim had conceded.

Swork was a locally owned coffee joint. WiFi brought in its share of hopeful screenwriters, and Occidental students looking to get caffeinated while they got their social media on. One corner was set aside for little kids: wood bricks, trains and tracks, baby dolls of every hue of human. Madsen sank into a comfortably over stuffed armchair. He took a sip of his café Americana. "Damn, that's good. Two shots espresso, cold water and ice, who'd have thought that would add up to ambrosia? Like it?"

Kazim took a sip, nodded without much enthusiasm. He started to speak, but Madsen jumped in. "Kazim, right? Tough time to be Syrian. And you're Muslim, I'm guessing?" Kazim was silent as a stone. "Syrian, Muslim and working for the rat squad. Homeland security didn't want you?"

"I didn't want them."

"No? So instead you chose IAG?"

"I chose Homicide." Kazim held out his hand, "I'm your new partner."

Madsen looked at the man's hand for a hard moment, then burst out a full laugh. "Son, what the hell did you do to deserve me?"

"Insubordination—their word—objective disregard for asinine directives would be closer to true."

"Well, Detective Kazim…" Madsen took Kazim's hand and shook it. "Welcome to the end of your career ascension."

"I was glad when I heard I was going to be your partner. I think I can learn a lot from you."

"Like what? How to shoot yourself in the foot, metaphorically?"

"I've heard all the rumors." Kazim took a long sip, savoring his coffee. "I also know you have the third highest clearance rate in the department."

"Third huh? Who's one and two?"

"A team out of Rampart. To be fair, they caught six softballs in a row."

"Good for them. Here's to softballs." Madsen raised his glass.

Kazim, looked at his watch, then at Madsen pointedly. "Feel like going to the scene and showing this poor acolyte how it's done?"

"Acolyte? You?" Madsen shook his head sadly. "Perfect." He dropped a few bucks in the tip jar, tipping his hat at the barely twenty-year old, fuchsia-haired barista. "That café Americana was good enough to raise the dead."

"Nice hat."

"Sarcasm?" Madsen asked.

"No, dude, I like it, the whole old guy *True Grit* vibe's cool."

Madsen cocked his head trying to decide if he should point out that forty wasn't old. Remembered when he was her age how old forty looked, and let it go.

On the sidewalk Madsen caught up to Kazim, eyeballing him up and down. "Change your name to Juan Sanchez you could pass for Mexican easy."

"True, and if you kept your mouth shut you could pass for woke."

"We all have our nondenominational interfaith crosses to bare, Detective Kazim."

Chapter 3

The Northeast Station was a two-story steel and glass nod to a sparkling clean, future Los Angeles. A future where cop shops looked like Abercrombie and Fitch. Next door, the original station stood to remind the officers of how lucky they were. It was a squat cement bomb shelter of a building. Crowded, peeling paint, it smelled permanently of sweat, testosterone, fear, and failure. On the upside suspects were incentivized to confess, if only to escape the funk.

Madsen parked his truck in the lot the city rented from a Korean Pentecostal church and took the shuttle the mile to the station. The new station was pristine, but the parking structure hadn't materialized, neither had the additional SMART teams promised, nor the bilingual Chinese and Thai officers needed to handle the flood of immigrants. In the face of those shortfalls, who the hell cared about parking?

Before leaving the crime scene, Madsen had told the officers to wrap it quickly. Kazim scanned the scene, shaking his head, "Something's off, I can smell it."

"That smell? It's is my scalp frying." Taking off his hat, Madsen mopped his brow with a bandana. "You know the elusive smoking gun we're always searching for? Francisco Gutierrez was holding it. We have the how and the who, we just need the why."

"Only if ballistics says Gutierrez' gun was the murder weapon. My gut tells me it's not."

"And my gut is saying, 'Niels, feed me a Tommy's double grease bomb.' I'm just not listening."

"A couple of hours too much?" Kazim stood legs set, unmovable.

"Either you're packing ostrich huevos or I'm getting weak."

"Both?" Kazim let a slight smile slip in.

"Fine, work the scene. I'll be back at the shop interviewing the suspect."

"Thanks."

"You want some old school detective wisdom?"

"I do. Please." Kazim spread out his hands graciously.

"Hydrate, and get a hat."

Fronted by thirty feet of soaring glass the station lobby was bright and cheerful, Sergeant Booker's expression was neither. He nabbed Madsen coming through the glass doors. "You got a second, Detective?" No waiting for an answer, Booker led Madsen to a corner off the lobby that was blocked from unwanted eyes by a potted ficus.

"Very clandestine, Bob, couldn't you just slip me a note in homeroom?"

"Not in the mood, Detective. Your boy, the Arab—"

"Syrian."

"Same thing. You better keep him on a choker, he demeans me in front my men again I'll kick his camel-jockey ass back to whatever sandbox he was born in."

"Burbank." Booker looked blank. "He was born in Burbank. And..." Niels stepped in, invading Booker's personal space. "Clock this, Bob, you or any of your minions fuck with Detective Kazim, I will take it personal. Got that?" He stayed close, his muscles taut, ready to strike, eyes locked on Booker who finally caved, backing up.

"All I'm saying is the guy needs to be schooled on command

structure."

"Or you could…" Madsen stopped himself. He took a deep breath and rolled his shoulders. "Screw it Sergeant, done's done."

"Sure. We okay Detective?"

"Copasetic." Madsen's eyes made a lie of his smile.

Up a flight of stairs was Homicide's bullpen. The space was clean, sterile, and effective, with none of the blemished poetry of bygone days.

"Anyone seen my suspect?" Madsen asked the room.

"Gilbert Grape's in six." Detective Hertzog had the sinewy body of a long distance runner.

"Anyone speak to him?"

"He's all yours. You do speak retarded, right?"

"Fluently. I understand you, right?"

"Nice, real nice. Remind me to bitch slap the hell out of you next time I get the chance."

"Roger that, pal."

On a TV monitor Madsen could see the interview room. Cisco sat in manacled to a table, staring slack-jawed at his fingers. A thin line of drool laced from chin to chest.

"Looks like you caught an easy closer." Deputy Chief Bette Fong stepped in behind Madsen.

"Maybe yes, maybe no. Thanks for the heads-up on the new partner."

"Any time." She flashed him a smile. "I hear he's both smart and troublesome."

"Yep and yep. He thinks maybe Gutierrez didn't do it."

Fong arched an eyebrow. She wore black Tom Ford high heels, a conservative but expertly tailored navy-blue suit, and on her lapel a small American flag. She looked both professional and stunning. "What do you think?"

"I'm not entirely clear what happened at that bus stop."

"You'll sort it out, I'm sure." She started to leave, at the door she turned back as if she had just remembered something, "Niels, one more thing. Word is you punched Mr. Gutierrez, twice."

"Nice false exit, Columbo." He shot her a wink.

"Is it true?"

"How did the officers on the scene call it?"

"Hill said you disarmed the suspect without incident. And that the suspect tripped. I call bullshit."

Madsen looked like a bad little boy caught with his dad's skin magazines. "Bette, come on, you know me."

"Yes, I do, that's the problem."

Madsen kept his eyes on the interview room, dropping his voice to a deep whisper. "You wanna discuss this over some Camarones a la Diabla and a bottle of Sierra Blanca?"

"That ship sunk." Fong looked at Cisco in the monitor. "Niels, what happened in Eagle Rock?"

"I stopped a rookie from killing our suspect. Anything else I say will destroy your plausible deniability. You want me to...?"

"No, but if I heard about it, then it is in the air." Her eyes went cold. "Wrap it up quickly, and quietly."

Watching her walk away, Madsen was taken by the juxtaposition of her ramrod posture and the delectable tiny sway of her hips. He wondered, not for the first time, if sleeping with his boss had been wise. Probably not, but given the green light again, he would push the pedal to the metal without a backward glance.

Cisco looked up slowly when Madsen entered the interview room. Madsen would tell any cop who wanted to be a detective to study acting.

Learn to become who the suspect, witness or even the victim, needed them to be. Father, confessor, compassionate mother, pal, whatever it took to gain their trust and loosen their tongues. Also, it didn't matter if the suspect was a baby-raper, wife-beater, whatever, you never showed revulsion or discomfort. Anger, sure, or compassion, even pity. Those came from places of strength. But letting a suspect make you uncomfortable gave them the power.

"Okay if I join you?" Madsen sat without waiting for Cisco to answer.

"Can I go home? I need my afternoon medication, two o'clock." Cisco's worried eyes darted around the room.

"Won't be too long, need to ask a couple questions. I'm Detective Madsen. Remember me?"

"Yes. I'm not dumb." Cisco stared defiantly at Madsen.

"No, you're not dumb. You're retarded."

"And you're an ass pool." Cisco's eyes flared.

"Excuse me?" Madsen stopped, reeled his ego back. Took a breath. "Retarded, that's the wrong word?"

Cisco stared at Madsen, slowly his face softened. "Correctomundo." He tried on Madsen's phrase.

"Ok. Help me out here, what should I say?"

"Retarded just means something is slower than something. Like my brain is slower than other people."

"Is it okay if I use it?" Madsen was trying his damnedest.

"Nope, sorry."

"Why?"

"Might hurt people's feelings. And that's bad."

"So what do I call you?"

"Cisco. That's my name."

"Okay, I can do that, Cisco."

"And you are Tricky. And you hit me, remember?"

"I think you're confused, you tripped."

"No, I…did I trip?"

"Sure did."

"No. That is not true. June says I don't remember thing so good. But I remember this."

"June, your mother?"

"I don't have a mother."

"So, who's June, sister, what?"

"I live at June's house, it's kinda my house too. I have a room with…" Cisco ran out of words.

Madsen sat a small digital voice recorder on the table. "Do you mind if I record this? It will make it go faster."

"Then I can go home?"

"Yep."

"Okay. I don't mind."

"Good." Madsen pressed the red record button. "This is Detective Niels Madsen of the LAPD interviewing Francisco Gutierrez—"

"Cisco."

"AKA Cisco. Date is July 12th at…" Madsen looked at his watch. "Two forty-seven p.m."

"It's okay." Cisco said as if answering a question only he heard asked.

"What's okay?"

"I forgive you, tricky man."

"Oh yeah, what for?"

"Hitting me. Tricking me. I forgive you. Maybe your June never told you about not hitting. Yeah, that's it, right?"

"That's it." Madsen looked down at the pad and scribbled a note. It was a stalling tactic, made the suspects think they were giving their game away. The ruse was lost on Cisco. "Tell me about David, does he live at June's house too?"

"He's my roommate…was. He *was* my roommate. He's dead, they put him in the van."

"Yes, they did. Do you know the phone number for June's house?"

"Phone numbers are hard. June wrote it on a card."

"Where is the card, wallet?"

"No, Tricky. On the dresser by my bed."

"That's a good place for it Cisco, can't lose it there."

"Right. I lose stuff sometimes. I had a watch once."

"So, how do you reach June?"

"I call her name." Cisco cupped his hand by his mouth and yelled, "June. Like that."

"What if you're not at home?"

"Then I talk to her when I get home."

"And how do you get home?"

"I take the bus, or sometimes an Access cab."

"Where?" Madsen was starting to get frustrated, his words coming harsher than intended. "Where do you take the cab to? Where?"

"June's home. You don't pay very good attention. Do you need your medication?" Cisco was smiling.

"No, I don't." Madsen exhaled his tension. "So, when you want to go home, what do you tell the cab driver?"

"Oh, I tell him the address."

"You know the address?"

"Of course, Tricky. How else could I get home?" Cisco shook his head at Madsen's lack of brains.

Madsen felt his cool evaporate into a pounding in his temples. "Any chance in hell you'll tell me the address?"

"Hell's a bad word."

"Yes, it is. Now, what is the address?"

"The address?"

"Yes."

"Oh...okay...." Cisco rattled off an address in Eagle Rock, saying it fast so it wouldn't slip away.

Madsen typed the address into his iPhone's map.

"Do you play Angry Birds?" Cisco eyed the phone.

"No, do you?"

"Come on Tricky, think." Cisco tapped his forehead, "I don't have a phone. Adair does, but I don't."

"Who the hell, sorry, *heck*, is Adair."

"Adair is Adair." Cisco shrugged.

"Wait." Madsen looked down at the map on his phone. "That address two blocks from the bus stop where David, um, where I met you. Right?"

"Yes." Cisco repeated the address in the same staccato rhythm.

Madsen click off the recorder and dropped it into his pocket. "I'll be right back."

"Do you have any juice? Orange is best."

"Sorry, we have a soda machine."

"June says sodas are bad. Juice is better."

"We don't have any juice. How about some water?"

"Okay. Tricky?"

"Yeah Cisco?"

"You have a headache?"

"Yes, I do."

"I get headaches." Cisco rubbed his burry scar ridden scalp. "Don't scrunch up your face, it makes it worse. And no soda, okay?"

Madsen closed the interview room door behind him. "Anyone have the new guy—Kazim's—number?"

"You lost your partner in less than a day?" Detective Mauk had a strong Germanic face, short blonde hair and the kind of muscles you needed if you were going to swim in the boys club of LAPD Homicide. "A new record. How many is that, Madsen?"

"Do you have his number?"

"Do I look like your secretary?"

"Kinda."

"Fuck off." She flipped him the bird.

"How about some aspirin?"

"That, I have." Mauk tossed him a bottle.

"Midol, really?"

"You seem like you're having a bad man-struation."

"Man-struation? Damn, that's good." Madsen said with genuine admiration. "You make that up on the fly?"

Mauk nodded. "Midol, it's acetaminophen and caffeine. Won't make you grow tits or nothing."

"Too bad, I always wanted a pair of my own."

"No, you don't. They come with a pay cut and a perceived intelligence drop of ten percent per cup size." She wasn't bitter, just stating a fact and fucking with Madsen.

"On the upside they're good for a free drink at most bars."

"Not worth it, trust me."

"I do." Madsen said and he did trust Mauk. She was a solid detective with a clear moral compass. Back against the wall he couldn't hope for a better cop by his side.

Hertzog sat near the back of the room, feet up on the desk. He was reading the *LA Times*, which he folded down, looked at the clock then at Madsen. "You get Gilbert Grape to confess already?"

"You know Gilbert Grape was the Johnny Depp character, DiCaprio played his brother."

"DiCaprio played the retarded one?"

"Grow up Hertzog. No one uses the R-word anymore." Mauk called out.

"Yeah, Ms. P.C.? So what am I supposed to call them?"

"*Them*?" Mauk shook her head. "Intellectually disabled is the preferred term."

"Intellectually disabled. Hmmm." Madsen tried it on.

"Yes, according to the federal government and any evolved human."

31

"Evolved?" Madsen asked. "Guess we both know that leaves Hertzog high and dry."

"What crawled up your ass?" Herzog asked Madsen.

"Your sister's index finger, and I liked it."

"Sick, Madsen, you are a sick bastard."

"Too true."

"So how long you gonna take to crack Gilbert Grape or his intellec-his little brother or whatever." Then under his breath so the others in the room couldn't hear, "I got twenty on five-thirty, so?"

"You suggesting I push for a confession, just so you can win a bet?"

"Isn't like he didn't do it. Gutierrez is one evil bastard."

"Really? Hmm, not sure evil is in his wheelhouse."

"Oh, it is. Sweet simple Cisco is playing you like a Stratocaster." Hertzog windmilled a Townshend air-guitar solo. "Man's a killer, cold blooded." He held up a computer printout.

"What you got there?"

"It was sent to me, for you." Madsen reached for the printout, Herzog yanked it out of reach. "This? You want this?"

Madsen got very still, arms at his side. His face went cold. Hertzog tried to play it light, failed. "Whatever, man. Here." Hertzog released the papers. "It's Gutierrez' jacket, and he's been a bad, bad boy. Read it, then tell me I'm wrong."

Madsen took the file to his desk. The first page showed a stone-faced young Latino's mug shot. From the thousand-yard stare to the bored fatalism he vibed mainline con. He looked nothing like the man in interrogation room six. Madsen rechecked the name, Francisco Gutierrez. The photo was almost ten years out of date, but it was Cisco. The differences were quickly evident, in the photo his shaved head lacked the network of scars. There was more, something intangible was missing from the man in photo. Something in his eyes was cold, almost dead. The Cisco locked up in interview room six looked lost, confused but very much alive.

The file was in reverse chronology. Madsen started at the back. On a handwritten form it stated Francisco Gutierrez had been arrested on October 31st, 1984 by LAPD officer Jamison, Badge 56883, Hollenbeck Division. Vehicle Code **VEH 23103** Reckless Driving. Vehicle Code VEH 10851 Vehicle Theft. CA Penal Code PC 192 Vehicular Manslaughter. The disposition of the charges were sealed because Gutierrez had been thirteen years old at the time of arrest. A note in the side margin stated, "Killed his passenger. Cold blooded." An asterisk led to the bottom of the page, "Gutierrez denied gang affiliation, lied. Cousin of Rafael Ortez, founding member of La Colina 13. Gutierrez found guilty. Pulled innocent kid act. Judge only gave him six months in Youth Authority. BULLSHIT."

Madsen flipped quickly through the file. May 12, 1985. PC 187, murder in the first-degree. Gutierrez, posing as a gay prostitute, lured a victim into an alley. He then shot the victim two times in the face with a .38 caliber revolver. He had been caught with both the murder weapon and the victim's wallet on him. Gutierrez had committed the crime one day after his fourteenth birthday, allowing the District Attorney to prosecute him as an adult. On December 20th of that same year, Francisco Gutierrez had been convicted and sentenced to serve twenty-five years-to-life in a California state prison; remanded to Pelican Bay. Another handwritten note, same hand, same pen, "While in Pelican Bay, it was rumored—but never proven—that Gutierrez became a hitter for Mexican Mafia. Gutted multiple Black Guerrilla Family soldiers. No witness came forward. Asshole only did nine years of his stint. Released on some bullshit clemency."

The following pages were filled with violent charges leveled but never proven, notes scrawled around each page. "Gutierrez is slippery as an eel." "Witness intimidation." "Threatened at least two jury members." "Witness' daughter disappeared." "Gutierrez is dirty as sin, and smart as Lucifer."

Motherfucker.

"I told you he was pure thug." Hertzog stood behind Madsen, looking over his shoulder.

"These files, the notations, who wrote them?" Madsen spoke without looking up from the files.

"No can say."

"Who sent them to you?"

"Wasson from the Sheriff's gang unit. He said Gutierrez was a card-carrying sociopath. Said the punk was playing mental now to keep out of the joint. Said we shouldn't believe a word comes out of his lying mouth."

"He said a lot. Wasson? Detective with the Sheriffs?"

"That's what I said. You going deaf as well as dumb?"

"He initiated, or you reached out?"

"He did. What?"

"Why you? Not your case." Madsen keeps it casual, not looking up.

"We worked a joint deal last year. What? Must have a red flag on Gutierrez. Maybe I was the only number he had."

"You say so, so it be." Taking the file Madsen headed back interview room six.

"W-w-why... I d-d-d-don't like this room." Cisco stumbled over his words as he tried to understand what he was doing in the interview room.

"No one does. Here." Madsen sat a Styrofoam cup full of water down by Cisco, who drank it down in one long steady pull. Smacking his lips when he was done.

"I was thirsty. Can I go now?"

Madsen turned on the recorder. "All you have to do is tell me why you shot David and we're done."

"I—no—I didn't shoot. David was my friend."

"The officers found you holding the murder weapon, standing

over the victim. Explain that?"

"I-I-I. Please." Cisco looked like he was deep in thought. "I don't remember."

"Don't remember?" Madsen's face was pure incredibility. "It was just a couple of hours ago. And he was your pal. But you don't remember?"

"No. I'm not lying."

"Really? Look, we all make mistakes. Time for you to man up, tell me why you shot him. I'm sure you had a reason. Tell me, and maybe I can help you out."

"I don't.. hurt people...don't. It's bad."

"Really? You want to play it that way? Cool beans." Madsen laid the print out on the desk, tapping on the mug shot. "Francisco Gutierrez, that's your name, right?"

"Yes, but you know I want to go home."

Madsen spun the file so the text was facing Cisco. "Can you read that?"

"No, maybe. No." He screwed up his eyes trying to make sense of the printed words. "A-a-agrrr-vay...aggravated..."

"*Assault*, aggravated assault three counts. One count extortion. You took a baseball bat to a store owner, ruptured his spleen."

"No."

"The wife? You gave her twenty-two stitches and a concussion. Ringing any bells?"

"I didn't. Tricky, believe me."

"Their son?" Madsen pointed at a picture of a young man on a stretcher, his leg is bent unnaturally. His face is pure animal pain.

"I didn't. No." Cisco is transfixed by the picture. "That isn't, that is wrong."

"Oh, wait, after you were arrested, the family changed their minds, said they misidentified you. But you and I know you did it."

"I don't remember."

"How about him?" Madsen pointed at a picture of a dead man in a West Hollywood alley. "You shot him twice in the face, must remember that."

"No. I-I-I, maybe. No. Please stop."

"I'm just getting started. Between '96 and 2013, you were a suspect in over fourteen violent crimes. We know you are an enforcer for La Colina 13."

"No."

"Yes." Madsen pointed to Cisco's arm, from wrist to elbow amongst the tattoos of jail bars, buxom señoritas and Pancho Villa was an AK47 with the words "La Colina 13" bannered across it. "What the hell is this? Not in La Colina 13? You think I'm an idiot?"

Cisco looked down at the tattoo, then back at Madsen. "I want to go home."

"Tell me why you shot David and this ends."

"I don't shoot…didn't. No."

"No?" Madsen looked down at the printout. "Two thousand and thirteen you were arrested for shooting Victor Black and a fifteen-month old baby."

"No."

"A *baby*." Madsen looked more sad than angry.

"That, that, I wasn't that."

"Oh, it was you. You skated, but we both know you killed them." Madsen suddenly leaned over the table, getting in Cisco's face. "Tell me, you son of a bitch. Why did you shoot David?" Spittle flew from his mouth.

Cisco looked too stunned to speak. He started to mumble "I'm not a bad man…"

"No one is fooled. No one. Why did you shoot David?"

"I…am…not…a…bad…man." Cisco clamped his mouth shut.

Madsen tried yelling louder. Slammed his palms onto the table. Cisco stared into the middle distance, almost peacefully detached from the rage around him. Madsen tried whispering, steam hissing anger with threat filled eyes. Cisco sat silent. He was done speaking.

Hertzog caught Madsen on his way out of the bullpen. "What you want me to do with your little pal? Book him? I know you don't want to kick him."

"Leave him hooked up. No one speaks to him. He needs to ponder his sins until I get back."

"And if our esteemed Deputy Chief wants to know what he's doing in there instead of a cell?"

"Tell her I got this one. He's gaming us, I know it." He stabbed Cisco's file with his finger. "This isn't the jacket of an idiot. A mean bastard, but smart. He's not gonna walk on this, regardless of how good his Gomer act is."

Chapter 4

Parking by the bus stop, Madsen stepped down from the pickup. The lowering afternoon sun did little or nothing to drop the temperature. The air was thick and cloying. He was sweating through his shirt, wanted to ditch his sport coat, but it covered his pistol so he didn't.

"Where the hell is Detective Kazim?" Madsen made the officer standing by the crime scene tape flinch.

"Mucho Macho Tacos, sir." He pointed to a food truck parked in a vacant lot across the street. It had a cartoon taco with massive biceps painted under the name.

Madsen put his head down and crossed the street like a bull stalking a china shop. "Detective Kazim?"

Kazim stuck his head out of the back of the truck, saw Madsen, took a bite of a taco. "Carne asada to kill for." He offered a taco to Madsen, who took it, turned, dropped it into a trash bin and recrossed Colorado.

"You celebrating solving the case?" Madsen said over his shoulder.

"Lunch, man. Late, but lunch none the less. Javier," Kazim motioned to the taco truck. "He knows Cisco and the victim. Said no way Cisco did the shooting."

"He said that, hmm? Then that's that." Madsen dusted his hands off. "Dang, I just remembered, the D.A. called, asked if we could build our cases on evidence, not the word of a taco chef. Did you find any witnesses?"

"No, but—"

"Any video?"

"No, but I—"

"Hush, unless the next thing you tell me is a solid fact, not a feeling, not a hunch, you really better keep your yap from flapping." The officer guarding the crime scene started to laugh, Madsen snapped him a look that shut him down. Back to Kazim, "I know you discovered that Gutierrez and the victim lived two blocks south of here, right? Your blank stare says no. Why not?"

"I was building a picture..."

"How about this for a picture, let's put a bow on this creep. Then get home in time for dinner."

A tall wooden fence blocked off the house from the street. A small sign over an intercom said *Bridge-Way Group Home.* Madsen pressed the buzzer and waited twenty seconds and buzzed again. On the third try a male voice answered "Hello." It took Madsen a moment to realize nothing else was forthcoming.

"Good afternoon, this is Detective Madsen from the LAPD. Could you please open the gate."

"Not supposed to."

More silence.

"Is there someone there who's authorized to let us in?"

"I don't..." The intercom was cut off and then picked up by a woman who apologized and opened the electric gate lock when she learned they were police.

Past the fence a sycamore spread its shade over the front yard. The large two-story Craftsman had a graceful porch and peeling forest green paint. The detectives were walking up a brick path when a woman's scream came from one of the upstairs windows. Madsen started to run, Kazim at his heels. Unsnapping the strap on his belt holster, Madsen wrapped his fingers around the grip of his pistol. Hand on gun, ready to pull, he pounded on the thick oak door. He identified himself as LAPD. He pounded again.

Above them, it sounded like the woman was being flayed. Then she stopped mid scream. All went quiet.

Madsen stepped back, readying himself to kick the door in when it swung open.

A calm woman in her mid-fifties looked at him and smiled. "Let me guess, Johnny at Le Petit Café called you. Even though I've asked that he talk to me first, gave him my cell number, still he calls you." She was dressed in jeans and a worn, button-down denim shirt. An oblong piece of polished turquoise hung around her neck. She was tan, and her sun-bleached hair was tied back in an utilitarian ponytail. "I'm June Cleaver—don't say it, heard them all. I'm the director of this bedlam." She reached out her hand.

The woman on the second floor started to scream again. Madsen moved in quickly. June let him pass with a slight smile.

"No one leaves." Madsen called to Kazim, taking the stairs two at a time. Following the woman's cries he pulled open a door. A young woman stood alone in a bedroom screaming at the wall. Seeing Madsen, she went instantly silent.

"Who are you?" She had wild unkempt long hair and smeared on make-up. Circles of pink on her cheeks. A smear of red lip stick went half an inch beyond her lip lines. Blue eyeshadow and black mascara ran down from her eyes.

"Detective Madsen. Are you alright ma'am?"

"No, I'm not. See what they did to me?" She held out her palms. There was nothing Madsen could see. "They cut me when I'm not looking. They hurt me bad."

"Who hurt you?"

"Staff, they don't like me. Say I'm too pretty to live. Like a butterfly on fire." Running her hands maniacally through her hair, her fingers got stuck in a tangle. "Damn! See what they did to me?"

"What do we say about fibbing, Pris?" June appeared behind Madsen.

"I'm not lying. Not a liar liar pants fall down."

"No, you're not." June stepped behind Pris and gently stroked her hair. Pris watched in the mirror as June picked a brush off the dresser and calmly started undoing the tangles. Slowly the anger retreated from Pris' eyes.

"I'm tired." Pris spoke through a yawn.

"I bet you are. Why don't you lay down for just a minute."

"Okay, but I won't sleep." Pris let June lead her to the bed. "They come and hurt me when I sleep."

"That's fine, you can stay awake if you like." It wasn't even a minute before Pris was lightly snoring. June backed out of the room, leaving the door open.

Madsen followed June down the stairs. "What's her problem?"

"Dear Pris, they're adjusting her meds. Never easy, but with her, the doctors can't seem to get even close. Sometimes I think treating brain chemistry is more intuition and alchemy than science. But you didn't come to hear me ramble. Pris has stopped screaming. So, if you will issue me the noise complaint or warning or whatever, we can both get on with our afternoons."

"We're not here about the screaming." Kazim said. Madsen shot him a look to shut him up. Then he mimed taking notes.

"I assumed..." June said.

Rashona, a strong Jamaican woman in animal print scrubs, joined them. Papers flapped in her hands when she spoke. "Intake forms, from that new woman, where do you want her?"

"Put her in with Janie." Rashona started to protest. "Don't say it, I

41

know. But Medicare won't pay for a private room. And we sure as heck can't subsidize it."

Madsen cleared his throat. "Is there someplace we can talk?"

"Here, we can talk here. I don't keep secrets from staff." June scribbled a signature, handing Rashona back the forms.

"I need your full attention." Madsen's head was starting to thrum again. "Please, an office, dining room, someplace we can shut the door."

An older man in a wheelchair rolled into the foyer. He wore goggles and a tee shirt proclaiming he was a member of the Star Wars Rebel X-Wing Starfighter Corps. His chair was decorated with Star Wars stickers. He had oxygen tubes running under his nose. "June, June, June."

"Donald, what is it?"

"June, June, June."

"What?" June smiled at Donald.

"Um I forgot. God damn it!"

"Language, Donald."

"Sorry, sorry, sorry."

"Rashona, can you take Donald into the kitchen?" June was direct, without a hint of bossiness.

"Want a snack, big man?" Rashona rolled Donald down the hall.

"Yes, yes, yes. Snickers?"

"No. Carrots I think."

June looked at Madsen and shrugged. "Come on, let's get this over with. I have the new intake to settle and our overnight staff has the flu, I need to find a sub, or I won't be sleeping tonight."

June's office was cramped and tiny, papers stacked on every surface. A framed poster of Anasazi ruins hung behind her. The chair she offered Madsen had multiple duct tape repairs. Kazim stood in the doorway pad and pen in hand.

"Glamorous, right?"

"I've seen worse shit holes." Madsen immediately wished he hadn't sworn.

June didn't raise an eyebrow. "Really, have you?"

"No, not really."

"Every time I set aside some money to fix it up, maybe expand a little, a client chips a tooth and Medi-Cal won't cover what they call a cosmetic procedure. Or one of them needs..." She raised her shoulders. "Nine hundred and fifteen dollars, that's what the Social Security Administration expects our clients to live on. Insanity. Oh, and if some Good Samaritan gives them anything, SSI cuts their check."

Madsen gave her a tired look that his returning headache may have made harsher than he intended.

"I'm back on my soapbox, right?" June smiled feebly. "What can I help you with?"

"I'm Detective Madsen, homicide. This Detective Kazim."

"Homicide?" The unflappable June Cleaver looked shaken.

"Do you have a client named David living here? Had Down syndrome?"

"Had? No. I was talking to David this morning." She glanced at a whiteboard chart with client's names and where they were. "David's at the Eagle Rock Mall, took the bus. He likes to sit in the air conditioning and talk to people." She looked at Madsen's face for an explanation of his mistake. None came. "He's...Oh, hell. No."

Madsen passed his iPhone to June, on it was a close up of David's dead face. "Is this him?"

June stared at the photo not speaking.

"He was found at the bus stop down Colorado. He died of multiple of gunshot wounds, that's pending the coroner's report. But it won't change."

"No." She looked past Madsen, into empty space. "When I started working, I was told to not get too attached to the Down babies, life expectancy was thought to be short. That's not true, not today. He was only twenty-five."

"I'll need to get his parents' or guardian's address, number. They'll need to make a final identification."

"Of course." She was on auto pilot. She had retreated into herself while her body went through the motions. She fired up her lap top. She printed out David Torres' mother's information.

Folding the paper, Madsen dropped it into his pocket. "One more thing, do you know Francisco Gutierrez?"

June froze, panicked. "Not Cisco. He can't be dead, too. No."

"He's alive."

"Thank God." June gulped a deep breath in.

"Did he go to the mall with David?"

Again, June checked the whiteboard. "Yes, they both signed out and left at eight forty-five."

"Was anyone with them, an aide?"

"No. This isn't a locked ward. The higher functioning clients have freedom."

"David and Cisco were high functioning?" Madsen steamrollered on. "How so?"

"What happened, Detective?" June was flustered.

"Did Cisco have a beef with David, anything?"

"No, no. They were roommates, friends."

"Never an argument, *nothing*? Come on, I'm not buying it. What did they fight about? A girl, messy sock drawer, what?"

"They're human, of course they had minor disagreements."

"What did they disagree about? You can't protect him."

"Protect him?" June tried to puzzle his questions out. "Where is Cisco?"

"Mr. Gutierrez is in custody for questioning."

"What? You have Cisco? Why?"

"He is being interviewed as a person of interest in the murder of David..." He looked at the folded paper, "Torres."

"That's insane. Cisco is incapable of hurting David or anyone else."

"Bullshit." Madsen's eyes went cold. "He's a killer and we both know it. What I don't know is why you're covering for him. He have something on you? He threaten you? I can keep you safe, but you have to talk to me."

June jumped up as if propelled onto her feet. "Out. Get the hell out."

"I'm trying to help. Trust me I'm not the enemy here."

June gabbed his shirt front forcing him to stand. "Don't come back without a warrant."

As the front door thudded shut behind them, Kazim looked at Madsen with no hint of asmile, "That went well."

"Go back to the shop. They get you a desk yet?"

"Yes, where are you going?"

"Get on the computer, find everything you can about Gutierrez." Madsen took Cisco's file off the passenger seat of his truck. "Verify that this file is legit. I want to know what a detective Wasson from the Sheriff's office has to do with Gutierrez. Go." Madsen shooed him away with a sweep of his open hand.

Holly Torres lived a few minute drive from Bridge-Way, in Highland Park. Like all of the Los Angeles basin, the area had been appropriated in a chain of legal land theft — as defined by the latest victor — from one culture to the next; from Chumash to Tonva, to Spanish, to Mexican, to American. By the beginning of the twentieth century Highland Park and its eastern neighbor, Pasadena, had become a home to artists and intellectuals, and together they birthed the Arts and Crafts Movement. In 1940, the Arroyo Seco Parkway, the first freeway in the western United States, opened with off ramps in Highland Park. Easy mobility brought change and white flight to the suburbs. By the mid 1960's, Highland Park's population was largely Latino. Fifty years later, gentrification was shifting the demographics once again.

Holly Torres answered the door of her small bungalow wearing a do-rag, jeans and a Rosie the Riveter t-shirt. The living room was clean and orderly. Decorated vintage cool, it felt like a 40's time capsule. She offered Madsen a seat in a floral print wing back chair that faced a sofa covered in the same upholstery.

"Would you like some iced tea, Detective?" She hovered.

"No thank you ma'am." She wouldn't meet his eyes. "You may want to take a seat."

"I'm fine standing... Lemonade? Fresh made."

"Ma'am, I'm sorry to have to tell you this—"

"An Arnold Palmer? Everyone loves those. Won't take a sec." She turned to leave.

"Your son David died this morning."

This stopped Holly. She stood in the kitchen doorway, back to Madsen. After collecting herself, she spoke, "Do you have any children, Detective?"

"No, ma'am."

"I was twenty-five when I had David. Special needs, that was the label, Down syndrome. Do you know what the odds are of a twenty-five-year-old having a baby with Down's?"

"I don't. Rare?"

"One in twelve hundred. I wasn't cursed, David was a great kid. Hank, the sperm donor, didn't see it that way. He took one look in the delivery room and burst into tears. Good old Hank lasted five months before he was in the wind." Her even monotone spoke of bitterness long faded unto numbness. "When David was in school, every back to school night, every bake sale, every...I was there. Who wasn't? Not one goddamn father. Special ed parents' nights are full of single moms. Men are weak." Turning back to the living room, she seemed not startled but close to it, when she saw Madsen. "Sorry, Detective, um, would you like something to drink?"

"I'm fine, thank you." Madsen picked up a glass paperweight off the coffee. Two sea horses swam frozen in the globe. Madsen focused on the glass, watching Holly in his peripheral vision. "You haven't asked me what happened to your son."

"Haven't I?" She looked vacant. Lost. A tear rolled down her face. She wiped it away. "I saw David Saturday. Took him for a haircut. He looks good, looked. He's...so many of his classmates died over the years, Jason, congenital heart defect. Kimberly was hit by a car. You get ready for...damn it." Tears started to flow, her shoulders shook. "I'm sorry."

"There's nothing to be sorry for."

"I...David was happy, you know, really happy. Why? Damn it, why?" She started sobbing, receding into her own personal place of pain. She didn't wipe the tears and snot away. She slumped down into a deep sofa, wrapped her arms around herself and rocked slowly.

Madsen gave her what space and privacy the small room could afford. His job was a balancing act. He was here to deliver the worst news a mother could receive. He was also here to see how she took it. Like it or not, most violent crimes are committed by people close to the victim. Citizens want to believe the threat to loved ones comes from monsters, gang members, terrorists, the other. Stats just don't bear that out.

Holly's crying slowed. Madsen stood, waited for her to look up before speaking, "Is there someone I can call?"

Holly thought for a long moment before speaking in a whisper, "*Who?* Who would I call?"

"A family member, friend. I can call victim services but honestly they're always backed up, so no telling."

Holly let out a long slow breath, then inhaled, gathering strength. "Where is my son?"

"He is with the county medical examiner."

"Medical examiner? You mean the morgue?"

47

"Yes."

"Why didn't you say that? Medical examiner? That supposed to soften the blow?" Her features crumbled from rigid back to lost. "I'm such a bitch. I'm sorry. Fuck. Why am I apologizing to you?"

"No need to." Moving into her small tidy kitchen, he found a glass and filled it with water. She looked at the glass like it might be filled with poison, decided it was fine and took a long drink.

"Thank you." She looked up at the tall cowboy detective and smiled. "I'm a mess."

"I've done this job a long time, only thing I've learned about grief is it's uniquely personal."

Holly nodded at the truth of his words. When she was done drinking her water she slowly set the glass down, started to speak, but stopped herself, then tried again. "How? How did David die?"

"Shot. He was shot."

"Who the hell would shoot my boy? Who?"

"We are working hard to find out, and we will, trust me on that." Giving her Cisco's name would do no good, and if by some slim chance he was wrong it could do immeasurable harm.

"What happens next..." She asked herself more than Madsen. He explained that the body would need to be identified, but not right away. June had given them a preliminary identification. He wrote his cell number on the back of his card and asked her to call if she needed anything. She didn't look up. He left the card on her coffee table. He said he would call in the morning to make arrangements for the viewing.

Pulling the front door closed he walked back towards his pickup. Anger flooded him. Murder almost always came down to domestic disputes or money or sex. Sometimes all three. David didn't seem to have any money. Sex? Unlikely. What then? Why had this woman's son died?

Chapter 5

"Who the fuck is in the interview room with my suspect?" Madsen stood at Kazim's desk, looking down on his new partner.

Kazim took his time looking up from his computer before answering, "You mean *our* suspect?"

"No, *my*. I'll tell you when it becomes ours." Madsen looked around the bullpen for support but was met by averted eyes, except Hertzog, who gave him a thumbs up. "We clear Detective New-Guy?"

"That's not actually how that works Detective Old-Guy. Partner, as in what's yours is mine, and what's mine is yours. As in, our case."

Madsen went from stony to a big smile. "How do you sneak up on anyone with the clanking of those big brass balls?"

"Padded Jockeys."

"That'd do it. So, partner, who may I ask is with our fucking suspect?"

"That would be his social worker." Kazim passed a business card. Madsen read it quickly.

"Adair Hettrick? He's not an attorney, so he has no right to be in the room."

"She. And, actually, she does."

"No, she doesn't."

"Ok, fine. Why don't you stomp in there and explain that to her?"

"Think I will."

"Have at it, partner."

"You aren't going to demand to come with me?"

"No, I think I'll sit this one out." Kazim turned back to the computer, typing rapidly with all ten fingers, putting Madsen's hunt and peck to shame.

"Would you mind observing, unless you're too busy showing off your secretarial skills?"

"Be glad to." Kazim stood, fighting not to look too gleeful. Taking a position behind the video monitor holding his pen and pad, at the ready.

The first thing Madsen noticed when he entered the interview room was her red hair, curls flung around her head with abandon. Next was her peaches and cream complexion to go with her slight Scottish accent. Riding over all this was flint-hard eyes. She looked thirtyish. Madsen had ten years and at least ten inches on her, but when their eyes locked she didn't blink.

He broke off and turned his attention on Cisco. "You look pale and sweaty. The room's cold, so what is it? Reality sinking in? You feeling guilty, Cisco?"

"Hi, Tricky." Cisco smiled up at Madsen. "This is Adair, she helps me with things."

"Cisco, remember?" Adair used an imaginary key to lock her lips, then tossed it over her shoulder.

"I forgot. Oops, I just forget a-again." Cisco locked his lips and threw away the key.

"Ma'am, you'll need to clear the room." Madsen came on hard. "You can meet with Mr. Gutierrez when he and I are done speaking."

"Detective," she had a slight Scottish accent. "We won't be speaking to you without counsel present."

"Ma'am...or would you prefer I call you Adair?"

"Ms. Hettrick."

"Okay, Adair, I mean, Ms. Hettrick." Madsen delivered his sheepish smile, the one designed to disarm and ingratiate. "I'm sure you mean well. And that Cisco wants you here, But I have to insist you step out into the hall." His words only served to harden her features, so he changed his tactic. "No? Okay. You may be new to all this legal stuff, but it's not my first rodeo. Should I call your supervisor, let him know one of his subordinates is obstructing an official police investigation? That's a crime. Please."

Shooing Adair away with his fingers, Madsen sat down across from Cisco and took out his digital recorder. After fiddling with the device for a moment he hit record and set it on the table. Looking up he seemed surprised that Adair hadn't left. "Feel free to have my partner find you a cup of coffee. I'll come get you as soon as Mr. Gutierrez and I are through."

"Ah, yes, and now is when I cave in to your superior strength, position, and wit."

"I can have you removed, I'd rather not, but..."

"Actually—and factually—you can't."

"Shall we find out?" Madsen turned to the camera ready to call Kazim in.

"Certainly, but only if you want to look the fool."

Cisco looked from Madsen to Adair and back again. Grinning like he was watching the best tennis match ever.

"Cisco is conserved. Do you know what that means, Detective?" Madsen stared at her, giving up nothing. "He is a ward of the court. You must know what that is?"

"Sure, I only look stupid."

"No, you don't. You look arrogant. Petulant. Clearly a man used to getting over on people. But not stupid."

Madsen fought back a smile. "Flattery buys you nothing. Again, why am I not bouncing you out that door?"

"I am Cisco's conservator, and as such, I legally speak for or sign

51

for him. Any permissions obtained without my consent shall be seen and treated as void. Clear enough, Detective?"

Madsen winked at Cisco. "She's a firecracker."

"Yep." Cisco realized he had spoken and instantly apologized to Adair. She patted his back, smiling. When she turned to Madsen her smile vanished.

"Patronize me, minimize me, just don't speak to my client without me."

"Well, we'll see." Madsen stood, tipped his Stetson and walked out.

Kazim buried his mirth when Madsen joined him monitor. "You catch any of that bullshit?"

"Actually, not bullshit, partner. Any statements obtained without the suspect's conservator present will be found inadmissible. Sorry, but it's a law thing."

"You're loving this, right?"

"A bit, yes."

Madsen rolled his eyes up, asking God to give him patience. "Okay, Detective Kazim, in between trying to protect the suspect's rights, did you do any LAPD work? Did you happen to notice if they have an attorney of record?"

"I did, and, no. She, Ms. Hettrick, asked to have us contact the Public Defender's office."

"Before we've charged the guy? Hmm. You haven't made that contact, have you?"

"Nope. We have no obligation to do so until and after he is booked."

"Well done. Did you call the D.A.?"

"I thought, first, we should get our collective ducks in a row, partner."

"Kid, at this moment I don't totally hate you. I can almost forgive you for letting that Scottish bulldog blindside me."

"I can live with almost." Kazim looked at Madsen, but his attention was on the screen. Adair was speaking to Cisco, her features softened and she was smiling as she patted down his sweaty forehead. Cisco looked spent, pale and weaker than before, what he didn't look was worried. He appeared not to have a care in the world. If he was faking it, he was damn good.

"Did you find Gutierrez's jacket?"

"I did."

"Were the files I gave you legit?"

"At a quick glance, yes."

"Do you hate definitive answers, or are you just trying to chafe my ass?"

"If precise language is a problem, I can keep my mouth shut."

"No, you couldn't, not on a dare."

"I couldn't, you're right." Kazim said, truthfully.

"That settled, guess it's time to make this little piggy squeal."

Adair's smile dropped when Madsen entered the room. "Is our attorney here yet?"

"No, they're not."

"Then we'll wait to speak to you."

"Fine with me. One quick question, why isn't a family member his conservator?"

"I can't disclose that to you."

"Are you a priest?"

"No. A social worker with ethics."

"All righty, then." Madsen sat, and turned his full attention on Cisco. "Hey, Bud, you need anything? Water?"

"I already…" Cisco started to speak before remembering and clamping his mouth closed.

"Sorry, I'm not trying to trick you." Madsen held out his hands, palms up to show his innocence. Cisco cocked an eyebrow in disbelief. "Really, Buddy, just want to be sure you know what is what. See the

53

way this deal works is, I can't call you an attorney until we arrest you. I know, unfair." Madsen seemed to be interpreting Cisco's expressions, "Maybe you're right, maybe you didn't shoot Davy, I mean David, Torres."

"I didn't do that." Words burst from Cisco. Adair patted his arm gently. "I know. No talking. But I didn't."

"I know you didn't. Cisco, it's alright. I'm here to help."

"Yes, you are." Madsen turned his focus from Adair back to Cisco. "Why don't I lay out the options and the two of you can chew on. Okay?" Madsen waited for Cisco to nod consent before continuing. "Okay, choice one is you cooperate, that means—"

"I know what cooperate means."

"Okay, what?"

"Means help, like doing what June asks me to."

"Right. So, I need you to help me, you need to tell me truthfully what happened today. Or—and to be honest—the second choice is kind of rough. See, I would have to arrest you..." Cisco's eyes shifted from Madsen to Adair. "Buddy, it's the only way we can get you a public defender. It gets worse, sorry, I'm not gonna lie to you, the Public Defender's office is backed up, could take a day or two to get to your case. Until then you'll be sent to county lockup."

"Lock..." Cisco was starting to look worried now.

"Jail. Can't be helped."

"That's not true, is it, Adair?"

"Tell him." Madsen kept focused on Cisco.

"Detective Madsen is telling the truth, Cisco, they can, but I don't think they will."

"We will. You've been to twin towers." Cisco shook his head. "Yes, you have, more than once. You know the drill, strip search, orange jumpsuit. I don't think the other inmates will like your tattoos."

"No." Cisco covered his forearm with his other hand.

"I have a feeling La Colina 13 has only enemies in the twin towers."

Madsen turned to Adair, mock helpful, "Impossible to hide gang affiliation in jail. You know what that means for our boy here? Cisco does."

Cisco was locked on Madsen. "No Tricky. I want to go home. I…" His upper lip was trembling.

"We'll do the best we can to keep you safe. But you've been in the joint, it's chaos, right?"

"No. I don't remember that. I'm a good man. I want to go home." Cisco's eyes were wild.

"Can't you see you're terrifying him?" Adair rubbed Cisco's shoulder. "It's going to be Okay?"

"I'm trying to help, Cisco. You're a drowning man and I'm trying to give you a life preserver."

"I am not a sailor. I told you, I am a good man." Cisco was ashen.

"I just need the truth. Why did you kill David? Tell me."

"I didn't." Cisco looked at Adair, suddenly unsure. "Did I?"

His body was starting to tremble harder. He went to wipe his face with his right hand, but the handcuff chained to the table stopped it midair. He panicked like a trapped wild animal. He yanked his hand against the chain.

"Come on Cisco, you know what happened to David. No one forgets something like that."

"No…I…" Cisco stopped speaking, his eyes seemed to lose focus. His free hand started to move slowly, rhythmically up and down.

"What the hell is this? You wanna talk, let's talk, but enough with the act."

"Detective, please, stop."

Madsen looked at Cisco unsure of his next move. Cisco's neck stiffened, and he started to arch his back.

The door banged open and Kazim ran in. "Madsen, he's having a seizure!"

Cisco's body went rigid as he convulsed. Shaking wildly his eyes rolled up into his skull. He stopped breathing. Air was forced from his lungs as his chest muscles contracted, making a groaning sound. His teeth clacked as his jaws snapped together. Arching back, he sent his chair skittering across the floor. Racking forward his head struck the table edge. A gash opened in his left eyebrow. Blood flowed.

Kazim gabbed Cisco, hugging him to his chest to keep him from dropping and fracturing his wrist in the handcuff. The chain snapped with every jerk. "Key, Madsen!"

Madsen fumbled to understand what was happening. Struggling the key out of his pocket, he worked to insert it into the moving manacle, finally unlocking Cisco's wrist.

Kazim sank down, lowering Cisco onto the floor. Turning him on his side, Kazim kept him from aspirating. He held Cisco's head on his lap to protect it from striking the floor as Cisco's legs and arms jerked rhythmically. Cisco was contracting and relaxing with increasing ferocity. He was gone from his body, leaving it on a wild and dangerous autopilot.

Madsen looked at the blood on Cisco's face and headed out the door. Adair called after him, asking where he was going.

He was gone without answering.

"Damn, Madsen, you go old-school full rubber hose when you're pissed." Hertzog said.

Madsen spun around searching. "Where the hell is the first aid kit?"

"The first aid station, obviously."

"Where?" Madsen's blood flooded his face and ear drums. He knew ripping Herzog apart was a bad plan, but it sure would be satisfying.

Hertzog almost made a tomato crack about Madsen's face, but decided on living instead. He pointed at the break room.

Returning to the interview room, Madsen found Kazim holding

Cisco loosely, protecting his head but not trying to control the movements. Adair knelt beside them, patting Cisco's hand and cooing quiet reassuring words. The seizure slowly crested and started to let go its hold of Cisco's motor control, leaving him limp in Kazim's lap. His face was pale and his lips were blue.

Crouching down Madsen inspected Cisco. "He'll need stitches." He pressed a sterile gauze patch to the cut, taping it in place to stanch the blood flowing down Cisco's face.

"Do I call 911?" Adair had her cellphone out, but was uncharacteristically unsure of how to proceed.

"No." Kazim said. "He needs to get to an E.R. fast. May need oxygen, anti-seizure medication." He shot Madsen a hard look.

"He's right." Madsen looked at Cisco's eyes. "Can he walk?"

"No chance." Kazim said.

"Don't you have a wheelchair?" Adair asked, realizing instantly they wouldn't.

Instead of answering her, Madsen took Cisco in his arms and lifted him like a drunken bride ready to cross the threshold. "Where's the unit parked?" He asked Kazim.

"Out back, but—"

"Keys." It wasn't a request. Kazim handed them over, "Stay here, keep digging."

Madsen moved quickly, Adair at his side holding Cisco's hand. As they crossed the squad room Hertzog jumped up, "What the hell, Madsen?"

"He had a seizure."

"Call the paramedics. You can't transport a prisoner like this."

"He's not a prisoner. Didn't book him."

"Then book him." Hertzog blocked Madsen from exiting.

Kazim stepped between them, calm. "Detective Hertzog, Mr. Gutierrez' social worker and conservator has asked us to drive him to a hospital."

"Well, fuck her. This guy is a killer." Hertzog turned from Madsen, challenging Kazim.

"Madsen, is it okay if I hit this guy?" Kazim asked with zero levity.

"Go for it." Madsen didn't' hesitate.

"Madsen, Deputy Chief, she'll take your nuts." Hertzog called past Kazim.

"I suspect so."

"She may take your badge too kid. You ready for that?" Hertzog asked Kazim.

"Come on man, look, he clearly needs a doctor." Kazim said trying to defuse the other detective.

"Fine, it's your neck, your razor." Hertzog turned away from Kazim. "Don't either of you pricks ask to borrow an umbrella when this shit storm hits."

Madsen mouthed "I'll call you," to Kazim on his way out the door.

Chapter 6

They made it down the stairs and out the back without further incident. Reaching the unmarked Ford, Madsen lay Cisco down in the back seat. Cisco's eyes were still closed and he was unresponsive. Adair climbed in the back, holding Cisco's head on her lap, staring down at his face.

"Cisco, can you hear me? Wake up please." She kept her panic well-hidden.

Cisco's eyes fluttered. A whisper was the best he could manage. "The walls are on fire."

"Here, Cisco? I don't see any fire."

"No, in the angry room. Fire on the walls." His lids slowly closed. Madsen flicked his eyes into the rearview mirror.

Adair looked from the man on her lap to the man in the rearview mirror. "He'll be okay, worst is past." She told Madsen, trying to sound like she didn't know seizures could happen in a cluster.

Another could strike any time.

Ten minutes later, when they reached Glendale Memorial's emergency entrance, Cisco was groggy but able to sit up.

"Can you walk?" Madsen opened the back door, not offering a hand.

Cisco's voice was shaky. "Sure, no problemo." He took one step and his knees buckled.

Madsen caught him under his arms and held him up.

"Thanks, Tricky." Cisco let Madsen walk him through the automatic door. When the nurse brought a wheelchair, Cisco sat down, smiling, "This is like Donald's," he patted the wheelchair's armrest. "Only Donald's has Star Wars stickers."

"Do you like Star Wars?" The nurse asked.

"Not really, don't tell Donald."

"It's our secret."

Adair was stalled at the admitting desk while an overzealous administrator asked her a stack of questions.

The nurse swiped her badge, opening the door out of the waiting room. She started to roll Cisco away. He looked over his shoulder, frightened. "Tricky?"

"What?"

Cisco look at the open door, then back at Madsen.

"You want me to come?"

"Yes." Cisco reached up to take Madsen's hand. Madsen was uncomfortable, he shoved his hand into his pocket. "You don't like me?"

"I don't know you."

"Yes, you do. I'm Cisco, remember?" His open smile was lost on Madsen. "You look mad."

The nurse is watching for Madsen's reaction. "That's just my face, Bud. Resting ass kicking face."

The nurse chuckled at that.

"Hey, Tricky?"

"What, Cisco?"

"I'm going to be okay, right?"

"Yeah, you'll be okay."

"You're not taking me to the bad place?"

"Not tonight."

"Not ever, right?"

"Sure." Madsen sold it like it was the truth.

Cisco scrunched up his face, worried, while the nurse put an oxygen mask on him and then took his vitals. He winced when an intern stuck a needle with lidocaine into his eyebrow. After it was numb the intern scrubbed out the wound. He was starting to put stitches in when Adair came through the curtain.

"Hi, Adair." Cisco waved his free hand. "This man is sewing me."

"I can see that. How're you feeling?"

"Like poop. How are *you* feeling?"

"Poop covers it nicely."

"That's not a bad word, right?"

"No, poop is accurate."

It took eleven stitches to close the gash. After tying off the last stitch the intern held up a hand mirror for Cisco.

"I'll have a scar, right?" Cisco eyed the stitches.

Madsen looked at scars in Cisco's scalp. "Yeah, another one."

"Cool."

"You like scars?"

"Lilly says they're pretty."

Before Madsen could ask who Lilly was, a busy neurologist bustled into the examining room. He had bed head and deep dark bags under his eyes. He took the chart from the nurse, looking at it while he spoke. "Mr. Gutierrez, I'm Doctor Wagner. Do you know what brought you in here tonight?"

"A black car." Cisco smiled, proud. The neurologist looked confused.

"He had a seizure." Madsen reported. "Lasted maybe forty-five to sixty seconds."

"What type of seizure?"

"The big type."

The doctor did a slight eye roll before continuing. "Did he lose

61

consciousness?"

"Briefly."

"What anti-seizure medications is he taking?"

Madsen had no idea. Adair called Bridge-Way "June said he takes 600 mg Gabapentin, three times a day. She wants to know why he didn't take his two o'clock meds."

The neurologist spoke very slowly and slightly louder to Cisco. "Did you forget your meds today?"

"No."

"Are you sure?"

"I didn't forget. Told Tricky. Two o'clock, three white pills."

"Your brother has a very serious condition." The neurologist said to Madsen.

Madsen wanted to say that they looked nothing alike. Cisco was clearly Latino while Madsen looked like he stepped out of a fjord.

"He thinks you're my brother, Tricky."

"I'm not." Madsen drew his badge. "LAPD. Homicide."

"Did you withhold this man's medication, officer?" The neurologist started to write in the chart.

"It's Detective, and it wasn't like that. Don't write that down."

"It was a miscommunication—a mistake." Adair sounded calm and reasonable as she explained that she was Cisco's social worker. That Madsen had no foreknowledge of Cisco's epilepsy. And that she thought he had gotten his afternoon medication at his group home.

"You are aware this man could have died?"

"Yes. It won't happen again."

Contrite didn't fit Adair. Had the neurologist been paying attention he would have heard the false tone. But he was busy comparing dick size with Madsen, his hand hovering over the chart like a threat.

"Screw this, Doc. Report what you want. See, who did what when means diddly. History." Madsen had edge in his voice. "What matters now is keeping Mr. Gutierrez from having another seizure. How's your malpractice insurance?"

"Massive." The neurologist passed the chart back to the nurse without writing on it. "600 mg Gabapentin onboard, right away. Intravenous fluids for dehydration. I want a CAT scan." The nurse started to ask a question, but the doctor was already heading out the door.

"He's busy." Cisco said.

"Yes, he is," the nurse said, "Now, you sit tight while I get your medication and schedule you a CAT scan."

"You know," Cisco paused, "I don't have a cat."

"No…it's a scan. Um…how we look at your brain."

"I know that." Cisco cracked a wide smile. "Not my first rodeo."

Madsen caught up with the busy neurologist as he rounded a hallway. "You have a moment?"

"Wagner, it's Dr. Wagner. And no, I don't have time." He looked away from Madsen, started to move but Madsen stepped into his path.

"Sorry about back there, hard day. But I really do need to ask you a few questions."

"And I need to be in on a consult in ten minutes."

"This will take two." Madsen stood immovably.

"Then you will let me get on with my afternoon?"

"Absolutely." Madsen was pure sincerity.

"Fine, what is it Detective?"

"Gutierrez, the man you just saw, he's a con man. I believe he faked that seizure."

"Not possible. Or, I should say, not remotely probable. Anything is possible."

Madsen shook his body and rolled his eyes into his skull.

"You can mimic the symptoms, the behaviors, yes. But before prescribing medication his doctor would have done an EEG and a CT

63

scan, at least. Those results can't be faked." Dr. Wagner stopped, he was intrigued by the puzzle. "There was a man in Scotland who could trigger a tonic-clonic seizure at will. He got clerks to yell at him and then he would seize."

"New take on the old slip and fall?"

"Something like that."

"How about memory loss? Can you test for that?"

"Memory loss, PTSD, some forms of brain injury, are all self-reported. Like drug addicts with soft tissue damage, no way to prove if they are suffering or conning. It comes down to the attending's call." He started to step away, then stopped. "There is an emerging specialty, neurological slash forensic psychologist. They claim to be able to test for all of the above. Several judges have allowed them to give testimony as expert witnesses. Workman's comp cases, mostly."

"I'm trying to wrap my head around this…a medical test? Could you do it?"

"No and no. It's psychology." Clearly a field the doctor found beneath him, "They ask questions. Questions that seem complicated on the surface but are actually simple to answer. A liar will not answer them correctly. A reverse fail, proving their intelligence." Looking at his watch he shook his head. "I'm sorry I—"

"Thank you for your time, one last thing…"

"Quickly, please."

"If you were to guess, is Gutierrez faking his brain condition?"

"I don't do guessing."

Cisco was on the exam table with a wet wash cloth over his face, not moving. Madsen walked through the doorway when his phone went off. It sounded like a klaxon. He didn't need to look, it was Deputy Chief Fong's ring tone. Hand in pocket, he hit ignore, silencing the call. Adair arched an eyebrow, questioningly.

"Nothing important." Madsen spoke quietly. "What's the word?"

"We're in line for a CT scan, thirty minutes, they think."

"Good." Madsen searched her face.

"What are you looking for, Detective?"

"Wondering, that's all."

"Wondering why I didn't jump on that doctor's side, help him bury you for withholding Cisco's medication?"

"Something like that."

"Because, you didn't know Cisco was epileptic, did you?"

"No. But…"

"I told him the truth. Not used to that? I find that people who distrust others are often distrustful themselves."

"That—or they're cops."

To his surprise she smirked.

"Adair?" Cisco called out from under the wet cloth.

"Do you need something, Cisco?" She asked.

"Can I take…" He searched unsuccessfully for a word. "…this… off?"

"Of course you can." She lifted it off him, looking into his face. "Better?"

"I feel tired and… my…" He scrunched his face. Adair smoothed the lines from his forehead.

"It's okay."

"My… my… words are missing."

"They'll come back. Truly. Close your eyes." She continues massaging his face until his breath slowed. Moving away she explained to Madsen that Cisco was postictal. After a seizure, it would take a while for him to be fully himself.

"How long?"

"Why, Detective, you in a hurry to get on with your waterboarding?"

"No, it wasn't like… you're screwing with me now."

She nodded. "I get you are doing a hard job. I do. But I've known

Cisco for over two years. I *know* him. And he didn't shoot anyone."

He thought, *Unless he has you completely snowed.* Then, he said, "I hear you. Now I just need to prove he didn't."

"Adair?" Cisco kept his eyes closed but clearly he hadn't been sleeping.

"Yes, Cisco?"

"The...the...the brain thing?"

"CATscan?"

"Yes. That." Cisco opened his eyes and looked to Adair, "Can Tricky come with me?"

"I don't know, you should ask him."

Before Cisco could speak, Madsen jumped in. "Sorry, no. I've got work to get done. What about Ms. Hettrick? She's here, willing and waiting."

Cisco chewed his lower lip thoughtfully. "You...you...coming back?"

"Yes. Ms. Hettrick can call when you're done and I'll come get you." Cisco watched Madsen go, worry clouding his face. "Tricky?"

Madsen turned back from the hallway. "What, Cisco?"

"I didn't..."

"Didn't...what?"

"Do...what you think."

"I don't know what I think, yet. Take it easy breezy, Bud. I'll see you later."

Madsen hated leaving the cool air of the hospital, but he finally had enough bars for a decent call. In the shade of the hospital's portico he called Kazim, tasking him with tracking down Cisco's prison medical records: "Find out what you can about his brain injury."

"Nice end run around medical records privacy."

"You moonlighting for the ACLU?"

66

"You think he faked that seizure?"

"Not any more. The rest of it? Could have."

"I'll see what I can find out. Now, I have a question for you."

On the other end Madsen let out a slow breath. Taking off his Stetson he wiped sweat from his forehead. "Shoot."

"Do you believe in coincidences?"

"Not much, why?"

"And yet you, a homicide detective, happened to drive by the murder scene."

"Okay, rare, but they do happen. Point?"

"Twice?"

"Stop being cryptic and get where you're getting."

"Fine. Do you know who called in the crime?" Madsen kept silent so he wouldn't explode. "You don't? Neither do I. That's because it wasn't called in. Patrol officers Hill and Russo just happened to be rolling by and saw the suspect standing over the body, gun in hand."

"No shit?"

"No shit. Weird, right?"

Chapter 7

Sergeant Booker stood at the urinal trying to relax sufficiently to release his bladder. The embarrassingly weak stream was a side effect of the surgery, along with the sexual problems he would never ever share with his fellow officers. Growing old sucked, but he guessed it beat being dead. A small dribble finally started when he heard metal scraping on tiles. Swiveling his head, his eyes went wide.

Madsen wedged a paper-towel filled trash bin against the door, effectively locking it.

"The hell you think-" Booker started but was cut off by a "Shhh."

Madsen moved down the stalls, checking each, making sure they were alone. "Sergeant, great to see you. A couple of quick questions."

"Here? Are you completely insane?"

"Not completely, no. Do you know Detective Wasson?"

"What?"

"Sheriff's department?"

"I don't need this crap." Booker headed for the door, but Madsen stepped in between him and the exit. "Step out of my way Detective or we will have a real problem." Booker squared his stance, tightened his fists. His body language said he was ready for a fight. His inability to hold Madsen's gaze made a mockery of his bravado.

"Simple question, yea or nay?" Booker almost imperceptibly shook his head. "Okay, next question, you think of any reason Russo and Hill would want to railroad Francisco Gutierrez?"

Booker dropped his fighting stance, his face growing serious. "They…what? You have any proof?"

"Not a shred. It's a working theory. I'm asking you your opinion."

Booker relaxed as it sunk in. Madsen hadn't blocked the door to keep him in, but to keep others out. Cops are notorious gossips, and in the current political climate even asking the question could end Russo and Hill's careers. "My opinion? Russo and Hill are both solid men. My further opinion is, that Mex banger is pulling a scam. I worked the Victor Black case, saw the child he shot."

"You know how he got all those head scars?"

"Don't. And don't care. Animals belong in cages, right?"

"Right. You hear anything?" Madsen said, moving the bin away from the front of the door.

"I'll tell you. And you pull this crap again, I will write you up."

"Ok, might want to close the barn door first."

Booker mirthlessly zipped up and walked out.

Madsen made it halfway up the stairs before Bette Fong appeared on the landing. She looked down on him, cold, deadly. She said his name, one word, a quiet hiss.

Then she turned.

She rightfully had every expectation he would follow her to the office reserved for her frequent visits. As he crossed the bullpen, Detective Mauk gave him a sympathetic smile. Hertzog's smile was pure gloat with zero sympathy. Hell, even Kazim treated Madsen like he was toxic. He kept his face down, eyes locked on what must have been the most interesting computer screen image ever. Madsen wanted to call Kazim out for cratering under political pressure.

Got my back partner? Really?

He wanted to say. Didn't. Kazim's was the smart play. Rule numero uno, keep your head down and shield wall up until you are ready to charge.

The office was officially a place for detectives to interview witnesses and victims. Comfortable sofa and chairs, a mini fridge stalked with bottled water and soda: plein-air paintings of Griffith Park. It was by design meant to make citizens comfortable and at ease.

Bette Fong stood looking out the window. Madsen wasn't sure she was aware of his presence until she spoke. "Close the door."

He did as told, then leaned against the door, keeping himself as far from her as possible.

For a long moment the room was silent.

If she wanted to play who would break and speak first, he was game. Folding his arms across his chest he started to hum, low, quiet. Bette Fong slowly turned around, her eyes stayed straight ahead, tracking with her body. It wasn't until she faced Madsen that she spoke. "What is that?"

"The song? Blaze Foley, Clay Pigeons?" He looked for recognition, got none, so he sang a few twangy lines about riding a greyhound bus back to Texas.

"God, you *are* a hick."

"I seem to remember you liking it."

"I faked it."

"Liking the song?"

"Yes, that too." She gave him a sweet smile that slid on and off on command.

"Ouch."

"Niels, I have a very simple concept for you. Ready?"

"Fire away."

"I am your supervisor, your boss, the person who can grease your path to success or destroy you."

"Grease my path?" Madsen lift the corner of his lip in a sexy sneer.

"When I call, you pick up."

"Sorry Bette, um Deputy Chief, been a crazy crazy day. I was at the hospital."

"Performing open heart surgery?"

"No."

"Then you should have picked up. Period." Taking a bottled water, she sat in an over stuffed chair, indicating Madsen take the sofa. "Sit. A drink?"

Hefting a chair, Madsen set it down facing Bette Fong. "Not unless they've started stocking Herradura."

"Seems unlikely." She fought back a grin. "Have you spoken to the D.A.'s office?"

"Nope, no ma'am. Something is hinky with this case."

"Hinky? Did I tell you to close it fast, or was that a dream?"

"You did and I will. But it's complex, not entirely sure Gutierrez is guilty."

"Do the math Niels, a known gang member was standing over a dead body, holding the murder weapon. Arrest him."

"The presumed murder weapon. If he's innocent?" Madsen focused on his scarred callused hands when he spoke, "We lock him up, he won't make it. Way he is, rival gangs will tear him up."

"When did you get soft?"

"I'm thinking of you, boss. The optics. An innocent retarded man dies on your watch. Bad."

"Intellectually disabled." She corrected him.

"Right, sorry. But still, bad press."

"We'll ask the Deputies to put him in protective custody. Okay?"

"The khaki crooks? Really?" The turf war between LAPD and the Los Angeles county Sheriff's department had been raging since 1869 with no truce in sight. "I wouldn't trust them to protect a nun in a brass chastity belt's virtue."

"Nice image, cute."

"Right? Okay, look, we don't know, not for certain, that the gun we recovered shot David Torres. Twenty-four hours Bette, give me that. Let's see if the ballistics match."

"You're reaching. There is no way the results will be ready in a day."

"Please." Taking her hand Madsen went for pure sincerity. "Trust me, he did this? I'll lock him up."

"Yes ,you will." She still loved looking into those blue eyes. "Damn you." She whispered as she reclaimed her hand and stood. "I have to run, dinner with the councilman."

"Still seeing Jerry, huh?" She'd been with the city councilman when she and Madsen tore up more than one hotel room. She said she would leave him if Madsen would only ask. He didn't…and she got tired of waiting.

"He's an adult, Niels."

"And I'm not?"

"You are a man-child. You are a shot of tequila and beer back. Jerry is a fine vintage port." Walking out she stopped with her hand on the doorknob. "Gutierrez flees, commits new crimes, spits on the sidewalk in view of a reporter, I will take your shield, gun, and pension." She left without turning to see if her threat had landed, she knew it had.

Madsen stood by the window waiting as Deputy Chief Fong exited the building before rejoining the bullpen. "You still work here?" Detective Mauk asked as she dropped a laptop into her leather messenger bag. "Or did that good-old-boy ah-shucks charm pull your fat out of the fire again?"

"Bought me a stay. Question: What the hell is wrong with tequila and beer?" Madsen asked.

"Nothing if you're a UCLA co-ed." After a quick smile she was gone.

Pulling a chair over Madsen sat down next to Kazim, who asked,

"I still have a partner?"

"That?" Madsen used his shoulder to motion to the room he and Fong had been in, "Nothing. I bought us a day before we need to kick or book Gutierrez."

"That's something."

"Something stupid? Tell me I'm not an idiot."

"Universally, no can do. Can say, I don't think you're an idiot this time."

"From your mouth to whatever god you heathens believe in."

"Are you a true believer, Detective Infidel?"

"I believe in the holy trinity, Detective Heathen. Fast horses, old whiskey and young women. Beyond that the whole deal is a crap shoot, and the odds are always stacked in the house's favor."

"The gospel according to Tom T. Hall, huh?"

"You like country, I may have judged you too harshly."

"Like it? No. Hate that corny crap. My dad, he loves it. My childhood road trips were all marred by Waylon and Willie and Glen Campbell. Dad would sing, 'Like a Muslim cowboy' until I wanted to stab my ear drums with a number two pencil."

Madsen looked like Kazim had just pissed in the communion wine. "You are a very sad young man. But your dad sounds like a hell of a guy."

"He is, disregarding his musical taste, truly amazing. Now would you like to discuss the relative merits of Kurt Cobain's lyrics vs. Willie Nelson's? Or shall I tell you what I've discovered?"

"The second, please. Save me from having to plead justifiable homicide when I shoot you in your blasphemous face."

Kazim stifled a smile. "Fair enough. A quick review of Francisco Gutierrez jacket shows that the files you were given were true." Reading notes off the screen, Kazim continued, "Couldn't confirm his juvenile court cases, sealed. But at fourteen years old he was tried, convicted, and sentenced for murder one as an adult."

"Do a big boy crime, do big boy time."

"That'd make a cute bumper sticker. But it's bullshit."

"He killed children."

"He was an adolescent locked up with mainline felons." Kazim's face flushed. He knew better than to argue prisoners' rights with a brother in blue. But that didn't stop him. "A kid, two years away from being able to drive. Probably never French-kissed a girl, and we're throwing him away."

"Boohoo, 'he was only a wee lad.' Try and sell that crap to his victims' families. See if *they* agree he was just a child." Madsen went cold. He had looked at too many faces and seen the devastation on hearing a loved one was never coming home.

"Net result of our enlightened judicial system?" Kazim turned back to the facts on his computer screen. "After nine rehabilitative years, Francisco Gutierrez returned to the streets a hardcore fully-trained gangster. A Phi Beta Kappa, PhD level criminal. In the next twenty-plus years he was arrested eleven times for violent crimes, with zero convictions."

"This is the son of a bitch you were defending?"

"Not defending. Pointing out that we have culpability. *We* sent him to gladiator school. He thrived and that's on us."

"That is a steaming pile of horse crap. In homicide, we speak for the dead. We collect evidence, help build a case. What happens after that is way above our pay grade."

"That's a convenient justification. Sleep well at night?"

"Like a baby. Wrap up this nasty fairy tale. What got us here?"

"Okay, here it gets a bit vague, speculation based on notes, subpoenas and search warrants requested. Looks like the sheriff's gang unit was building a RICO case against him. It would be his third strike."

"Detective this ain't a strip tease show. What happened?"

"Two years ago, they're about to drop the net on Cisco. Before they can arrest him, he's found dumped in an alley in Pico Rivera. Beaten severely enough to put him in a coma for…" Kazim scanned his notes again. "Here, um, six weeks. Broken right leg, both feet, right arm and extensive brain trauma caused by multiple blows to the skull."

"Who delivered this karmic justice?"

"They interviewed members of La Colina 13. One vetrano implied that Gutierrez was drawing too much heat. The ultimate judgment was 'No Humans Involved.' Sheriff deputies didn't break a sweat trying to solve it."

"And our boy?"

"When Francisco Gutierrez woke up, he couldn't remember his prior life."

"Horse shit."

"Not horse shit. Stress, fear, or a concussion can screw up memory."

"So, we hit Speedy Gonzales with a shovel again and he remembers?"

"This isn't a cartoon." Kazim couldn't tell if Madsen was screwing with him, so he continued sincerely, "More head trauma will only lead to more brain damage."

"I can live with that." Madsen saw Kazim's shock. "Kidding. No, I'm not. Yes, I'm kidding…I think."

"Do you want to know what I discovered? Or can I go home to my wife."

"Please Professor Kazim, shoot."

"According to hospital records obtained by the D.A., his cognitive functioning was assessed at the level of intellectual disability, or an I.Q. of under seventy."

"Doctor told me those tests can be gamed."

"Cisco would need to be brilliant, and possibly have a degree in developmental psychology to fake the results and not get caught."

"So, he's either dull as a doorpost, or he's…what?" Madsen mumbled, teasing it out.

"Moriarty." Kazim said.

"Who?"

"Professor Moriarty? Sherlock Holmes' nemesis?" Kazim caught a look from Madsen, "You know who he is."

"I do have some of that book learnin'." Madsen laid the hick on heavy. "'Sides, didn't they make a moving picture about Sherlock?"

"Asshole. So, and this last part is pure conjecture, I think the D.A., in light of the brain damage, decided not to pursue the RICO case against Mr. Gutierrez."

"And the Teflon banger skates again. Ain't this a jug fuck of a case. A criminal genius or?"

"Exactly, or…"

Madsen filled a mug with cold coffee. Gulping it down he hoped to slow the headache that was returning with a vengeance. Madsen's cell chirped, he put it on speaker, holding it between himself and Kazim.

"Hi, Tricky. It's me Cisco. I'm in the hospital." Cisco sounded dopey, like he was drifting on the edge of sleep. "Did you know blue Jello is called Berry Blue?"

"No, I didn't."

"Why doesn't it taste like berry?"

"I don't know, Bud."

"You sure you're a detective?"

"Pretty sure. Is Ms. Hettrick there?"

"Yes. I can't use her phone when she's not here."

"Fair point. Can I speak to her?"

Once on the line, Adair said Cisco was almost done, but Madsen needn't pick them up. "I can take a Lyft back to my car."

"What sort of gentleman would I be if I let you do that?"

"The sort that saves gas by not driving in circles."

"I'm on my way." Madsen covered the phone to muffle the sound. "Getting in my car as I speak."

"Really not necessary."

"You're breaking up. I'm about—" Madsen abruptly ended the call. Dropping the cell back into his pocket, he picked up Cisco's file.

"How do you want how handle the investigation?" Kazim asked.

"Like all of them: run each theory down until it's proven true or false."

"I guess I meant how are you going to handle Cisco?"

"He's a forked theory. So, I'll follow both paths, treat him as if he is both a victim and a suspect."

"You can do that?"

"If he turns out to be innocent he better hope so."

"Madsen, I really don't think Cisco did this."

"I know you don't. And partner, that is why I laid my long neck down on the Deputy Chief's chopping block."

"What if I'm wrong?"

"Then I won't be needing any new hats."

Chapter 8

"Nothing good happens late at night." Cisco said as they rolled towards Eagle Rock. Madsen's attention moved from windshield, to rearview mirror, to side windows, and back out front.

Leaving the hospital, Madsen felt a tingle at the base of his skull. Someone was watching him. Glancing casually over his shoulder he clocked a late model Dodge Charger parked in the ambulance-only spot, engine running. Flat black paint and wheels. It was de-badged, with all the chrome trim painted black. Limousine tint hid the occupants. Driving out of the parking lot Madsen noticed the Dodge pull out. Could be a coincidence, but he didn't think so. When Madsen drifted into a left turn-only lane, the Dodge—two cars back—did the same. On the green, Madsen blasted straight, merging gracelessly to a chorus of horn blasts. The driver of the Dodge was forced to turn or blow their cover.

Three miles later there was still no sign of them.

"...that's what she said. Tricky? Tricky, I'm talking."

"Huh?" Madsen wondered how long Cisco had been speaking.

"Do you have earwax?"

"Ear...what?"

"Maybe you need June to clean out your ears. She uses warm water. Feels funny."

Baffled, Madsen looked to Adair. "You have any clue what he's talking about?"

"He's letting you know it is past his bedtime."

"Lights out, nine. Not ten twenty-two. That is what I'm talking about." Cisco tapped the digital clock on the dashboard. "June says rules are rules."

"I'm sure she'll understand."

"No. Nine. Lights out."

"Got it. Be there soon. I..." Across the street from the Bridge-Way sat a '71 Monte Carlo. Green pearl paint, gold-leaf pinstripes, lace stenciled roof, a classic lowrider. Slammed to its frame and rolling gold spokes with 520s. This wasn't some hipster's nod to East Los, it was a legit gangster ranfla. The Monte Carlo's roof blocked Madsen's view of its interior. If not for the glow and waft of smoke exiting the driver's side window he would have assumed it was empty. Locking his eyes forward and keeping his speed steady, Madsen drove past the bus stop.

"Tricky, you missed June's. It's there." Cisco pointed out the rear window.

"She have a back door?"

"We can't use it. For deliveries, not people."

"I don't think anyone will mind." Madsen turned right at the next corner, left again down the alley running behind Bridge-Way. Its pavement was cracked and scattered with deep potholes. Cyclone fencing and rolled razor wire protected the parking areas and loading docks. Lack of streetlights left lots of shadows to hide in.

"Back door's not for people."

"We're in luck, then. I'm not people, I'm a cop." Madsen killed the engine, gliding to a stop under a NO PARKING sign. Turning off the headlights, he rolled down his window, listening as he waited for his eyes to adjust. A gray tomcat dropped from a fence, landing on a dumpster. Nothing else moved.

Cisco looked from Madsen out the window then back to Madsen, unable to hide his dissatisfaction.

"Yes?" Madsen spoke without taking his eyes off the alley.

"You don't do rules very good."

"Sometimes rules need to be bent, just a little."

"That is not how rules work. Rules keep us safe. Don't you want to be safe?"

"I want you and Ms. Hettrick to be safe." Madsen turned off the interior lights before opening the door. "Stay here. I'll be back."

Cisco started to object, but Adair convinced him it was better for them to wait. "It's all right for Detective Madsen to go in. June won't mind."

"Promise?" For an answer Adair hooked her pinky around Cisco's, shaking it once.

"Okay. Wait. Tell June I was at the hospital, okay Tricky? And tell her I told you the rules." Madsen nodded as he closed the door.

Being ordered around by a banger suspect. Way to control the situation, Madsen.

Through the glass, Madsen caught Adair's eye, one quick severe glance let her know that she needed to keep Cisco in the truck.

The wooden gate under a "Deliveries Only" sign creaked loudly when Madsen pushed it. He froze. Waited. Pushed again more slowly, lowering the squeal to a soft growl. The backyard was small. A ten-by-twelve Tuff Shed took up most of the real estate. Light spilled out of the kitchen windows. Madsen moved stealthily across the yard. Pressing himself against the house's back wall he slowed his breathing.

Ridiculous. Spooked by a couple of mean old cars. It's nothing.

Up three brick steps Madsen paused.

Or it's a La Colina 13 shooter coming to finish the job on Cisco.

Testing the backdoor he discovered it was unlocked. No noise came from the kitchen.

Cowboy up, Madsen.

Stepping in, he pivoted from corner to corner.

Nothing leapt out and shot him.

Thing about cop-instincts is sometimes they're bullshit. Or worse, an excuse for being a scaredy-cat.

The kitchen smelled of fresh baked bread. A large butcher block table was scattered with chopped vegetables, jars of peanut butter and strawberry jelly. A whistle jerked Madsen around. A kettle on the shiny new industrial stovetop shot steam. Behind him, a pantry door flew open. In his peripheral vision a shape swung something club-like at his skull.

"W-w-w-wait!" Cisco's cry stopped the assailant.

Madsen turned around to face a rolling pin held over Rashona's head. She looked from Cisco to Madsen, trying to determine the threat level.

"Tricky is a friend. I told him deliveries, not people."

"He did." Madsen played it cool and easy, "Sorry to frighten you."

"Frighten *me*?" She let out a percussive laugh. "Boy, I grew up in Trenchtown. Frighten me?"

Adair hung back in the doorway, embarrassed. She answered Madsen's "what the fuck" look with a shrug. "He jumped out. I couldn't stop him."

"Sorry, Tricky. Don't be mad."

"You saved my brains from getting dented."

"That would be bad." Cisco rubbed his scar riddled head.

"Yes, it would."

The hall door swung open and June strode in. "Ro we need to—" Seeing Madsen she flared. "You. Did your goons forget to break something?"

"I don't—" Madsen was cut off by Cisco stepping past him.

"Hi, June. I was at the hospital. I'm sorry. Nine, lights out. Nothing good happens late at night."

"You aren't in trouble." June dropped the irritation from her voice. "You're a good man, Cisco."

81

"I am a good man."

June inspected Cisco's face, noting the bruise and stitches. "Did the detective hurt you?" Turning on Madsen she asked, "Did you?"

"Tricky? He's my friend. He gets grumpy sometimes, but he's a good man, too." June looked at Madsen, incredulous.

"I didn't hurt him, he tripped."

"Same thing Adam said when God asked him how Eve got that black eye."

"It's what happened."

"So you say. Is Cisco under arrest?"

"Not yet."

"Do you have a warrant?"

"No, do I need one?"

"Your storm troopers didn't seem to when they tore up his room. I'll be calling the ACLU tomorrow."

"*What?*" Madsen didn't try to cover his confusion. "Who was here?"

"Cops. Cisco has rights, you know."

"I know he does."

"My room?" Cisco looked up at the ceiling.

Madsen turned from Cisco to June, "Were they uniforms?"

"No, suits like you. Only not so… cowboy."

"Tricky's a horse-boy. He doesn't have any cows." Cisco's grin destroyed June's scowl.

"All hat, no cattle, eh Detective?"

"Something like that." Madsen slipped on his guaranteed to disarm, little boy grin. "I apologize for any distress caused, but I swear those men weren't mine."

"You swear, huh?" June's softening was slight, but a softening nonetheless.

Madsen crossed his heart, "My word is my bond."

"I'm hungry." Cisco tapped Madsen's shoulder to get his attention.

"What's for dinner?"

"Bit late, Bud." At the hospital Madsen had brought dinner for Cisco from Sonic. He watched with dismay and amazement as Cisco had wolfed his way through a double cheeseburger, fries and a chocolate shake. "Can't be hungry again."

"June says I have a fast mataba-thingy."

"He does. Want a snack?" Cisco nodded yes. "Adair?"

"Famished."

When Madsen asked to see Cisco and David's room, June waited until Cisco said it was fine with him, before she relented. "I neither like nor trust you." June told Madsen, "But Cisco does. He's a good judge of character. That buys you one shot."

"I'll take that." Madsen played it sincere, a hint of his smile in reserve. "Ma'am I really am only trying to discover what happened to David Torres."

While Rashona fed Cisco and Adair, June led Madsen up the stairs.

"We'll see." On the upper landing, June paused and took a long measure of Madsen. "Character is a funny thing. A person's true nature comes out, sometimes quickly, sometimes slowly, but it always shows itself."

Madsen didn't know what to do with that, so he went all business. "These men, did they show you badges?"

"Nope. Bulled their way in. When I asked to see a warrant, they said the home was part of an ongoing investigation so they didn't need one. Didn't seem right, but the living room was full of clients, a Zoomba class, I didn't want to disrupt them any more than your friends already had."

"No uniforms, no badges? How are you so sure they were police?"

"The mix of Axe body spray, stale cigarette smoke and officious attitudes gave them away."

Madsen nodded, he knew the type. "You get their names?"

"No."

"Did they leave a card?"

"You really didn't send them?" June started to worry. "Then who? What aren't you telling me?"

"Probably nothing. LA county is huge. Left hand doesn't always know the right…you know?"

"Interdepartmental miscommunication? Are you serious?"

"Serious as a ghost chili chimichanga." Madsen made it hard to stay angry with him. June was trying and failing.

As June led Madsen down the hall, Donald rolled out of his room mumbling quickly about his teeth hurting and his radio being broken. "It's after lights out, Donald."

"I-I-I-I yes. Heard voices. Cisco is up."

"Yes, he is. But you need to get back in bed now." June used her chin to point out Cisco's room to Madsen before rolling Donald out of the hallway.

Stepping into Cisco and David's room it was clear it had been tossed, and not gently. Both single beds had mattresses hanging off their box-springs. Drawers full of clothing had been dumped on the floor. Comic books were scattered. On a bedside table, he found a pair of hearing aids. A photo of Cisco and David hung crookedly on the wall. They had their arms over each other's shoulders, broad grins graced their faces. Peeking out of the curtain, Madsen could see over the bus stop and across Colorado. The low rider, like a bad habit, was hanging around. It was parked in the perfect spot to see anyone coming or going from the group home.

"Are you police?" A young woman with black hair in a pixy cut and Hello Kitty pajamas stood in the doorway.

"I'm a detective, and you are?"

"Lilly. My room is down the hall. Cisco didn't do it."

"Didn't do what?"

"Anything. Whatever you think he did."

"What makes you think I think he did anything?"

84

"Well…" Lilly screwed up her face. "One, I saw him in the police car. Two, he did not come home all day. Three, you messed up his room. Four…um, four…wait…four, I'll think of it."

"That's okay, I get your point. I didn't arrest Cisco. I didn't mess up his room. Are you friends with Cisco."

"I'm his girlfriend." She beamed. "I think he's beautiful."

"Did David and Cisco get along?"

"Everyone likes Cisco. Do you like him?"

"I just met him today."

"That's all it takes. Maybe you think too much." She scrunched up her eyes, mimicking over concentration. "It is okay to trust."

"Lilly are you in bed?" June called from the hall.

"Yes."

"No, you're not. Come on now."

"I'm coming." Lilly rolled her eyes, then turned back to Madsen. "I work at Vons. I help people."

"That's great." Madsen winked. "Better head to bed, don't want to be tired at work."

"No, I don't. I have to be alert." Lilly started to leave then came back. "Cisco really didn't do whatever it is. Promise."

"Okay."

She nodded thoughtfully. Was about to speak, then forgot what she was going to say. She had been gone a couple of minutes when Cisco came in. He looked around the room, eyes wide with shock.

"Oh no. Someone trashed my room."

"Sure did. Any idea what they were looking for?"

"No."

"If I knew what they were thinking, it might help your case."

"Tricky, I don't know them. How would I know what they think?"

"Okay, how about this, can you tell me what's missing? Did they take anything?"

Cisco looked around, confusion clouding his face. "Nothing's where it should be." Picking up a pile of t-shirts he looked at a dresser centered under a sign with his name spelled out in wooden letters, the drawers were on the floor. "Not good."

"I get it, Bud." Madsen picked up a drawer and slid it in. "I always need to clean up my desk before I start work."

"I don't have a desk."

"No, you don't." Madsen continued replacing drawers in the dresser.

Adair stood in the hallway, leaning against the wall so that she could hear them without being seen.

"Look around." Madsen told Cisco. "Take it slow. Anything you can think of, anything."

Cisco moved around the room, shuffling his feet, not wanting to step on any of the clothes or comic books. At David's dresser he stopped, gently tracing the wooden letters on his sign. The sock drawer hung open and off its runners. Below a pair of gym socks was a cache of shiny objects, a rhinestone barrette, silver whistle, soup spoon, a makeup compact.

"What you got there?"

"I didn't lose my watch, see?" Cisco lifted a scratched Timex out of the drawer and held it up for Madsen to see. "I thought…but, nope. David had it."

Madsen looked into the drawer, "Are those things David's?"

"No. But…he wasn't a bad guy."

"He stole your watch. Did that make you mad?"

"He's my friend. It's just stuff."

Madsen nodded, let it pass. One more loose puzzle piece to rattle around his brain.

Cisco turned in a slow circle. Not seeing what he was looking for, he frowned. David's dresser had been pulled away from the wall, Cisco crawled behind it but, no luck.

"What, Bud? Something missing?"

"Yes…no, here it is." Cisco lifted up a blue plastic binder that lay under a pillow on the floor. It had "X-MEN" in Sharpie on the cover. Opening it, he showed Madsen sheet after sheet of clear plastic holders filled with X-Men trading cards.

"These yours?"

"No, David's. He's really proud of them. Gambit hologram card, hard to find. Iceman is…" He suddenly looked deeply sad. He set the binder down on top of the dresser.

"What?"

"David. He's never coming back."

"No, he's not."

"Not fair. Tricky?"

"Yes?"

"I miss him." Tears brimmed in Cisco's eyes, he let them spill down his cheeks without wiping them. "Does it have to hurt so bad?"

"I think it does, Bud." Madsen handed his bandana to Cisco, who blew his nose and handed it back. Madsen hid his slight disgust and dropped the cloth into his pocket.

"Oh no…" Cisco leaned back behind the dresser. "David kept his treasure behind the dresser. Said it was safe from robbers."

"Treasure? Like in his drawer?"

"No. Not sparkles. *Treasure.* X-Men cards and money."

"Money?"

"Yes, Tricky. Sometimes you don't listen too good."

Madsen pulled the dresser farther out from the wall. "Did he keep it in a wallet?"

"Like this." Cisco pointed at the binder. "Only red." Cisco slumped down onto his bed. He picked a Wolverine action figure up off the floor. He stared at it, lost in sad thoughts. "Did you know Wolverine heals himself?"

"Hard to hurt him huh?"

"No, he hurts, but he doesn't die. I wish David was a wolverine. Do you think they have X-Men cards in heaven?"

"Sure they do. Can't think of any reason they wouldn't." Madsen lied, truth was he had little belief in heaven or God or any other religious hokum. Veteran homicide detectives fell a couple of ways; Deacons, they clung to religion as a way to give meaning to the mess, God's will is final and not ours to question. God Haters, they thought any God that could watch the atrocities people visited on each other and not step in was either nonexistent, or just plain cruel. Then there were Party Boys, their motto, drink like no one is watching and live like you don't give a fuck. They lost themselves in the arms of a pretty skirt or a shot of tequila and left theology to priests and philosophers. Madsen, if he thought about it, was a strange mix of all three, mostly he believed in chaos and serendipity. He believed in cowboy karma: if you acted with honor good things came your way, except for when they didn't, and that's when you had to put your head down and keep pushing on.

That was theoretical. Cisco wanted concrete. Unless he was a ghetto Moriarty, and this was a ruse. And if he was what he seemed, what was Madsen going to say? Life is fragile. Death is a mean bastard that leaves you not wanting to care about anyone or anything. It is also inevitable, so it's best to say screw it and move on down the road? No. So he kept his mouth closed and helped straighten up the room. He put the beds back. He replaced drawers. He picked up clothes and Cisco told him where they went.

Madsen held up a small stack of comic books.

"Those are X-Men, David's." Cisco pointed to a low bookshelf on David's side of the room. "Justice League are mine, also Nick Cruz, he's police."

"Yeah? Never heard of him."

"He's not real. A comic? He's dead. Kinda a ghost. Is David a ghost?"

"I don't know."

"I hope if he is, he isn't a scary one, he didn't like scary things."

Piece by piece, they brought order back to the room. The last thing Cisco did was to straighten the photo of him and David on the wall. "I know what's missing."

"What's that Bud?"

"David."

"Yep."

"And his special money. Someone took that, right?"

"Looks that way."

"Bad people?"

"Yes." Madsen knew the world was much more complex than bad guys versus good ones. Humans were driven by an infinite number of needs and desires. They did horrible things for good reasons, and acts of generosity for purely evil reasons. It was his job to discover who did what and leave judgement to the courts.

Moving to the window, Madsen peeked out through the curtains. The low rider hadn't moved. He motioned for Cisco to take a look, showed him how to use the curtain so he wasn't seen, like hide and seek.

"Dark. I don't see anyone."

"Across the street. The car."

"It's…oh I—" Inside the low rider a Zippo flared exposing a vetrano. Silver hair buzzed tight and covered by a black bandana. Plaid shirt with only the top button closed. Goatee. After firing up a Tiparillo, he let smoke dribble out of his mouth and nostrils, this and the flickering flame lighting him from below made him look like a horror show Satan. Cisco jerked away from the window. "Th-th-that is….no."

"Do you know the man in that car?"

"No…yes." Cisco was pale and trembling. "Raf…Rafael?"

"That his name? Do you remember him?"

"Maybe…"

"Stick with me." Madsen held Cisco's shoulders with eyes locked.

89

"You can do this." Cords popped out on Cisco's neck as he strained to think.

"No...I don't...I..." Cisco's face went lax as he gave up trying. He slid down the wall until he was sitting on the floor. Head down he stared at his hands folded on his lap. "Sorry, Tricky."

"That's okay, Bud." Madsen sat down next to Cisco. It had been one long hot mother of a day. "You like to swim?"

Cisco mulled this over for a moment before speaking, "Yes. Water, right?"

"Can't swim without it. We have a pool up at my house, not fancy or big but it gets the job done." Madsen could see Cisco still wasn't sold, "Pancakes. We have pancakes for breakfast."

"Syrup?"

"Wouldn't be pancakes without syrup. What'd you say, one night?"

"Is Joker there?"

"Who's Joker?"

"Don't know. Think he's a bad man."

"Then, no way José. Only horses and me and my grandpa, he can be crotchety but he's not bad man."

"Good." Cisco relaxed enough to show a hint of a smile. "You know my name's not José, right?"

Madsen assured Cisco that he knew his name. He found a backpack in the closet, it had the Dark Knight on it, Cisco said it was his. Together they gathered up a few days worth of socks, underwear, and t-shirts. Cisco wanted to bring his comic collection. Madsen said there wasn't room, but Cisco convinced him to let him take a few of his favorites. As they were leaving, he picked up the Wolverine action figure.

"Will David mind?"

"He'd be glad you have it."

"Okay." Cisco tucked the tiny superhero into his shirt pocket, leaving his arms and head sticking out.

Chapter 9

A crescent moon hung over Tujunga, its pale light fighting to be seen past the haze and city's light pollution. The name Tujunga comes from a Gabrieliño Indian myth, meaning old woman. The chief's wife, stricken with grief over a lost daughter walked into the hills above the village. Her sadness and unwillingness to accept the loss caused her to turn to stone. Not that most modern Angelenos knew or cared much about history. To them, Tujunga was one more of LA's many oddities. It was horse country, complete with ranches, country western bars and working cowboys slapped down in the north east corner of the suburban hell known as the San Fernando Valley. Its relatively rural areas attracted horse people, bikers, meth-heads, and naturalists. Of late, monied families priced out of trendier locales added to the demographics. "The Madsen spread," as Grandpa Hem had ironically called it, was two and a half acres of dust, hard-pack and scrub oak, a small barn and a corral. It backed up against national forest land, giving it wide open views.

Hemming Madsen and his wife Grace were teenagers when they had migrated from a small town in the Texas Panhandle to Southern California. The unspoken reason for the move was teen passion in a hayloft, and lack of protection. "Everyone knows you can't get knocked up the first time. Right?" To escape the wrath of her Baptist family, who would shun her more for laying with a Lutheran than for the unplanned pregnancy, they headed west. Los Angeles, paradise by the sea. Oranges hanging in arm's reach.

Eighteen year-old Hem discovered quickly that paradise had a price. With a family to support and no real job skills he took what he could get, janitor for a bank, gas jockey, door to door Hoover sales. Two, three jobs at a time. When a neighbor mentioned LAPD was looking for recruits, he scoffed. When he heard they paid $116 a week plus benefits he ran to apply. That chance conversation led to a lifetime career, his path a series of unplanned events. "Life is a fickle pony. Sweet and calm one moment, bucking like a banshee the next. Best to keep the saddle cinched tight, always be ready to hang the hell on and when you get thrown, dust yourself off and climb back on."

Madsen checked his rearview mirror one last time, all was clear. Gravel crunched under the Ford's tires as they drove down the driveway. Cisco stirred but didn't wake. He had passed out on Adair's shoulder minutes after climbing in the truck. The battle to convince June that Cisco would be safer with Madsen was epic. She called Madsen a bully with a badge, a fascist who cared more about closing his case than he did about Cisco's wellbeing. Madsen tried going soft, tried charm, when all else failed he went hard. "Lady you have zero idea what I'm capable of. You don't like me? I don't care. Whoever tossed Cisco and David's room may be back. If he's here? Best case they're cops and they arrest him. Worst case? They're not cops and he disappears."

"Why would I trust you?"

"Don't. Call 911. They will pick Cisco up and drop him in a cell. His death will be on you."

It was Adair who broke the stalemate. As Cisco's conservator the decision was hers to make. She agreed too many people knew where Cisco lived, and he would be safer with Madsen, with one caveat: she would go with them. Before they left, June gave Adair five days-worth of bubble-packed medication. "If you need to know when he takes what, it's all written across the top of each sheet, above the pills."

"Or ask me. I always know when to take my pills."

"He does." June concurred.

After they left Bridge-Way Madsen asked Adair if he could drop her at her car, adding, "I got this."

"I don't know you, what you will or won't do. What I do know is, you pushed Cisco to a seizure whilst you were interrogating him." She had a point, he couldn't deny it or disagree.

Moving down Madsen's long dark driveway she was reconsidering the wisdom of her choice. "Do you have neighbors?"

"Worried no one will hear you scream?"

"Should I be?"

"Depends, does western decor or ornery old men make you scream?" Madsen checked to see if she was smiling. She wasn't. "We have neighbors on both sides, they're just hidden by the brush. You're safe."

"Never doubted it."

"You kinda did."

"Yes," Adair smiled at herself, "I guess I did. It's been a difficult day."

"No arguing that." The headlights swept across a low ranch style home, complete with wagon wheel hitching post and board and batten shutters. Parking, Madsen asked Adair to wait a minute.

On a wide front porch Nat sat, his chair leaning back against the wall. Hearing Madsen's boots on the walkway he tilted back the cowboy hat covering his eyes. He was edging towards seventy, but his smooth black skin made him look much younger.

"Hard day, young man?" Nat asked.

"I've had easier ones, that's a fact." Madsen plucked three twenties out of his wallet and passed them to Nat. IHSS covered in-home care, but Madsen also paid Nat for helping out with the horses and such. "How's Hem?"

"Sleeping. Better day than some. Remembered who I was for the most part." Nat stood stretching out his arms so that his shoulders and back crackled and popped. "We're down to a single bag of oats."

"Alright. Thanks, for…Hell, everything."

"My pleasure. Not for your grandfather I'd be bones in a shallow grave, or dug up and scattered by a coyote." With a tip of his hat Nat walked into the shadows. He lived a few miles down the road and always refused a ride saying he needed the walk.

Cisco mumbled, but never fully woke when Madsen carried him into the house. His eyes opened briefly when he was laid in Madsen's bed, he smiled and was out again. The house was cold, the way Grandpa Hem liked it. The utility bills were large. The all too necessary air con's compressor's bearings were starting to growl and groan. Madsen would never mention any of this. Grandpa Hem protected him from the knowledge of the hours of overtime worked to pay for raising him up. Now it was his turn to keep silent

.

Adair stared at steer horns hanging over the fireplace. The house was decorated in "old west frat house." A large Texas flag hung next to a dart board, a 4H placard draped with red ribbons and a rodeo poster took up one wall, another was claimed by book shelves stuffed with paperbacks. TV trays sat in front of two duct tape-patched recliners. The dining room table was covered with horse tack in the process of being cleaned, and a torn apart lawn mower engine.

"You bring women here often?" Adair asked Madsen when he returned.

94

"Did."

"And how did that work out?"

"The past tense should tell you. Can I get you a drink?"

"I'd murder a whiskey. Two fingers and a bit of ice, if it's no bother."

Madsen removed a basket of clean laundry and week-old newspapers from their only couch, motioning for her to sit. Adair used her work phone to clear emails and check voice messages. Her caseload hadn't eased up because she was away from the office. She answered the emails she could, and made a to do/call list with the rest. She'd just finished when Madsen set a tray down on a cluttered coffee table. He'd prepared an eclectic spread. Ritz crackers, sliced cheese and salami, a bowl of pico de gallo, various pickled vegetables and chilies, and most importantly, two tumblers of amber liquid over ice.

"Wow, Detective, you went all out." Adair went straight for the liquor.

"Sorry for the…um I can run out to—"

"Gah." Adair spit her drink back into the tumbler, looking like it had bit her. "What is that?"

"Wild Turkey, Kentucky's finest. Not a fan? Or is that how you enjoy whiskey, spit and smell?"

"I was born in Scotland, where whisky was invented, and that sir is not even close to whisky." She sniffed it, crinkled her nose and took a second drink. Holding this one in she actually smiled. "Too sweet and too potent." She noticed Madsen's frown. "But not half bad, long as you're not expecting a smooth water of life taste."

"You say so."

Adair took another sip, followed by cheese on a Ritz. Leaning back, she exhaled a deep breath, allowing her shoulders to relax. Above them she noticed a dog fight of model airplanes taking place. "Yours?"

"Grandpa and I made those when I was a kid. I went through a flyboy stage at nine or ten."

Adair took another sip, starting to actually enjoy the flavor. "Are you're from Texas, or do you just like playing cowboy."

"Second generation Angeleno."

"Nooo."

"Scout's honor." He gave her a three-finger salute.

"So, this, um, *look*, is it to impress the women?"

"Are you impressed?"

"No, not much."

"Then no. Try the salsa, we grow the chilis."

"Are they hot?"

"Absolutely."

"Good." Adair scooped some pico de gallo onto a cracker. Her eyes lit up at the taste. She gasped and took a long pull of the bourbon, coughed. "Well done, Detective. Thank you."

"Any time." He sipped his drink contented to watch her.

"All this, um, interior design, I take it your grandmother is not around?"

Madsen thought about the question, then shook his head, clearing a bad memory. "She's been gone forever, or at least as long as I can remember. Grandpa Hem and me do fine."

"And your family? Father? Mother?"

"Gone, too. All three died when I was six."

"I'm sorry. I didn't mean to..."

"Was what it was. Now it's just something that happened." Looking out into the darkness, Madsen could feel her eyes on him.

"How very stoic."

"H.G. Wells, Diana Gabaldon, Richard Matheson, even Mark Twain. They all wrote about time travel. Why do you think people are so fascinated with the concept?"

"Haven't a clue." She continued to watch the side of his face. He was handsome in a rugged marauder sort of way. His nose had been broken and set crooked. His blue eyes seemed to look past the horizon at some yet to be discovered land.

"The one thing we have no control over is history. Once it's past, it's untouchable. The fantasy is we can go back, we can change it, make different choices." Turning he found her staring at him. She didn't look away or shield herself from him. She didn't play coy.

"Why didn't you arrest Cisco?"

"He would be eaten alive in county lockup."

"But why do you care about him?"

"I don't."

"Then?" She stared him down, unwilling to let it go.

"He's a criminal. A killer. His past? He's going to have to pay for that one day. But I don't know if he killed David Torres. If he goes down for that falsely, the real killer skates." She just kept staring at him. "If he did do it? I'll sure as hell see he ends up in a cage."

"You believe in justice."

"Is that a question?"

"A statement, Detective."

"Niels. If you're going to sleep over, don't you think you should call me Niels?" Trying to change gears, he gave her one of his best grins.

"I bet you're used to women dropping their knickers when they see that smile."

"Nah, you misjudge me. I'm a sheep in wolf's clothing. All snarl and gnash, no bite." Still he held the grin.

"Liar." She said with less conviction than she hoped for. Leaning forward Madsen reached out, using his index finger he moved a red curl off her cheek. "Nice move, Detective." She found it hard to speak above a breathy whisper. "About Cisco…"

"He's asleep. Nothing in his case will change tonight." He was inches from her face. His eyes flicked to her bow-shaped lips, up to her eyes, then back to her lips.

"You are a dangerous man. I know who you are…what you are…" She was leaning in when she caught herself and sat back, shaking the moment off. "This isn't going to happen."

"You sure?" It was a real question.

"Really. Flattered and all, but no."

"Okay." Settling back in his chair he let out a low laugh. "So that moment? I misread it?"

"I didn't say that, Detective." Her smile was neither sexy nor sly, it was simply a smile. "Thing is…I don't believe this is the time or place for, um, romance."

"Romance? Ma'am you misjudged my intentions."

"Oh, did I?"

"All I was fishing for was a quick tumble on the table. No romance involved."

"Well, in that case…no thanks." She was enjoying his light banter.

"And, given your disdain for my rather grand offer, why am I letting you stay?"

"I didn't give you an option."

"Must be it." Madsen relaxed. When he went to pour Adair a second drink she declined, telling him she needed to be coherent in case Cisco needed her. She took her charge seriously. Lulled by food and general exhaustion they talked easily. She told him she'd come from Edinburgh when she was eighteen and never left. She liked being a social worker. He liked being a cop—some days. They both loved books. He told her he was enamored with poetry.

"No. Cowboy poets? Limericks? Once was a man from Dunblock?" She teased.

He countered with, "A stranger has come to share my room in the house not right in the head. A girl mad as birds."

"Dylan Thomas, well done. Bit obvious but still solid points for going Welsh. Gone with Burns and I'd have been obliged to take you to bed."

"Too late for a redo?"

"Afraid so. Here is the real test. When no one is watching, what do you read?"

"You want my guilty pleasure, huh?"

"Get this correct and I'm yours."

"Really?" He was enjoying the hell out of her.

"Say and find out."

"Tell anyone and you might end up in tomorrow's tacos." He bit his cheek before speaking, "Ok. Epic fantasy. Swords and sorcery."

"No. *Game of Thrones* caught you too? Dog." She was laughing, "Is it the beautiful naked women or the sex, or the sex with the beautiful women?"

"Reductive take, but not entirely untrue—and no. It wasn't around when I was a kid. Tolkien, and then later Tad Williams were the writers who flew me far from home and my life."

"Damn, sorry, but no thumping mad bunny style for you tonight."

"Really, alrighty then. So, spill it, your guilty pleasure."

"Crime fiction. Stuart Neville is great for a Mick, but it's Rankin, Denise Mina, Jay Stringer that really take me to town."

Madsen broke out laughing. "Old blood and guts Hettrick. Did not see that coming."

"You were expecting bodice rippers?"

"More hoping than expecting."

"Sorry to disappoint." Her smile faded, she looked away not wanting to see his eyes. "What happens to Cisco tomorrow?"

"That depends on him—and me, I guess. He needs to tell me how he wound up standing over a dead man with a gun in his hand."

"Did you ask him?"

"Claims not to remember."

"His memory is faulty, particularly when stressed."

"Convenient."

"It's how he's wired. If you want to know the truth you need to keep calm. Cisco tells the truth, but, he won't make logic leaps, he's a literalist. He will answer the question you ask and not be able to see an implied question. You ask did he see a car, he will say 'no' but not say

99

he did see a truck." She reached out lightly running a finger along his hand. "Niels, he didn't kill David."

"Someone did." Madsen pulled his hand away and stood up. He loved the way his name sounded in her mouth. But he hated being played.

"Niels?"

"Here." He dropped a quilt, pillow, and towel on the couch. "Bathroom's on the left."

"Where will you sleep?" Did she choose that moment to lower her voice to make it sexier, or was it the effect of the whiskey? Madsen wasn't sure. Was it an offer or a simple question?

"Out front. If anyone comes for Cisco, they come through me." He stepped outside closing the door before she could speak and change his mind.

Chapter 10

One a.m. and it was eighty degrees outside. A forest fire on the desert side the San Gabriel Mountains backlit the peaks with an apocalyptic orange glow. Over a thousand acres blackened so far. If the fire crews couldn't contain it, it would be snowing ash in the foothills by dawn. Horses in their paddocks sensed the coming smoke. They snorted and stomped the earth. Madsen rested in a hammock on the front porch trying to quiet his mind and zen the hell out of the heat.

Let go of attachment to concepts like, sweaty pits are nasty. Pain is caused by holding onto suffering or some such crap. Fuck it's hot.

His bumpersticker zen was proving ineffective. He cadged it from a self-help book he bought from the Bodhi Tree. He was trying to impress, charm and maybe understand a nouveau hippy he had dated a few years back. She had taught him that vegan burritos didn't suck. He had taught her not to judge a guy by his boots. He had been with her for several months but never introduced her to Hem, either because he didn't want to hear Hem's view of her lifestyle, or he didn't want to get too close so when they inevitably split it wouldn't hurt. He had taken her camping and fishing on the Kern river. They had spent a star-filled weekend camping in Joshua Tree. Other than that, they always made love in her apartment, and he never stayed the night. When she grew tired of waiting to be invited into his life, she had left, taking his interest in the Tao of Pooh with her.

Madsen liked—hell, loved—women, in the abstract. Some men had a very narrow bandwidth of what they found sexy. Not Madsen. Lithe or zoftig, dusky or pale, book smart or street smart, down to earth or wild, he loved them all. But he had never gotten close to marrying. Excuses went like this, he needed to take care of his grandfather, or he had just joined the LAPD and needed to put his full attention on his career, or he hadn't found the right woman. Regardless, he loved women, they could sense this and returned the feeling. He had the build of a Nordic farmhand, capable of plowing a field or building a ship and rowing it to far off lands. His sandy blond hair refused to stay combed and brought out their nurturing side. His easy smile and willing laugh sealed the deal. From across a barroom or Trader Joe's produce section he looked like a catch and a half. They took his inability to commit as either a challenge or a blessing. If there was some deep psychology at play in all of this, he had neither the desire nor the courage to dig into it.

Thoughts of Adair's bow-shaped mouth came to him unbidden. She lay ten feet away, just the other side of the front door. Flipping mental channels, he forced himself to think about the case. Who had motive to kill David Torres? Could Cisco have shot him and not remembered it? If so why? Was Cisco playing him? Was Adair playing him? Was Adair Cisco's accomplice? He had made the mistake of confusing attraction with trustworthiness before. Her eyes were the color of exotic minerals, brown streaked green rock with flecks of gold.

Reeling in his mind, Madsen concentrated on the here and now. He felt the rubber grip of the handgun resting on his lap. The milled aluminum and heft of the Mag-Lite. Working from the hammock out he focused on the darkness around him, shadows under trees and brush created inky nothing. He listened past the silence. A breeze rustling leaves. An owl called. Distant tires rolling on the 210 freeway sounded like a mechanized river. A horse blew out its breath. Metallic clicks followed by a car's door chime. A car door slamming shut. He waited for footsteps, but heard none.

The car sounded close, the street beyond the driveway or next door.

Slipping off the porch, Madsen crept quietly into the trees. He didn't need light to move through the familiar shadows. He headed toward the road, where he imagined the sound might have come from. His pistol was in his belt hidden by an untucked shirt. Freaking out civilians never played well with his bosses. Through the branches he was sure he could make out a parked car. The silhouette could be a Dodge Charger. Movement snapped Madsen's head around. Ten feet to his right a hulking figure leaned back, separating itself from the shadows.

Madsen froze.

The figure rocked. It quietly hummed a melody that was lost in the air.

Madsen reached under his shirt, resting his hand on his pistol's grip.

The sound of liquid hitting a tree trunk made Madsen smile. The guy was pissing, didn't mean he hadn't come to take out Cisco, but it did lower the odds. Pros pissed before going on a hit, or so Madsen imagined.

Madsen waited until the man was done, zipped, and walking toward the road before he moved. The man's shuffling branch-breaking gait covered any noise Madsen made. The man stepped across a culvert, opened the door and slid into the driver's seat of a blacked-out Dodge Charger. Illuminated by the interior lights was a beefy round-faced man, with a fringe of dark hair circling his bald pate. He vibed cop, if he wasn't on the job, he had been. The car door closed. The lights went out.

Madsen waited.

Nothing moved.

Twenty minutes later, the car still sat. Whoever was in there followed Madsen from the hospital. But not up here, he was sure of that. Like most cops, Madsen's address and number were unlisted. Hard for a gangster to find, easy for a fellow officer. Either Bette Fong had sent him to surveil Madsen, or this case was more complicated than it appeared.

Fuck it, only one way to find out who this guy was.

Madsen broke through the tree line running crouched toward the Dodge.

The man saw Madsen and cranked the massive Hemi to life.

Madsen stood tall in front of the hood. Clearing his holster he took aim through the windshield. "Freeze."

The Dodge's tires smoked as it roared in reverse.

Madsen moved his finger off the trigger. Pissed as he was that somebody was snooping on him, it didn't constitute eminent danger.

The Dodge screamed as it whipped a 180 and powered down the road.

Madsen holstered the pistol. The car was gone around the corner before Madsen could make out the license plate. He stood beside the road waiting for the night sounds to reclaim the silence before returning home and back to his hammock.

In the gray predawn light Madsen woke to the smell of distant fires and Grandpa Hem and Cisco chatting.

"It's gonna be hotter than two rats fucking in a wool sock."

"That's a bad word."

"Rat or hot?"

"No, *that* bad word."

"Which one?"

"I can't say it, you know."

Slitting his eyes, Madsen could see their backs as they walked way. He waited until they disappeared into the barn before sitting up. For the last five hours he had drifted between sleep and wakefulness, listening for any out of place sounds. Finding his cell, he located the number he needed in his history and called it.

"Who the mother-fuck is this?" Kazim asked, his voice slurred with sleep.

"Nice way to greet your partner. You kiss your mother with that mouth?"

"She's dead, so no. Do you sleep?"

"Not much. I need you to check something out for me. I was tailed by a big middle-aged white guy in a murdered-out Dodge Charger."

"Murdered, *what*?"

"Blacked out, de-chromed. Late model."

"Hold on..." Kazim sat up, found a pad. "License number?"

"Don't know, plate light was off."

"Then...?"

"The whole thing vibed cop. Sniff around see if you can find out if Fong or anyone else put a tail on me." Madsen also gave him the Monte Carlo's description, "Could be owned by a vetrano, first name Rafael."

"A low rider, driven by a Latino named Rafael? That narrows it down to a hundred thousand, give or take a few."

"He's connected to Cisco, start with known members of La Colina 13." Over the cell Madsen heard a muffled female voice. "Are you in bed with a woman?"

"My wife, she wants me to suggest you buy a watch so you can tell when it's an appropriate time to call a co-worker's home. Her words."

"A ball buster huh? I like her already." Madsen hung up and climbed out of the hammock.

In the living room, he found Adair snoring on the couch. *Coffee*, his brain screamed for it. He set a kettle on the stove, took the coffee

105

pot and filter holder out of the sink and washed them. Searching the cabinet, he discovered zero filters. On the shopping list by the fridge he added filters. Paper towels weren't ideal, but he filled one with Folgers and poured hot water in anyway.

"Mmm, that smells good." Adair sat up, looking rumpled in a causal good way.

"Cream, sugar?" Madsen filled two mugs.

"Black's fine, thank you." She shut her eyes tight, and opened them looking out the front window. "What time is it?"

"Early." Madsen checked his wrist watch. "Five twenty-two."

"Yes, that definitely *is* early." Adair took a swallow of coffee, made a face and picked a couple of grounds off her tongue. "Umm, chunky."

"There's a Starbucks five-and-a-half miles that way." Madsen pointed out the front door. "If you fancy a morning stroll."

"No need, I like it chunky, added roughage's always a good thing." Her smile wasn't met by the same from Madsen. "Niels, did I do something wrong?"

"No ma'am." He drank his coffee looking past her.

"You're sure we're okay?"

"Right as rain."

"Are you angry because I didn't...?" She waggled her eyebrows at him playfully.

"We met yesterday, I'm not sure you're my type."

"You have a type other than female and available?"

"Yes. And what gave you that idea?"

"You are a man."

"Ouch." Madsen pulled an invisible arrow from his heart. "My requirements are simple: she must be pretty, smart, funny, worldly without being snotty."

"Is that all?"

Madsen spoke as he walked out of the living room. "She must be supportive, but not clingy, well read, sexy but not...." Closing the bathroom door he mumbled the last words. He dropped his clothes into a hamper and stepped into the shower. With no hot added the water came out tepid. Not refreshing but it did the job of washing off the previous day's stink.

Madsen was pulling on a pair of jeans when Cisco bumped through the door into Madsen's bedroom. "Whoa, Cisco, I'm getting dressed."

"I know. It's okay Tricky, we're both boys."

"Point." Madsen pulled on his boots and a loose fitting short-sleeved western shirt. He clipped on his belt holster and pulled his shirt over the pistol.

"You going to shoot someone, Tricky?"

"Not planning to."

"Then why do you need it?"

"In case."

"In case you have to shoot someone?"

"Yeah, I guess." He watched Cisco who was pulling underwear, socks and comic books out of his backpack and not finding what he was looking for. "Can I help you, Bud?"

"I forgot." He pointed to a brown stain on his tee shirt. "Always pack a clean shirt. Always."

"How did you...?"

"I guess I don't like coffee. It happens." He shrugged.

"No big thing." Madsen reached into his closet. "This should work." He held out a red Hawaiian shirt decorated with hibiscus flowers.

"That's ugly."

"There's nothing wrong with it."

"Then *you* wear it." Cisco was smiling.

"Okay, how's this?" Madsen pulled out a short-sleeved western shirt like the one he was wearing.

"That looks good." Cisco pulled off his t-shit exposing several long, ragged scars across his back and belly. Dropping the western shirt over his head, he looked in the mirror and grinned. "We're both cowboys

107

now, right?"

"I thought I was a horse-boy."

"Grandpa Hem said that wasn't right. Said you don't need cows to be a cowboy. True?"

"If Grandpa Hem said it, it's true."

"So it is hotter than two rats-—

"Hold on there, Bud, true don't mean you need to repeat it."

"I know." Cisco's serious expression broke into a grin. "Got you."

"Yes, yes you did."

While Cisco was in the bathroom, Madsen stood in the hall watching Grandpa Hem in his La-Z-Boy drinking coffee and talking to Adair. Pushing seventy-six, he was all bone, sinew and attitude. Whiskey and time left his nose bulbous and bloodshot. Niels had no memories of a life before he had come to live with his paternal grandfather. He had never asked Grandpa Hem what it had been like for him, at first because he was a kid and not fully aware that adults have feelings, and later because men didn't talk about those things. With one swat of God's left hand Grandpa Hem lost his wife, son, and daughter in-law. He never let the grief spill onto Niels' childhood. He stuffed it down into that steamer sized lockbox in his chest and kept moving forward, knocking out the bills and caring the best he knew how to for his grandson. When the pain tried to pull a Houdini, he'd tamp it down with Lone Star and Cuervo. Niels had many memories of helping the old man off the floor and into bed, but not one of him crying. "Carry your own water, do your duty, laugh when you can and sleep when you die. That, my boy, is the Texan way." Niels remembered Grandpa Hem telling him.

"You screwing my grandson?" Grandpa Hem asked Adair.

"What?"

"You and him, are you doing the horizontal bop?"

"We just met."

"Okay. I ever tell you about the time Chief Gates took a date to a drug raid?"

"I don't think so." Adair wasn't thrown by non sequiturs, she spoke crazy fluently.

"Old rod up his ass took Nancy Reagan to a crack house bust. Hot Lips Houlihan herself. She primped and preened, cooing over the chief like he was sex on a stick. A photo op, that's what it was. Horse shit. Chief Parker would have puked up a cat, had he been around to see that. Parker was a real cop, you know? After witnessing the sideshow Gates called Operation Hammer…I almost quit. Lutz convinced me to put in for homicide." Grandpa Hem was partly telling the story, and partly reliving it. "Lutz, he was my partner, good man. Had a pretty little Mexican wife. What happened to Lutz?"

Adair was about to speak when Madsen stepped in, "He died in '98."

"Hell yes he did. Think I'd forget my partner died?"

"Didn't say that. Want some eggs?"

"That'd be good. We have any fat back?"

"I'll see." When Madsen stepped into the kitchen, Grandpa Hem turned to Adair, as if seeing her for the first time.

"Well, aren't you a pretty little thing. You dating my Niels?"

"Not yet, no."

"Playing hard to get, huh? Smart move. Harder the chase the better that rabbit tastes."

Madsen groaned. Maybe this was why he never brought women home. He broke two eggs into a frying pan greased with bacon fat. The sizzling drowned out whatever Grandpa Hem said next. He pushed two pieces of wheat bread into the toaster. Cisco walked in, drying his hands on his pants, looked at what was cooking and his face dropped.

"You said pancakes. Not eggs. Pancakes."

"I don't have pancakes, you want eggs?"

109

"No. Tricky, a promise is a promise. And you said syrup."

"You remember that easy enough, but you don't remember what happened to David?"

"I'm hungry. I don't think too good when I'm hungry."

"Don't play me."

"I'm not. Pancakes were *your* plan."

"Enough about pancakes." Madsen felt his blood rising. He took a calming breath before continuing. "I'll find you pancakes after we talk about David."

"Nope, not smart." Cisco wagged his finger. "I thought you were smart, Tricky."

"Please, Cisco, just give it a shot."

"I hate shots."

"No, it's an expression."

"It's silly. Pancakes, please."

Madsen knew it was pointless to continue any questioning. Cisco was mostly charming and funny, but his single mindedness could be irritating. The deputies had one opinion of him, his caregivers had an opposite one. Madsen needed to talk to someone on neither side.

While Cisco and Adair were in the front yard Madsen hunched down beside his grandfather. "Hem, you know anyone who worked Pelican Bay in the mid 80s 90s?"

"Yes, sure do." Hem cocked his head trying to remember. Worry drifted off his face momentarily then was replaced by a pleasant smile. "Did you say something, Niels?"

"Not important, Grandpa. I'm heading out, have a good day."

"Well, I will. I think your mother made a pie." Hem sniffed the air smelling a phantom pie baking. "Cherry, I do believe."

"You know I love cherry pie." Madsen kissed Hem on the forehead and stepped into the building heat of the day.

Chapter 11

Pat and Lorraine's coffee shop was famous for two things: Tarantino shot some scenes there in *Reservoir Dogs*, and for being the best mixture of diner Americana and authentic Mexican meals in LA Madsen parked in the back, hiding the pickup behind a jacked-up SUV. No cars followed them—none he saw—didn't mean they weren't there.

Holding the door open, Madsen graciously motioned for Cisco and Adair to enter. The air was rich with grease and peppers. "Smell that Cisco? They make some huevos rancheros good enough to make a grown man cry."

Cisco squinted, Eastwood style, "You said pancakes."

"Yes I did." He turned to Adair, "Nothing wrong with his memory when it comes to breakfast."

"That..tht-hat's because…" Cisco searched for a reason.

"Because breakfast is the most important meal of the day." Adair stepped up to rescue Cisco.

Before Madsen could push for more about Cisco's memory, the hostess arrived. Her nametag announced her as Sofia, a soft name for a hard woman. She had white hair, deep wrinkles and an ample bosom spilling out of her white shirt. Her stern face transformed into a smile when she saw Madsen.

"Niels, come here." She took his face in her hands and standing on tip-toes she planted a kiss on his lips. Madsen wasn't a casual hugger let

111

alone a lip kisser, but he knew better than to pull back. Releasing him, she appraised his companions. "These two work or friends?"

"Friends." Cisco beamed his infectious smile. Apparently, Sofia had been inoculated, she fixed Cisco with a hard look. "You don't scare me." He told her.

"No? Why not?" Sofia asked.

"Tricky likes you. He doesn't like bad people."

"Tricky?" Sofia looked to Madsen.

"Long story."

"It fits, though, eh, Niels?" Seating them at a four-top she asked about Hem, the sparkle in her eyes spoke of more than friendship.

"Hem's tough enough for any ten men. Riding, roping and living the good life." Madsen lied.

"You tell him I'm keeping a special piece of cherry pie for him. And to get down here, we miss him."

Cisco almost squealed when a small tower of pancakes was set down for him. Next came a plate of bacon and a glass of orange juice. Closing his eyes, Cisco bowed his head. "Bless this food, that I am about to eat, thanks Lord." Crossing himself he opened his eyes and enthusiastically attacked his meal.

Adair lifted a sloppy fork full of huevos rancheros into her mouth. She gasped as the flavors struck her tongue.

"Good, right?" Madsen asked.

"I lack the superlatives to express how good."

"Better than haggis?"

"Ignorant man. Only those who haven't been initiated to true highland haggis make jokes about it." She took another healthy bite. Madsen started to ask her another question, but a cocked eyebrow told him to let her eat.

Madsen only ordered coffee, but that didn't stop Sofia from setting a pan dulce cuernos in front of him. Nibbling at the sweet bread he tried to ask Cisco questions, but it was a no go until he cleaned his plate. Multitasking was not Cisco's strong suit.

After the last bite, Cisco sat back, rubbing his belly with satisfaction. A loud burp escaped his mouth. He looked as surprised as anyone by the sound. His smile turned to embarrassment. He covered his mouth and spoke through his hand, "Sorry. That was not good. Lilly says burps are gross."

"True, they are not polite." Adair stiffened her back, sitting up like a proper lady. "One should never—" She cut herself off with a bullfrog deep wail of a burp. It went on for a full three seconds. "That was a seven-point-five. With extra points for depth and breadth."

"You two are a couple of damn hobos," Madsen scowled, "Here I take you to a nice restaurant and you—" A burp rumbled out of him. What it lacked in duration it made up for in pure bass tone. Sofia stood above them, scowling eyes flicking from one to the other. All three held their breath until she dropped a check on the table and walked away. Only then did the laughs burst free.

"Cisco, you full?" Madsen looked at the empty plate.

"Full, yes."

"Good. Adair?"

"Yes, thank you, those were fine huevos rancheros."

"Huevos is eggs." Cisco informed her.

"That's right, you are a very smart man." Cisco beamed under her compliment.

Madsen stared at Cisco until he felt the gaze and turned to look at Madsen, "What?"

"We need to talk, and I need you to tell me the truth."

"Okay, Tricky. But, um, you look upset."

"I'm not. I'm worried, this is serious business. Right?"

"Right." Cisco started to fidget. Adair took his hand gently stroking it.

"Ok Bud, you remember the gun you had at the bus stop?"

Cisco's face clouded over. "That was scary."

"Did you fire the gun you had at the bus stop?"

"No...no." Cisco shook his head.

"Are you sure? You don't look sure."

"I'm not. I don't think I did."

"Where did you get the gun?"

"I don't...was it on the ground?"

"You tell me."

"Maybe...maybe it was by David. Maybe I didn't want anyone to find it. Guns hurt people."

"Yes, they do." Madsen kept his tone calm and passive. "Who shot David?"

Cisco dragged a fork tine in the syrupy residue on his plate, studying the patterns as if the answers might be there.

"Did you see who shot David?"

"I think...I don't remember. You angry, Tricky?"

"A little bit, yeah."

"Me too. I'm angry at me." Cisco sat up. "Wait. I remember a mustache and yelling. Spitting." He slumped over, out of steam.

"Where? Was this at the bus stop?"

"I...don't...maybe...or..."

"A mustache? Who had a mustache?" Madsen's intensity was ramping as adrenaline hit his system.

"I don't, I'm not sure."

"Think hard. Anything will help."

Cisco screwed up his face and tapped his temple with his finger. He squeezed his eyes closed. After a moment he opened them, relaxing his face. "Sorry, Tricky."

Madsen took a deep breath, consciously slowing his pulse. "It's cool, Bud. No problemo. You want some more O.J.?"

"Lots of sugar in O.J."

"Yes there is. Water?"

"I don't want to have to pee. They have a bathroom, right?"

114

"You need to go?"

"No. It's good to know, case I need it. Right?"

"Sure is." Madsen smiled lazily. "Here's a question, one that's been bothering me, why didn't you drop the gun when Officer Russo asked you to?" Nonchalant, no pressure. "I mean you didn't do anything wrong, so why not drop the gun?"

"I don't want to be dead." Cisco looked away from Madsen and back to the lines his fork was making in the syrup.

"You knew he was a police officer?"

"Police shoot people."

"Bad people, they shoot bad people. Are you bad?" Madsen's tension was back, floating just under his skin. "Are you?"

"I-I-I…" Cisco stammered, searching for a way through Madsen's emotional minefield.

"You don't have to answer that, Cisco." Adair's voice was calm and reassuring.

Cisco looked up at Madsen, his eyes filling with tears. "I'm a good man."

"So you keep saying." Madsen took the bill to the cash register and paid it. He kept his back to Cisco, letting his frustration dissipate. If Cisco was faking, Madsen knew he'd need to keep the pressure up. If Cisco actually had brain damage, well then, Madsen was a total asshole.

While Cisco used the restroom, Madsen stepped into the parking lot and called Kazim's cell. The young detective picked up on the second ring, "Hello, Mom, can't talk, I'm at work."

"I must be in a bag of trouble. Deputy Chief there?"

"Yes, I know. Sometimes it's best to leave Dad alone. Let him cool down."

"Got it. I'm going radio silent."

"Ok, Mom, I'll call when I get a break."

Clicking off his phone, Madsen turned in a slow 360. He wasn't sure what he was looking for, but something felt off, violence seemed to lurk just beyond his peripheral vision.

The plan was to retrace Cisco's day. See if they could jog his memory. It had been Adair's idea, Cisco's memory was better when given context. Madsen didn't know about that, but maybe he could build a timeline leading up to the shooting that would either clear or sink Cisco.

"Seatbelt, Bud." Madsen said when they climbed into the truck.

"I know the rule." Cisco said, then creased his forehead with a thought, "How come they don't have seatbelts on the bus?"

"Good question, I don't know."

"Me neither." Cisco shook his head, he looked to Adair but her full attention was on her phone as she texted her office.

Interrogations were like taking a fighting fish with too light a line, you gave them room to move while slowly pulling them closer to the gaff. "I met your girlfriend last night."

"Who?"

"Lilly, she's cute." Madsen kept it easy breezy.

"She's not my girlfriend." Cisco was smiling bashfully.

"You sure? You're blushing."

"No, I'm not."

"You kind of are." Adair said, looking up from her phone.

"Not."

"Play it any way you want, Bud, I was just saying she seems like a nice girl."

"She is."

"All right, then." Madsen winked at Cisco.

"Change of plans." Adair told them she needed to pick up her car from the station parking lot. One of her clients went off her meds and tore up the cereal aisle of a Super A Market. Adair needed to check in on her, make sure the doctors and nurses in the psych ward had her most recent records, make sure they were treating her with dignity. That they knew someone on the outside was watching. On her medication, the woman was rational, kind, and easygoing. She said the meds dulled her feelings, her creative urges. She was a TV writer who at twenty-six developed schizoaffective disorder. She went from living in a house in the Hollywood Hills to a mental hospital, to a studio apartment in Glendale. She'd had seven good months on the meds—now this.

Madsen was glad to have time alone with Cisco. He promised Adair they were only getting background, and he understood anything said without her present was inadmissible.

As they neared the station Cisco's breath came hard and fast. "You taking me to the angry room?" He was panicking. "I'll be good."

"I'm not taking you there."

"Promise, Tricky? Promise."

"I promise."

Cisco slowed his breathing. "Good. I don't like it there."

Madsen passed the parking lot once, scanning, then around the block before pulling in. If anyone was looking for him, this would be a logical place for a stakeout.

Adair got out, then leaned back in the open door. "Take care of him."

"I will." Cisco said, he hadn't seen she was speaking to Madsen.

"Yeah, he will. Now go." Madsen said.

Adair walked across the lot, heat waves dancing around her. Madsen waited while she climbed into her older Honda Civic, blue paint fading to white on the roof and hood.

Madsen followed her for several miles until he was sure she was wasn't being tailed. He peeled off when she merged onto the freeway.

"Tricky, you know Dora the Explorer?" Cisco asked as they drove back towards Eagle Rock.

"Don't think so. Who is she?"

"A show. Nickelodeon. Hello."

117

"Any good?"

"She travels. Okay, easy one, do you know SpongeBob?"

"A cartoon, right."

"Good job, Tricky. Patrick the Starfish is his best friend. I don't have a best friend anymore. I was thinking. You have a best friend?"

"My grandpa, I guess." Madsen's eyes flicked to the rearview mirror. No one followed them.

"He's a grandpa, not a best friend."

"Yeah, you're right."

"David died."

"That's true, too."

"Maybe we could be best friends. Right, Tricky?"

"I don't know, Bud. We'll see." Madsen was only half-listening, thinking he saw a Dodge behind them. Cisco mimicked Madsen, looking out the window, then out the mirror, back out the window. Madsen looked at him. Then looked back out. Cisco copied him again.

"What are we doing?" Cisco asked.

"Making sure we aren't followed." In the rearview mirror the Dodge turned out to be a black Camaro.

"Oh. The green car is following us."

Madsen clocked a green Fiat Spider with its top down. The driver, a young man with slicked hair and a lumberjack's beard. "I think he's just going the same direction as us."

"Okay." Cisco stopped looking around and thought deeply. After a moment he spoke, "Is Adair your girlfriend?"

"No, she's not."

"You don't like her?"

"Like her just fine."

"Do you have a girlfriend?"

"Nope."

"That's something else we have in common, right Tricky?"

"Right, Bud."

Chapter 12

Eagle Rock Plaza was years past its prime. Built too early to get in on the mixed use, outdoor small town park setting style that attracted modern shoppers. Chain stores defected leaving knock-offs. Target moved in and became the anchor that kept the mall from drifting away. A Filipino market on the lower level added a constant fish smell to the air. "We went to Tar-jay." Cisco said, "Took the bus..." He was remembering or guessing. Hard to tell.

"What did you buy?" Madsen asked as they entered the megastore.

"Nothing. I can't always buy something. I'm not rich."

"Did David buy anything?"

"No..." Cisco searched, looking for the ghost traces of himself and David. "Yes. Not here." He led Madsen out into the greater mall. Passing an arcade, his body moved forward but his head pivoted to keep his eyes on the games and flashing lights.

"Whoa." Madsen put a hand on Cisco's shoulder. "Did you go in there?"

"No...I don't think..." Cisco moved into the arcade. "Do you like air hockey?" As if by suction he was drawn to a neon-green air hockey table. A woman in her early twenties stepped out from behind the cash register. She had blonde dreadlocks and was wearing denim overalls with a big pot leaf embroidered on the front. Out of a white wife-beater,

119

a tattooed dragon climbed up and over her shoulder.

"We're just looking around." Madsen said.

"Hey, Cisco, five-o bothering you?" She had a slight Texas accent.

"Hey, Serenity. Tricky is my friend. He's okay."

She looked Madsen up and down, undecided how she felt about him. "Table's yours Cisco. Show us how you do it."

"You want to play?" Madsen asked Cisco, when he nodded, Madsen held a ten dollar bill up to the girl, "Change?"

"No. The air hockey wizard slides for free." She used a passkey to turn on the table. It hummed to life lifting the paddles onto a bed of compressed air.

"Come on, Tricky, it's easy." Cisco leaned over one of the goals, bouncing the paddle between his hands.

"Just a second, Bud." Madsen turned to Serenity. "Was Cisco or his friend David in yesterday?"

"Come on five-o. He wants to slide." She motioned to Cisco, who was staring intently down at the game top. "You beat Cisco, I'll answer your question."

"It's easy, Tricky. Don't let the puck into your goal. You can do it." Cisco took a puck from the return and set it a few feet from his goal.

Madsen shrugged, took the paddle up and moved it on the air in front of his goal. Cisco slammed into the puck and sent it flying down the table. It banked off the left wall, sailed past Madsen's hand and sunk into his goal with a satisfying thunk. The score board lit up. Cisco grinned broadly, setting the puck back down he sent it speeding across the table. This time Madsen was able to block it, sending it back to Cisco who sliced the side of it. It spun wildly past Madsen's hand and into the goal.

"Tricky, you're supposed to keep it out of the goal."

"I'm trying."

"Maybe try harder." Cisco laughed gleefully and sunk another puck.

Madsen started out playing easy, letting Cisco win a few goals. Now, down three, he tried to block, but another puck sailed past him. And another. And another. Madsen's competitive side took over. No way was Cisco going to take him down without a fight. He swung wildly, driving the puck back to Cisco. The volleyed puck moved faster and faster, clacking loudly as it struck their paddles. Cisco feinted left then struck it right. It bounced off the wall and almost took flight. Slamming into Madsen's goal the scoreboard buzzed and flashed its red and blue lights, declaring Cisco the champion. 7-0. Cisco was beaming.

"The reigning champ!" Serenity took Cisco's hand and raised it over his head. "Way to sling 'em, wizard."

"I've been hustled." Madsen wiped sweat off his forehead with his bandanna.

Cisco bounced on the balls of his feet. It was the most lighthearted Madsen had seen him. They were in a bubble—tragedy, death, and threats of prison lay outside the door. For a moment, amongst the beeps and clangs of the arcade they were just a couple of guys having a good time.

Madsen asked Cisco if he wanted to play a different game, whack-a-mole, skee-ball, pinball. Without thinking he pointed out a shooter game called *Armed and Dangerous.* Cisco shook his head, air hockey was his game. Madsen agreed to play another round if Cisco took it easy on him. Cisco said he would, but as soon at the puck started moving he couldn't help himself. He sunk goal after goal. Madsen finally drove the puck past Cisco's paddle and into the goal. He did a small tight armed victory dance.

"Go crazy five-o." Serenity let out a laugh.

They played two more games. Cisco won 7-2 and 7-3. Madsen was getting incrementally better. Cisco was a star. It was as if his muscles knew what to do and his mind was just along for the ride. They were both sweaty and thirsty. Madsen headed for a soda machine, but was stopped by Cisco's shaking head.

"Water or juice, Tricky. Soda, no. It's the rule."

"Thanks for reminding me."

"That's what friends do. They remind the other guy of stuff."

"Yes, they do."

Serenity brought them plastic cups of water from a Sparkletts machine in the back room. Cisco drank his in one long steady gulp.

"Thanks." Madsen took a drink.

"You're alright five-o."

"Though I didn't win, or come close, or even have a hope in Hell, do you think you could tell me if Cisco or David were here yesterday?"

"You having memory trouble again, Cisco?" Serenity asked Cisco, without a trace of judgement.

"Yep." Cisco shrugged.

"But you never forget me, right?"

"Serenity, you're my friend, I don't forget friends."

"And that's what counts." She looked at Madsen and shook her head. "Cisco was here waiting when I opened the door, nine-thirty-ish."

"And David?"

"Nope, he was a no show all day."

"But you're sure Cisco was here?"

"Absatively. Days Cisco comes by are gold star days. Right, wizard?"

"Right, gold star." Serenity kissed Cisco on the cheek. He looked flustered, but happy.

"How long did Cisco stay?"

"That is, was, umm." Serenity thought a moment. "Tyrell from BMI was here fixing the Moto GP…umm, nope I didn't see Cisco leave. Sorry."

They walked the entire mall without discovering any memories. "Sorry, Tricky." Cisco said clicking on his seatbelt.

"That's okay, Bud."

"It happens." Cisco gave his signature shrug. "Tricky, can I ask you something?"

"Shoot."

"Why do you call me Bud? You forget my name is Cisco?"

"I remember. You want me to stop?"

"No, I don't mind."

"Alright then, Bud, that's decided." Before merging with the traffic on Colorado Blvd, Madsen looked both ways. Not seeing a murdered-out Dodge or a low rider he pulled confidently out.

"You and David been friends a long while." It was time to attack this from another direction, slide up on Cisco instead of full frontal on his memory.

"Yeah…" Cisco scrunched his brow. "Forever, I think. Or a year. Time is weird, right?"

"Can be." Madsen felt himself slipping down the rabbit hole. Grasping, he pulled back. "Did David have a girlfriend?"

"No." Cisco rolled his eyes at what was clearly the stupidest question ever.

"You have a girlfriend, why not David?"

"First, no I don't, remember? Second, David's gay."

"Really?" Madsen kept it flat, hiding the surprise, "Who's his boyfriend?"

"Doesn't have one."

"But he's gay?"

"You don't have to be gay *with* someone to be gay, come on Tricky, everybody knows that."

Madsen did know it. Sort of. Lately he wasn't sure what he knew. A couple months back he'd arrested a transgender gay man, "How's that work?" he'd said to Mauk. "She's into men. She has the correct equipment for sex with men. She turns into a man, but still wants to be with men. Seems like a lot of work just to get back to where she started."

"For a smart man, sometimes." She shook her head. "For starters, she's a *he*. Affectional orientation, who we want to be with, isn't the same as gender identification, who we *are*. You look confused, want me to draw a diagram?"

"Might help. No, I get that." He was able to wrap his head around that. Then she threw in the fluid nature of the spectrum of human sexuality.

"It's a continuum with entirely heterosexual on one end and entirely gay on the other. We all move back and forth on that line through our lifetime."

"And in the middle?"

"Bi, I guess."

"Wanting to be with men and women is just greedy, if you ask me." He said with a laugh. Raised by and spending most of his free time with a man born in the 1940s had left some gaps in his sex education. Now this. Why did adding an intellectual disability into the equation throw him off? It shouldn't, but it did. Thinking of a person with Down syndrome having sex was like thinking of a child doing it. The whole business made him queasy.

He was saved from any deeper thoughts on the subject by a call from Hem, who sounded pleasantly excited. "Niels, I remembered, Harry Mapu."

"Great. But, I need a little context here."

"You asked about Pelican Bay?"

"I did."

"Sure did. Harry Mapu. Big Samoan guy. Lives in Santa Clarita with his wife and a herd of rug rats." Hem sounded clear and sure. But Madsen knew odds were Mapu was retired, or dead, or a character on *Dragnet*.

Chapter 13

City Terrace rests in unincorporated East Los Angeles. It was developed in the 1920s by the Leimert family. An early advert for property heralded "moderate building restrictions" as well as "strict race restrictions." This being East Los, that didn't hold. Mexicans had lived there since the formation of Mexico. By the 1950s it was largely populated by wealthy Mexican American musicians and artists. In the 1960s it established itself as a mecca for the exploding Chicano art scene. In the 1970s and 1980s City Terrace was home to many of the epic punk rock backyard parties.

The City Terrace Madsen drove through was in a ground war. Folks with cash were fighting house to house, street to street in their drive to sanitize East LA Flipped homes sold for 650k a block away from addresses no richster would dare walk by. Gentrification, good news for those who took down over a 100k a year and wanted a home with that old East. LA feel. Good news for old time residents who owned their homes, they sold high and retired to the Inland Empire. Bad news for renters. They were screwed. Working class Mexican Americans could no longer afford the part of LA they had always lived in. In barrios dotting the hillsides they had survived Spaniards, Yankee repatriation, developers, gang bangers, and cops. But it was richsters, who dug their graffiti, sugar skulls, and dive bars that would deliver their eviction notices.

Brass filled Ranchero leaked out of The Bueno Borracho onto the slow-moving traffic. "This ringing any bells?" Madsen asked.

"Bells?" Cisco tilted his head out the window, listening. "Nope. No bells."

They were headed for the last known address for Rafael Ortiz AKA Joker, vetrano in La Colina 13 and owner of a bitchin green '71 Monte Carlo. Madsen had gotten the address from Kazim who spoke to Hertzog who spoke to his buddy in the sheriff's gang task force.

Being unincorporated, City Terrace was policed by the Sheriff's Department. Madsen should have reached out to their liaison before entering, but unless they were going to make a bust, most LAPD detectives didn't bother. Jurisdictional battles came down only if there was blame, glory, or funding on the line. Chatting with Rafael Ortiz didn't look like it would ping any of the above.

Cisco searched the streets for familiarity. Colorful murals were splashed across walls and store fronts. Quetzalcoatl, the Aztec snake god, wrapped entirely around one building. Another was painted to look like the wall had cracked and large sad people were coming out of the building. "Have I been here?"

"Sure. You grew up around here."

"I did?"

"Yes, sir, you did."

"I don't think so." Cisco squinted, scratched his scalp, tapped his toe to a rhythm only he heard.

Kazim and Madsen had a two-prong plan for the day. "Look into David Torres, see why in the hell anyone would want him dead. Insurance? He's heir to a tortilla factory? He pissed off the wrong person?"

"Caught a random bullet?" Kazim said without any real hope.

"I don't care if little green men did it, long as we have evidence to prove it."

"Got it. S.O.P. You want me to question Patrolmen Hill and Russo?"

"No. They're cops."

"So they get a pass?" Kazim tried to sound calm. Failed.

"No one gets a pass. But we need to be damn sure before we toss a grenade down that well."

"Yes, of course, I didn't mean to…"

"You did. It's okay. Now we're clear." Madsen then told Kazim he would be with Cisco. "I'll either jog his memory, or catch him in a lie."

"Where do I tell the Deputy Chief you are? She'll ask."

"Tell her I'm in the wind."

"She won't like that."

"Then make some shit up."

"She's pissed I'm not with you. 'A smart young man should keep his eyes and ears open, if he wants advancement.'" Kazim's impression of Fong was spot-on. "Said your mistakes would reflect on me."

"Wants you to be my handler?"

"More like a babysitter, I think."

"Screw her. She gave me until tonight, I don't have time to hold her hand." Tough talk that Madsen knew meant nothing. Power balance was all on Fong's side. She could burn him if she chose. She was also a decent woman who all things being equal would rather do the right thing. It was up to Madsen to make sure all things were equal.

The twisting hilly roads were easy to get lost in. Madsen had to back up, back track, and mumble obscenities under his breath until he found the street he was looking for, a cul-de-sac with six homes on it. It sat on top of hill, and on a clear day you could see all the way to Torrance. Young Chicano men in chinos, wife beaters and plaid shirts cluttered the porches, curbs and parked cars. With angry nonchalance, they watched Madsen roll past them.

The thrum of glass packs pulled Madsen's attention to the rearview mirror. A primer-gray Grand National stopped in the middle of the street, blocking Madsen's exit. Cisco started to tremble, eyes flitting over the gangsters without rest. Madsen touched Cisco's shoulder, refocusing his attention. "You're safe, I won't let anything happen to you."

"Y-y-you d-d-don't know."

"Don't know what?"

"A-a-a-anything." Cisco clamped his lips shut. His hand white knuckling the door handle.

"Stay here." Madsen said unnecessarily. Stepping down from the Ford he was met by two prison hard gangsters.

"You take a wrong turn, Honkie?" The more sane looking of the two asked.

"Honky? Really? You a *Starsky and Hutch* fan?"

"Who?" Confusion only pissed the man off.

"Nothing." Madsen kept his voice easy.

"Didn't think so." The less sane man had La Colina 13 tattooed across his forehead, and eyeballs on his eyelids, so that even when he blinked his crazy eyes didn't disappear. "Think a badge gonna keep you safe?" He invaded Madsen's space. His breath smelled of beer, pot, and decay. "You not safe."

Madsen used two stiff fingers in an attempt to push the man out of his face. It was like trying to move a granite boulder. "You are one fit son of a bitch." He said with respect. "You got a membership to the Pelican Bay Gym?"

The man grinned, exposing a mess of gold and broken teeth. "Funny guy." The grin fell away. "Why don't I bend you over, ride your joto ass?"

"Go for it." Madsen shrugged, casual. Then in a high-speed magic trick, he pulled the man's attention by slapping his shoulder with his left hand while his right locked onto Crazy's throat. Clamping down he cut off the man's breath.

The saner man pulled a large caliber automatic and aimed it at Madsen's face. The cul-de-sac snapped to attention. Assault rifles, handguns, and cut down shotguns appeared. They surrounded the truck. If they opened fire they would surely kill Madsen and Cisco, they would also hit each other. Not that that seemed to bother them.

Crazy's crazy eyes bulged. He struggled to pry Madsen's fingers off. Madsen held tight. He spoke loud and clearly. "I am here to talk to Rafael Ortiz, just talk. That can happen, or you can shoot me and this whole deali-o goes all helicopters and SWAT teams."

"Shhoot him." Crazy croaked.

"Not today." Rafael Ortiz stepped off the porch of the largest house on the street, and the only one that didn't have any cars parked on its lawn. He wasn't tall or overly muscular, he had no weapon and yet he was clearly the most dangerous person in the cul-de-sac. Stepping up, the younger gangsters parted for him. Looking from Madsen to his grip on Crazy's throat he shook his head. "Why don't you ease up Detective Madsen. Let Casper go."

"Casper? As in the friendly ghost?" Madsen released the man's neck. "One of those ironic names? You don't look too friendly."

Crazy stared fire and hate, his body rigid, read to go off. Rafael raised his palm to Crazy and blew on it like he was spreading ash. He snapped his fingers and the men surrounding them lowered their guns. Crazy said nothing, walking backwards he shot finger pistols at Madsen.

Madsen let his body relax. "Nice street."

"It's ours." Rafael covered his eyes to see past the glare on the truck's windshield. "That you, Primo?" Cisco looked away, like maybe if he couldn't see Joker, then Joker couldn't see him. Madsen just watched as Rafael opened the driver's door and leaned in. "Cisco, we're family, you're safe here."

Cisco looked past Rafael to Madsen. "For true, Tricky, safe?"

"I don't know, Bud." Madsen shifted his gaze. "We got your word Mr. Ortiz? Clean passage?"

"Don't need it, but you got it."

Chapter 14

From the J.F.K. and Jackie commemorative plates to the milky plastic covering the crushed velvet sofa and chair set, Rafael Ortiz's home was a 1970s East Los time capsule, curated and kept spotless by his eighty-six year old mother. She poured iced tea into tall amber colored ripple glass tumblers. Setting one in Cisco's hand, she traced his cheek with equal parts love and concern. "Mi sobrino, te echamos de menos. ¿Por qué te alejaste?"

"¿Te conozco?" Cisco said, confused.

"No hay necesidad de preocuparse. Estás en casa." The old woman kissed Cisco's forehead before fading back into the kitchen.

"Remember your Tía?" Rafael asked. Cisco didn't answer. He looked down, afraid to meet Rafael's eyes. "Primo, I'm the last person you need to fear." Turning on Madsen a glimmer of anger escaped before he covered it. "What you been telling him about me?"

"Don't know anything to tell."

"Good, cool." Rafael's peaceful confidence was back. "Drink up, Primo."

Cisco traced perspiration down the glass, looking to Madsen for permission.

"Go on." Madsen nodded consent.

"Caffeine, not good, makes me jumpy." Cisco's concern rang false.

"You want something stronger? Mezcal, no ice, no glass, no chaser. Right, Primo?" A smirk hid behind Rafael's goatee. "Time was, Cisco took all comers. He was a motherfucking monster, right?"

Cisco looked up confused, then was distracted by movement from outside. White gauze curtains partially obscured the backyard. Every surface was clean cement or whitewashed wood. A sitting man glided gracefully past the window. "Chuy…" Cisco said to himself.

"That's right Primo, Chuy's my boy."

"Can he fly?" Cisco didn't take his eyes off the window.

"Only in his dreams. Come on, say hello." Rafael led them through french doors and back into the heat. Chuy was in his mid-twenties, round and soft from years in a chair.

"Yo Chuy, I know you didn't forget tu primo, Cisco." Rafael slid edge in, silent subtext. If the man in the chair held animosity towards Cisco or the detective he didn't show it. With index finger and thumb he steered over to them.

"Cool chair. You like Star Wars?" Cisco asked.

Chuy tapped a key pad and a computer generated voice said, "Por qué, ése?"

"Lots of people in chairs like Star Wars."

"Verdad?"

"Verdad." Cisco nodded, a broad grin on his face.

Chuy typed and the voice said, "Want to see my race track?"

"Oh, oh, yes. Tricky I'm going to see a race track, okay?"

"Knock yourself out, Bud."

"But then I won't see it." Cisco held a straight face for maybe two seconds then broke into a smile.

Rafael waited until Cisco and his son disappeared into a freestanding garage before speaking, "He under arrest?"

"Not yet. When we rolled up, you knew my name. Have we met?"

"I know miles of things. Word out says you think Cisco killed that boy."

"Word out is wrong." Madsen finished his tea in one long swallow. He turned to face Rafael. "They say you or your baby Gs did that to him." Madsen swirled his finger around his head.

"*They?*" Rafael went glacier.

"They. They also say you were afraid he was going to flip."

"Why? Cisco did eleven hard with his lips tight. He's blood."

"Yet, you've been stalking him. Don't look surprised, I clocked you."

"I saw you seeing me. What? I want to blend, I drive my Prius."

Made sense. Only a wannabe or a poser did a stakeout in a car-show qualifier. The Monte Carlo was a rolling statement of wealth and power. The rims alone were worth more than Madsen's truck. "Say I eat what you're serving, what were you doing there?"

"Families, they are complicated, no?"

"Don't have one."

"Then, Detective, you are a lucky soul. Even when they break your heart, you stand by them." Rafael stroked his beard, deciding what to share. "Cisco was a sweet kid when he went down. La Colina 13, we had no juice. They ate him and spit out the bones. Came out stone cold. That was my jolt he rode. He never said a word. Family."

"You let a kid carry your weight?"

"I was nineteen, he was fourteen. Thought he'd do juvie camp." Rafael was lost looking into the shadows of his past. "Cisco never raised up. His body made it home, not his soul…scary motherfucker."

"Chuy?"

"Yeah, I guess you *are* a detective. Cisco took him on a run. A roll and scare, let rivals know La Colina 13 ain't afraid of boo. No shooting. No killing. Cruise by and home. Someone stepped off, threw a beer bottle at our boy's car. Cisco let rip. Four of them down before he released the trigger."

"Chuy?"

"One shot from a dying man's hand. Through the trunk, back seat and my son's spine." Rafael didn't blame Cisco, or maybe he did but he could live with it. They all made choices with permanent consequences. If Rafael hadn't let Cisco take his fall, maybe he wouldn't have become the kind of man who killed over being disrespected. Maybe Chuy would be running track and chatting up blondes at USC. Permanent consequences.

Whether driven by guilt, gangster code, or family connections, Madsen believed the vetrano when he said he was only there to be sure his cousin wasn't railroaded, "Cops got some shady history around here. Never know what they're willing to do."

Madsen could argue that those days were in the past. That the new LAPD didn't send gang bangers away for a five dollar crack rock while Hollywood actors did community service for a gram of coke. He could argue all that, but he didn't like to lie.

"What happened to Cisco's birth family?" Madsen asked.

"Father pulled a vanishing act when he was young."

"Mother?"

"You'd have to ask her. I haven't talked to her since he went down."

"You have an address?"

"I think she moved to Highland Park, or Cypress Park or some other bullshit park. Don't know and care even less."

"Wanna tell me why the rift, given your views on family?"

"No." A wall around Rafael slammed shut.

"I'm not trying to stitch Cisco up."

"Words. Worth less than the air it took you to make them." Rafael walked toward the garage, making it clear he was done talking to the detective.

From the garage side-door Madsen and Rafael watched as a 1/24 scale '64 Impala raced a '55 Chevy around the slot car track circling the inner wall of the garage. Cisco and Chuy piloted the cars with deep concentration. Rounding the final curve Chuy goosed the power and the Impala's rear kicked out. Its trunk collided with the Chevy and sent it careening off the track. A checkered flag popped up, then the Impala crossed the finish line. Chuy grinned, typing into his tablet. "Eat my shorts."

"No way, sick." Cisco was laughing with an abandon Madsen hadn't witnessed.

"De nuevo pendejo?" Chuy challenged.

"Can I drive the Impala?"

"Estas Loco, Guey! Nobody drives my woman or my short."

"Okay." Cisco looked like he hadn't a clue what that meant. Didn't matter, he ran happily to pick up the fallen Chevy and replace it on the track. Standing up he saw Madsen, his smile dropped. "We have to go, right?"

"That's right, Bud. I'm still on the clock."

Cisco set the car controller on the track. He scrunched down beside Chuy and said, "That was fun…thanks."

Chuy typed, "Next time, maybe I let you win."

"No cheating." Cisco shook his head solemnly.

"You say so." Chuy lifted his hand in a fist. Cisco bumped it, started to leave then had a thought, "Chuy, you play ai -hockey?"

"No."

"I'll teach you." Cisco said with a slightly gleeful smile.

As they were climbing into the truck, Rafael leaned in to Madsen. "La Colina 13 forgets nothing. Fuck this up, you'll watch your grandfather die." His voice was quiet so Cisco wouldn't hear him, and hard so Madsen would be clear it wasn't hyperbole. The threat also imparted that Rafael and his crew knew who mattered to Madsen. What it didn't say, and Madsen was left to interpret was what constituted fucking it up. Did they, as Rafael said, want Cisco cleared? Or did it not

135

really matter as long as it didn't lead back to them?

Turning the pickup around, Madsen discovered their escape still blocked by the Grand National. Casper leaned on the car's hood grinning like a hungry hyena. Madsen's horn tap brought a laugh from the man but no movement. He slipped his pistol from his hip holster and rested it between his legs. "Seatbelt on, Bud?"

"Yes. Safety first, remember?"

"That's right." Madsen moved the transmission into neutral and revved the engine once. It wasn't as menacing a sound as he wished but it got the message across. Casper just kept smiling. Madsen had had enough bullshit for one day. Putting the truck in drive he prepared to take off. Upside to pulling a kamikaze, live or die the human jack-o'-lantern was going to be a smear on the truck's bumper. Downside, dying.

Rafael stepped in front of the truck, slow, like he had an eternity, like the world waited on him. And in this small corner, it did. He gave an almost imperceptible nod. Casper slapped the Grand National's hood and cleared the road. Driving out, Madsen wondered if Rafael had intervened to help them, or to flash his muscle.

Cisco was uncharacteristically silent as they drove out of City Terrace. He traced the assault rifle tattooed on his forearm mouthing "La Colina 13." He scrunched his eyes closed, opened them disappointed to see the tattoo still under his finger. It wasn't until they were on the freeway that he spoke, "Those were scary people. Are they my family like he said?"

"Some are. Some not. You remember any of them?"

"They hurt people, right?"

"Yes, they do. Do you remember anything?"

"Chuy…maybe."

"Anything else?"

Cisco looked out the window. "No." He said quiet as a whisper.

"Yes, you do. I need to know what you remember. All of it."

"I don't." The scars on the back of Cisco's head jumped, he trembled but would not look at Madsen.

"Yes, you do." Madsen whispered.

Chapter 15

By the time Cisco plowed through a Tommy's double chili cheese burger and a pile of greasy fries, Kazim had called with an address for Cisco's mother, Zyanya Gutierrez. Rafael was either wrong, or purposefully trying to obfuscate her address, she lived in neither Highland Park nor Cypress Park but instead was ten minutes from Rafael's block—in Boyle Heights.

East LA was a collection of small towns and neighborhoods, each with a distinct look and feel. Some began as barrios in the days of the Spanish ranchos, others were created by the post-Mexican American war bigotry that drove Mexican Americans out of central Los Angeles, across the LA river and into what became East LA. These origin histories affected the inhabitants, kept them from blending into the monolithic East LA portrayed in films and TV. Because of village tribalism or financial inability or gang boundaries, the result was that many of the residents never left the six blocks that made up their neighborhood. Born and raised eighteen miles from Santa Monica, many had never seen the beach.

"Nope..." Cisco looked up at the three-story brick apartment building. "No bells ringing."

"Your mother move here after you left home?"

"My mother?" Cisco couldn't wrap his head around the idea. "June takes care of me."

"Yes, she does. But she's not your mom. Right?" Madsen spoke soft, not pushing.

"Right, yes...but I don't know about this." Cisco swept his hand to take in the building and street around it. He stopped moving.

"What's up?"

"It's my choice."

"Yes, it is." Madsen nodded thoughtfully. "It will be okay, Bud, I'll stand beside you, the minute you want to split, tell me and we're in the wind. How's that sound?"

"For real, right?"

"For real." Madsen held out his hand and Cisco took it, shaking it once, sealing the deal.

Zyanya Gutierrez looked baffled to find these two strangers in the hall when she opened her door. In her mid-sixties, she had a silver-laced black mane falling down her back. Her eyes locked on Madsen, cold fire. "Police? I don't care what Mr. Gilmore said, I will pay the rent in full after he fixes the kitchen sink."

"Ma'am, we aren't here about the rent. I'm a detective and would like to ask you a few questions. Can we come in?"

"Do you have a warrant?"

"No, ma'am."

"Then, no." She started to close the door but when her gaze shifted from the cop to the tattooed man she froze. Cisco looked openly at her with no sign of recognition.

"Ma'am, you're not in any trouble. I just want to talk to you about your son."

"I have no son." Zyanya's eyes didn't stray from Cisco's face.

"Fransisco Gutierrez isn't your son?"

"Fransisco is dead." She crossed herself. Cisco stared at her, his face starting to fall before her undercurrent of anger and pain. "He died when he was fourteen. They just never put him in the ground."

Cisco turned from her and clung to Madsen's arm. He mumbled and stuttered without coherence. His eyes screamed the message he couldn't find words for.

Madsen worked his jaw. He wanted to explode—and would have if he had been alone. Instead he handed her his card. "Sorry for the... inconvenience." He led Cisco away. Zyanya didn't close the door or take her eyes off Cisco until he disappeared down the stairs.

Leaving the building, Cisco was pale and trembling. Madsen said nothing. He led Cisco down the street to a park bench on the edge of Mariachi Plaza. It was a place musicians came to look for work, or to find bands to play with. An older man with a guitarrón was teaching a much younger man a section of a ballad. A regal gentleman in black gaucho pants trimmed with silver conchos lifted his trumpet and let pure beauty flow free. Cisco's face remained blank, his shoulders hunched. It seemed unlikely he saw or heard the mariachis. A plump older woman pushed a snow cone cart, calling out "Raspa, raspa." Madsen motioned to Cisco, to see if he wanted one. Cisco looked at the woman but didn't respond.

"Really? You're not hungry?" Madsen asked.

"No." Cisco stared off into space.

"You want to talk about it, Bud? Do you remember your mom?"

Cisco looked up at Madsen as if decoding him. "Sh-sh-she hates me. I must be a bad man if my mother hates me.... Right? Bad man."

"No. Fuck her. Really, Bud, fuck her. I don't remember my mother, never did, and I turned out okay."

"You don't? But... You didn't hurt your head, right?" Slowly, Cisco was backing away from the pain.

"No, nothing like that. She died when I was a little kid, so I don't remember her. I have Grandpa Hem though."

"He is not a mother." Cisco patted Madsen's hand. "June is good

140

with things like food and making you not feel sad if you can't sleep. You can borrow her sometimes if you want."

"That sounds like a hell of a plan."

Cisco looked around smiling at the gayly dressed mariachis. "Hey, Tricky?"

"Yeah, Bud?"

"I didn't die, like she said, did I?"

"No way, José."

"Good. That would be weird, right? If I was a ghost."

"Sure would."

"But then I could hang out with David. I'd like that part." He sat back and closed his eyes listening to the music. A peaceful smile gradually returned to his face.

Climbing into the pick-up, Madsen got a call from Holly Torres, "I need to see David, his body. I just..." Her voice drifted off.

"You don't have to explain. I can meet you at coroner's office in forty-five minutes. That work?" She said yes, but sound unsure. She both needed and didn't want physical evidence of her son's death.

Ending the call, Hem found Cisco staring at him.

"Who was you talking to?" Cisco arched his eyebrow raising the bandage.

"David's mom."

"She's a nice lady. Bought me a Slurpee—blue."

"Nice." Madsen asked Cisco to stay in the truck. Stepping onto the sidewalk, he called Adair and was told to leave a message. "Adair, sorry, never mind."

"You're supposed to leave your name." Cisco stood on the sidewalk behind Madsen.

"And you were supposed to stay in the truck."

"Tricky, if you don't leave your name how's she gonna know it was you?"

Madsen started to explain that a caller's number came through with the message, then stopped himself. He need a place to stash Cisco while he went to the morgue. Bridge-Way wasn't secure. If he took him the station Bette Fong could give his case to someone willing to book Cisco and be done with it. As long as Madsen had Cisco, he controlled the case.

"Bud, how'd you like to spend some time with Grandpa Hem?"

"Does he know about medicine?"

"I'll make sure Nat knows."

"Not forever right?"

"Couple hours."

Josh Stallings

Chapter 16

Built in 1912, the gothic red and sand-colored brick building was home to the M.E. administration's offices. It's labs and personnel were used by both LAPD and the Sheriff's Department.

Madsen saw Holly Torres by the front door, she grabbed the door's handle, started to open it, released it, turned away, turned back, stuck in the moment. She jumped when Madsen touched her shoulder. "Who the fuck?" Her arm was cocked.

"Whoa, it's me." Madsen held his hands up, palms facing her.

"Sorry Detective...damn....I'm, well—" Holly eased out of her battle stance. "I don't know how to do any of this."

"No one does." Madsen said.

"No. There aren't practice sessions for the unimaginable." Holly had aged overnight. She clearly hadn't slept. Her eyes were puffy from crying. She was holding it together, but just. Madsen offered her his hand. She shook it. She seemed glad for the formality. A hug might have broken her.

"Before we go in, is it okay if I ask you a couple of questions?"

"Okay." She seemed relieved to not have to enter the building yet.

Finding some shade under a tree, they sat on a retaining wall. Madsen spoke without looking at her. "Have you been able to think of anyone who might want to do David harm?"

143

"No, he was loved. I know all mothers say that, but with him it was true. He wasn't a saint, but he was kind. You know? Really kind."

"You were aware David thought he was gay?"

"*Thought?* From when he was a kid." She let out a laugh at a memory. "We were watching reruns of *Baywatch*—the show not that goofy movie—I noticed he really perked up when Hasselhoff was on screen and couldn't give a shit about Pamela Anderson's bouncing breasts."

"Sounds definitive." Madsen smiled. "Did David have a boyfriend?"

"Sex for him was more conceptual than practical. I hoped one day he might meet someone." The thought brought a tear rolling down her cheek. Madsen waited silently until she found a tissue and dried her eyes. Only then did he speak.

"Did David have any money?"

"Money? No. I mean he had a special needs trust. My father created it for him. But David didn't have access to it."

"Who did?"

"Me. Used it to buy him things SSI wouldn't cover—like pretty much everything."

"Did anyone else have access to the funds?"

"Access? After he moved into Bridge-Way I made June a signer on his account. It was simpler that way." Speaking about the administrivia of running David's life was pulling Holly back from heartbreaking grief.

"How much are we talking about?"

"Excuse me?"

"The trust fund, how much was in it?"

"My father opened it with four hundred thousand dollars. That was ten years ago. I don't know what exactly is left. Most of the principal I'd think."

"You do have oversight, right?"

"I guess, yes. I don't check it very often. I trust June, she's good people."

"With him gone, what happens to the remaining funds?" Madsen was treading lightly.

"I don't know. I'm his only family." She stopped speaking, then shifted gears. "Where are you heading with this?"

"Nowhere, I'm trying to get a complete picture."

"Do I need a lawyer?"

"No."

"I didn't kill my son."

"I can't imagine you did."

"I don't care about money. My father gave it to my son, not me. Now I guess I'll leave it to Bridge-Way, in David's name."

"Your father, David's grandfather, are you close?"

"Oh no. My father was strict Catholic. Old school. When David was born outside the sacrament of marriage I was written off."

"And David? When did your father create his trust fund?"

"After I had him baptized. Father was...accepting of David. But then, he hasn't seen David in years." Her shoulders sank. She looked past Madsen into an unfocused distance.

"Did David need a hearing aid?" Madsen backed out of the emotional mine field.

"He had what they called a profound hearing loss."

"Can you think of a reason he wasn't wearing his on the day he died?"

"He was always forgetting them, nothing more nefarious than that. Is there anything else, before we...."

"One last thing, minor, I was told David had a binder full of money. Does that make any sense to you?"

"No, it doesn't. Ludicrous." Holly sounded nervous. She was covering something. "Whoever said that was completely mistaken."

Madsen was no closer to understanding what happened to David Torres. He'd seen family members kill each other for a lot less than

400k. Was June skimming from the trust fund? Did she kill, or have David killed, to cover up missing money? Did Cisco still have the killer in him, hidden even from himself? Had he shot David and didn't—or couldn't—remember it?

Leading Holly to the Deputy Medical Examiner's office, Madsen was glad to find Clarence Collins had caught the case. Madsen and Collins had come up at the same time. Madsen liked that he was a no-bullshit man of science in a field full of bureaucrats.

Collins laid a photograph of David's face on the desk before Holly. She winced, then nodded. "That's my son, David."

"Thank you for coming down today."

"Where is he? My son, where is he?"

"He is still in an examining room. We should be able to release him to your funeral director tomorrow."

"I want to see him."

"We aren't set up for viewing, best to leave that to the funeral home."

"I don't care what's best. I need to see my son." Her face was frozen and fragile. "Until he moved out last year, he was never out of my sight for more than six hours at a time. Now I'm told I won't ever see him again. No. I need to look at him *today*."

Collins knew the rules, the procedures, but he also knew what was important. There is right and wrong, and then there is the gray area wherein most of life takes place. Madsen and Collins both knew it was also in the gray that most good was done.

Collins had one of the morgue attendants cover David to the neck with a sheet, hiding the incisions and stitches. Madsen held Holly's arm, feeling her stumble as her knees weakened. Straightening up, she pulled away from him and went to her son's side. She brushed his bangs up off his forehead. She whispered words only she could hear. Finally, she kissed her son goodbye and walked out. She thanked Madsen and Collins, told them she was aware they didn't have to do this for her.

"I'll find whoever did this. I won't stop until I do." Madsen said.

"Will that bring my son back?"

"No, but it might bring you some peace."

"It won't." Holly looked at Madsen for a long moment, then turned and walked out into the harsh Los Angeles sunlight.

Madsen followed his friend back towards his office. "Clarence, does forensics have a gun or bullet match yet?"

"You know I was told not to speak to you."

"This is my case. Who would tell you that?"

"Someone with a lot more juice than either of us lowly worker bees."

"You gonna listen to them?"

"Why would I start now? Hang tight." Collins called the lab. He looked concerned when he hung up. "They say they never received the bullets for testing."

"Who sent them up?"

"Me, Niels. Me. I tagged, bagged and sent them up last night." With evidence, chain of custody was everything. If evidence was unaccounted for, for even an hour, it could be kicked out of court as tainted.

"Can you at least tell me if it was a .38?"

Collins opened a file scanning down. "Bullets weighed 124 grains. Their size was consistent with a .38 or a 9mm. That's as close to definitive as I can get."

"As long as you're not sharing info with me, what else don't we know?"

"Two bullets entered the victim's chest less than an inch apart, suggesting they were fired in rapid succession. First shot pierced his heart. No gunshot residue, so it was fired from over five feet. Anything else would be guess work."

"When those bullets turn up, please call me."

"You know I will, long as you promise to forget it was me who

147

called."

"Done. Clarence, when this is over, if either of us still has their job, I'll buy you a beer."

"Keep your head down, Niels."

"Wish I could."

After being in the frozen ME's office, the air outside felt like an oven set on broil. Madsen's pocket vibrated as he crossed into the parking lot. "Is this the Niels Madsen ex-employee of the LAPD?" Fong spoke with a calm coolness that Madsen knew meant real danger. After avoiding four calls from her he knew it was time to take what he had coming.

"Bette—"

"Deputy Chief, Detective."

"Deputy Chief, I just got the word that the ME isn't supposed to talk to me."

"Who said that?"

"The ME. Do you know who put the stink on me?"

"No," Fong adjusted from cold bureaucrat to co-conspirator. "Niels, what did you step in?"

"Gets better, the bullets that killed David Torres are missing." Fong went silent, only her breathing let Madsen know she hadn't hung up. "Bette, what the hell's going on?"

"I'm going to tell you something, if you mention you've heard it, you could end my career. This morning I got an email from Sheriff White inquiring into the Gutierrez case. Said if he was in jail it would be a personal favor to White. And if he was cut loose it would be taken as an affront to the Sheriff's Department."

"What do you want me to do Bette? No shit, jerk the leash and I'll heel."

"Give me something, Niels. Something to hold them off."

"Cisco is starting to remember. Bits and pieces, for now. I think I can get him to recall what happened to David Torres."

"Any chance he's playing you?"

"Always a chance, but I don't think so."

"Officially, if anyone asks, I told you to book him."

"Privately?"

"Find out who killed David Torres, fast." They were about to hang up when Madsen called her name. "What? I need to go lie to the chief of police."

"Is Kazim working for *you*?"

"According to the chain of command you all are."

"Is he spying on me, for you?"

"I asked him to keep an eye on you, report back if you crossed any lines. Standard speech I give all your partners."

"That supposed to make me feel better?"

"Huh, turns out I don't care how it makes you feel Detective." She hung up before he could come up with a smart-ass retort.

Did someone from the Sheriff's Department tamper with evidence? Wouldn't be the first, or even the hundredth time they stepped over the line. The problems were systemic. A previous sheriff and his entire command staff went down under a federal rap. Orders had come down that deputies were to beat and hide an informer who was set to testify about prisoner abuse. They were no-shit, fuck-you-up dangerous. Madsen knew if he was smart he would arrest Cisco, go home and pull the blanket over his head.

He wasn't smart.

Never had been.

Instead, he called Kazim and filled him in on his meeting with La Colina 13, the missing bullets, and the possible depth of their fuckedness with the powers that be.

"So, if we discover the murder is linked to La Colina 13, we're dead?"

"Yep, us and the people we love, well people *I* love, not sure they tied you into the shit storm yet."

"And if the trail leads back to the Sheriff's Department our careers are over."

"Possibly, plus criminal charges if they can make 'em stick. Or they skip all that and we wind up in shallow graves in the desert."

"Any good news?"

"Not a scrap. Kazim, if you want to bail, I'll understand."

"Not in my nature. Have you seen my file?"

"No, I've been busy."

"If you had, you would know that when I see an opportunity to screw up my career, I go for it. Always."

"Consistency is damn admirable." Madsen was starting to like his young partner. Given ten or fifteen years, he might even learn to trust him. He asked Kazim what he had found out so far.

"I got nowhere with David Torres' financials. But the gun that Cisco allegedly shot him with was a Colt Detective Special with gold-plated cylinder, ejector rod, cylinder latch, and high end pearl handle."

"You're losing me, Kazim. Unless this has something to do with solving our case best save it for your gun enthusiasts chatroom."

"What? No, it is germane. The gun is a Bijan Limited Edition. Sold exclusively at House of Bijan on Rodeo Drive. Very rare. Christie's sold one for over fifty grand."

Madsen let out a low whistle. "Not your average pop and drop. Where did Cisco come up with a piece like that?"

"Exactly my question. The guns were numbered one through a hundred. Ours was sold at auction in 2002. And it has never been listed as stolen."

"You going to tell me who bought it, or should I swing by the office and beat it out of you?"

"It's registered to Edward Torres."

"Related to David Torres, how?"

"His grandfather."

Chapter 17

San Marino is a city of wealth equaling Beverly Hills, but the money is older. It rests surrounded by Pasadena, Alhambra, and San Gabriel. City names in Southern California tell the story of the messy, sometimes bloody recent past. San Marino started as a Gabrieleño-Tongva tribal village. The Spanish used monks and muskets to invade and occupy, thus it became part of the Mission San Gabriel Arcángel. After the Mexicans won independence from Spain, they claimed the land from the church and gave it as a land grant to Dona Victoria Bartolomea Reid, creating Rancho Huerta de Cuati. The 1846 Mexican American war delivered a California entirely free from Mexican domination. The dons retained their massive rancheros. In 1873, James DeBarth Shorb renamed Rancho Huerta de Cuati, San Marino after his grandfather's plantation in Maryland that had in turn been named for an Italian Republic.

Madsen looked out the passenger window of the unmarked Ford Interceptor and wondered if the men working the massive hedges and rolling lawns knew that at one time this was all theirs.

"The Torres family owns the local Spanish language newspaper." Kazim reported from behind the steering wheel. "Eduardo Torres dragged them into modern times when he created two Spanish language radio stations and a cable network."

"How rich we talking here? Ferrari and Gucci rich? Private jet rich? They named the university after you because you built it for them rich?"

"I'm going to say Ferrari leaning toward jet, but that's speculation. Zillow valued his home at twelve plus."

"Twelve?"

"Million."

"For a house? Better be one hell of a place to hang a hat."

It was. Two blocks from the Huntington library and gardens. A cobblestone drive fronted the Spanish Revival mansion. Two stories of pale pink stucco, deep set arched windows, wrought-iron scrolled rails, and topped with a rustic terra cotta tile roof. 9,760 feet of old-world opulence.

The woman who answered the door echoed the pueblo and mesas of her ancestors. Her obsidian eyes remembered a time before European invasion. Her starched white uniform made clear that how she felt carried no weight. After seeing the detective's badges she ushered them in to the grand foyer. She instructed them to wait. No chairs. No offer of refreshments. No pleasantries. "Wait here." Curt. Final.

Madsen reflected back at himself in the polished marble floor. Lack of sleep gave him haggard bags and sags. The heat left him drooping. He held his Stetson in his hand. Kazim openly gawked at the room. A wide, dark wood staircase swept to the second floor. It's wrought iron banister had so many graceful spirals and curlicues it was less Spanish and more baroque. Iron and gold were the unifying features of the décor. They had fifteen minutes to study all this before the housekeeper returned. "Mr. Torres will see you now." She turned, not waiting for— or expecting—a response, and led them deeper into the house.

Torres' office overlooked a brilliant green lawn that defied any notion of summer or drought. It stretched around an Olympic-sized swimming pool, past a rose garden and ended at a red clay tennis court. Torres was an elegant seventy, salt and pepper capping a fit form. When the detectives entered, he held up one finger, his attention focused on a file on his desk. They waited again, five minutes this time, while he finished reading.

"Have you discovered why my grandson was murdered?"

No hello. No nice to meet you.

"Good looking spread you got here." Madsen laid the drawl on thick and wide.

"I asked you a simple question."

"Yes, sir, you did."

"I am accustomed to being answered."

"I'm sure you are." Madsen lifted a gold letter opener off the desk, examining it while he spoke. "Problem is, see, that's not the way this works. Do you own a Colt Detective Model serial number..." he looked to Kazim.

"Bee jay zero one seven." Kazim read from his note book.

"As you can see, I own many things. More than I can keep track of."

"This was a special gun, gold over black blue steel. Some might call it tacky, or pimped-out." Madsen looked around the room with undisguised derision. "It would fit in here perfectly."

Torres turned from them, tapped an intercom twice. "Jill, please get the mayor on the phone."

"Santori?" A tinny female voice said.

"No, of Los Angeles. The mayor of Los Angles, not San Marino." Torres kept his back to the detectives while he waited.

"He's not in sir, shall I have him call back?"

"Yes. Of course have him call back." He clicked off, dismissing her without a word. Turning back, he gave Madsen a triumphant yet condescending smile. "Do you have information for me, or shall I get it from the mayor?"

"We seem to have gotten off to a bad start." Madsen snapped his hand down burying the tip of the letter opener in Torres' burl desk top. He followed it with a set of handcuffs that he placed on the desk with enough force to scratch the finish. "I don't give two shakes of a parakeet's tiny testicles who you know. You can talk to us here, or in the box, don't matter, 'cause you *will* talk to us."

Eduardo Torres had one more arrow in his quiver. The "I'm going to call my oh so important shark lawyer and you will tremble before his mighty sword of justice" maneuver. Madsen didn't blink. Told the multimillionaire to have his attorney meet them at the station. It took Madsen getting out the handcuffs and starting around the desk for Torres to finally get that this hick cop would not be cowed. Raising his hands, he first tried to play it off as a joke, then gave a weak apology, "I am so angry about what happened to my grandson. Not an excuse, but it's true."

"Understood. No hard feelings. We're here to find out who killed David, plain and simple." Madsen didn't feel the need to point out that the moment someone says something is 'not an excuse,' it surely is one. "The Colt?"

"House of Bijan limited edition?" Kazim added.

"Yes. Yes. The Bijan, a great example of 1990s extreme. What has it got to do with Davey's murder?"

"Is it in your possession?" Madsen asked, ignoring Torres' question.

"Of course. But you still haven't—"

"May we see it?" Madsen knew the trick with bullies was to yield them no ground on which to fight, without being aggressive.

Judging from the vault-like door and thumbprint scan lock the trophy room could easily do double duty as a safe room for Torres and a dozen of his close friends. It was a large, comfortable windowless room, more library or private museum than strongbox. Leather club chairs and a sofa circled an oak coffee table. Velvet-topped display tables showed off antique firearms, gems, Spanish doubloons, Roman, and Greek coins. The wall held bookshelves full of rare books. All of it meant to impress visitors into submission. Whatever you might be trying to sell, Torres already had two of them.

On a table groaning with handguns, arranged historically from matchlock to laser-sighted FN Five-Seven, Torres found the Baccarat case the Colt originally came in. Opening the lid, he lifted out a mink pouch, he seemed shocked to find it empty. He stared again at the case as if enough attention might make the revolver reappear. "It's missing. It was…."

Kazim stepped forward, giving Madsen a chance to browse the room. "When was the last time you saw the gun?"

Torres looked from Kazim's face to Madsen's and back, "What was the question?"

"Last time you saw the Bijan Colt?"

"I don't…. Odd thing, and I should have noticed, I kept the case open, Colt on the fur. It really is a lovely gun."

"Who has access to this room?"

"No one."

"The housekeeper?"

"No. Only my fingerprint opens the door."

From across the room Madsen lifted a leather-bound binder off a bookshelf. Plastic sleeves held mint condition rare coins. "Did your grandson collect coins?"

"I don't…yes, not valuable ones. I give him state quarters, circulated buffalo nickels. Why?"

"Do you know Francisco Gutierrez?" Kazim asked.

"Who?" Torres was getting flustered.

"Cisco Gutierrez," Madsen called from across the room. "Does he work for you?"

"No, I'm…Roberto Betto would know, he oversees daily operations."

"We'll give him a call." Madsen said, never intending to. "Did you see your grandson often?"

"Sundays I was in town. I would take him to church, and then he'd spend the afternoon here with me."

"Really?" Madsen rubbed his chin slowly. "Why do you think your daughter is under the impression you haven't seen him for a long time?"

"I have no idea. You'll have to ask Holly."

Kazim snapped his fingers to get the older man's attention. "You wrote an op-ed piece threatening to leave the Catholic church if Pope Francis didn't harden his stance on the LGBTQ community."

"Is that a question?"

"No. A fact. I wondered if it is your true belief or public posturing?"

"Are you a Catholic, Detective....?"

"Kazim, and no I'm not."

"Then you've no reason to care what I think of papal positions."

"David did." Madsen crossed the room, watching Torres for a reaction. "Did you know your grandson was gay?"

"Don't be absurd. My grandson was retarded."

"And gay."

"He wasn't. You've been speaking to my daughter." Torres was starting to turn red in the face. "Gay is a set of aberrant external activities. End of subject. No one is gay in their soul. No one is *born* gay."

Kazim read coolly from his notes. "You support ending same sex marriage with both large sums of money and editorial space."

"Marriage is a sacrament between a man and a woman, who God commands to be fertile and multiply. God's law stands above not beside the laws of man."

"Is that why Holly said she hasn't got any family?" Madsen said.

"I don't know what—"

"You're still the president of the Council for Decency, right?" Kazim said.

"Isn't that something," Madsen let out a lazy whistle. "Bet they'd run you out on a rail, they found out you had a gay grandson."

"He's not—" the veins in Torres' temples throbbed.

"-Did you personally or someone in your employ kill David Torres?" Kazim snapped off crisply.

"Did you murder your grandson?" Madsen shouted over his partner.

"No." Torres crumpled onto the sofa. Tears ran unnoticed down his cheeks. "I love Davey. *Loved* Davey."

Chapter 18

"That was fun." Kazim said as they drove away from the Torres estate.

"You know how to swamp out a horse stall?"

"No. The relevance of that question is?"

"If you did, I could hire you, you know, once we get fired for accusing one of the mayor's pals of murder."

"The victim was shot with his gun."

"Prove it without the bullets, then prove his gun wasn't missing slash stolen." Madsen wasn't saying anything they didn't know, but said out loud it was clearly both foolish and dangerous. "Gut check, you think he did it?"

"Do you?" Kazim asked.

"He could have."

"You saying that because he's an overbearing privileged homophobe?"

"You left out braggart and bully. But point taken."

"If he did, how did Cisco end up holding his revolver? Could Cisco be faking his disability to disguise that he's a hitman for Eduardo Torres?"

"Hell if I know." Madsen leaned his head back, closed his eyes and tried to go blank. Tried to let the answers present themselves. After fifteen minutes nothing floated out of the ether, nothing got clearer. Too many possible suspects and none looking any more or less guilty than the others.

"You coming in to the station?" Kazim double parked beside Madsen's truck.

"Nah, Fong gave me a soft pass on bringing Cisco in. Think I'll keep a low profile, case she changes her mind."

"I'll tell her you are....?"

"Chasing a wild hare down a blind alley."

"Oh, yeah, that will get the job done." Kazim smiled. "You hate me. Right?"

"Not nearly as much as I thought I would."

Above the front door to Super Hero Central hung a life-sized Spider-Man. It was an old school comic shop. Dealing in second hand comic books, trading cards and action figures, it was a throwback to a time before eBooks and PlayStations and virtual reality goggles. Mr. K perched on a stool by the cash register, his hair was pure white and tied back in a ponytail. He was Ichabod Crane lanky. Bright eyes darted and danced behind his rose-colored pince-nez. He was orating at a ten year-old girl in a Strong Female Character t-shirt.

"She Hulk, Spider-Woman, etc....they are simply female iterations of male paradigms. For real feminist views, here." Mr. K slapped a book on the counter. "The Unbeatable Squirrel Girl. Heard of her?"

"No, I don't...." The girl picked up the comic, eyes going drifty as she looked at the cover.

"You'll love her. You don't, you can always trade it in for Jem and the Holograms, but you *will* love her. Get through Unbeatable Squirrel Girl and we'll see about Ms. Marvel."

"Okay." She dropped a small pile of bills. In her excitement she didn't count them, just emptied her pocket onto the glass counter top.

"Shel, that's too much." Mr. K gave the girl back three bills. "Attention costs nothing." He tapped a finger against his temple. "Inattention can be very expensive."

"I know, I know." Stuffing the change into her pocket she picked up the comic with a reverence usually reserved for holy relics.

Madsen waited until the girl left and the bell over the door had settled before moving on Mr. K. "Nice girl. Seem to remember, when I was her age only boys were into comics."

"There was nothing written for women in the so-called 'golden era.' They only came in three flavors, sexy sidekicks, sexy girlfriends or sexy villains. Often—" Catching himself, he stepped off the soap box. He appraised Madsen in two quick eye flicks. "You aren't a collector or a fanboy. Cop?"

"Bingo. Do you know David Torres?"

"Ah, yes." Mr. K slipped off the stool and knelt beneath the counter and out of Madsen's view. "I would have thought you'd be here sooner."

"Why is that?" Madsen spoke to the empty space where the man had been.

"They had to come from somewhere. Don't get me wrong, David is a great guy, but not real money savvy." With the deep metallic *thunk* of a safe closing, Mr. K stood up with an envelope in hand. "I kept them, knowing sooner or later someone would be missing them."

"Makes sense." Madsen said, but it didn't.

"David loves Jim Lee's X-Men trading cards. Gambit is his favorite. Seems an odd choice. I get his love for Wolverine, sure, antihero with a heart of adamantium. But Gambit is just a thief who throws exploding cards. His relationship with the tragic Rogue is compelling...." Mr. K saw the detective's eyes glassing over. "No idea what I'm talking about?"

"Not a clue. What's in the envelope?"

"David always pays with coins. I thought he was raiding his piggy bank. Not uncommon with my younger customers. Didn't really even notice it until he started bringing these in." Tilting the envelope, he

160

poured out a small group of antique coins. Silver and gold. "I told him I couldn't take these, but when he got upset, I relented."

"How valuable are we talking?" Madsen lifted a gold Liberty Head dollar.

"That, in your hand, maybe two-fifty. None are pristine or profoundly rare, but still."

"Worth more than the cards he bought?"

"Ten to twenty times more." Mr. K pointed to the coins. "I never sold one of them. I wouldn't cheat a comic lover. Kept them separated."

"You never reported them, right? Tried to find out where Torres got them?" Madsen let the questions carry the weight of accusation without adding any emotional juice to his tone.

"Wait. I didn't do anything wrong or inappropriate."

"Probably not."

"I kept the coins, knowing—or thinking I guess—that June from Bridge-Way would stop by."

"But she hasn't?"

"Not yet."

"And you haven't reached out to her, right?"

"I did nothing wrong."

"You said that."

"I wouldn't."

"Said that too." Madsen believed all people were innocent until proven guilty and that everyone was guilty of something. Most lied as easy as breathing. His job was to discern big lies and criminality from everyday human indiscretions.

Mr. K moved his hand over the coins, like a magician hoping to make them disappear. "Did David steal these?"

"Why would you think that?"

"Because…well, why else send a detective to investigate?"

"Was David Torres in your shop yesterday?"

"No…no, definitely not." Mr. K was starting to be concerned, or *more* concerned with where this was leading. "Why are you asking these questions?"

"How about Fransisco Gutierrez?"

"Cisco?"

"Was he in yesterday?"

"No. He only comes in with David."

"Were they good friends?"

"Cisco and David? Thick as thieves. Sure, they disagree about X-Men vs. Justice League, but…this isn't about the coins."

"No. David Torres was murdered yesterday." Madsen dropped the news blunt, sharp edges exposed, watching to see how it hit the comic store owner. It hit hard. Mr. K gasped. Covered his mouth with a fist. Dropped onto his stool, holding the counter to keep from falling. He gulped breath. Eyes darted to Madsen hoping for a sign that he had heard incorrectly. Madsen shook his head, mouthing, "Sorry."

"How?" Mr. K asked.

Madsen explained he couldn't speak about an ongoing investigation. He swept the coins into an evidence bag. Mr. K looked blankly at the receipt Madsen set on the counter. There are moments when the fabric of normal life is torn, exposing something more primal, painful, and real. Depending on the depth of the relationship to the deceased, or maybe the depth of one's character, these rips repair themselves quickly, slowly or not at all.

The ringing bell announced two teenage boys entering the store. Mr. K slipped his public face back on. Madsen left Super Hero Central holding one more puzzle piece with no obvious place to attach it. Pinning the coins to the cork-board in his mind he looked for any pattern. The coins more than likely came from the grandfather. Why did Holly lie about David not seeing her father? How did that shiny pimped out .38 get into Cisco's hand?

Madsen's phone was buzzing when he climbed into the truck. He checked the number before picking up. "Detective Kazim, tell me you solved this case so I can get out of the furnace and into a cold beer."

"Wish I could. I found information on Harry Mapu, the Pelican Bay C.O.."

"Really?" Madsen had almost written Mapu off as a Grandpa Hem fantasy.

"Wasn't easy. Been retired a while now. Mapu wasn't in Santa Clarita. So I did a name search in Hawaiian Gardens, a lot of Samoans live there. And a surprising amount with the last name Mapu."

"And? Did you find him? And make it brief, it's too damn hot for a long-winded answer."

"No, I did not. But then I had a bright idea, I reached out to CalPERS. Harold Mapu receives his retirement checks at a trailer park in Azusa."

Chapter 19

"Damn, boy, you look like Hem." Harry Mapu was a large man in every sense of the word. His personality filled the cafeteria. Not tall, but stocky and muscular. He wore his long white hair in a ponytail. "Think Hem was about your age last time I saw him. You were all he talked about. You never made the NFL, huh?"

"Didn't try. Hem wanted me to play ball."

"What did *you* want?"

Madsen took a long drink of iced tea, thinking. "To be a cop like Hem, I guess."

"How's that working out?"

"It has its days."

Harry barked a staccato laugh. "It do that."

When Madsen had called the retired prison guard he'd dropped Hem's name. It had worked, like it so often did with cops of a certain age. His grandfather's reputation for decency and solid work were both Madsen's moral North Star, and the key that opened many locked doors.

"How's Hem doing? Not dead, right?"

"Far from it." Madsen knew that if Hem wanted his mental state spoken of, he'd do it himself. "Forty years on the street didn't kill him, doubt retirement has a shot."

164

"Good to hear. Tell him to holler at me. I could teach him how to play golf."

"I'm not saying you can't teach an old dog new tricks, but...."

"That wannabe cowboy's never going to play the sport of kings?"

"Never's a long time, but, no." Madsen inadvertently glanced at his watch.

"Detective, I have a sense you didn't drive to the Valley's armpit in this heat to listen to an old man ramble. I'm sure you can get that at home."

"Yes sir, I can. Look, it's a long shot, but do you remember a prisoner named Francisco Gutierrez?"

Harry went very still. He let out a breath. Looked out the window, then finally back at Madsen. His words came out quiet and deep. "Bad days, those. Sacramento's tough-on-crime sons of bitches decided if a teenager did an adult crime they should do adult time. We housed boys, fourteen, tossed them in with the main pop. Did what we could to protect them. We were grossly outnumbered. Most days we just kept a finger on the pulse of the chaos and prayed a riot wouldn't hit us."

"Francisco Gutierrez?"

"I remember him. Terrified kid, all eyes and trembling when we dropped him in that roiling soup. Forty-eight hours. Two days. That's all it took for him to be eaten up. Saw him in the infirmary. Broken bones and teeth. Torn rectum." Harry gulped down water, focusing on it to keep from crying. "Hardest part? Watching the light leave his eyes, replaced by something cold. He'd catch me looking at him and his face would reconfigure into that innocent kid. But I knew that kid died two days after being incarcerated."

"Do you think he's capable of convincing medical professionals that he is retar...brain damaged?"

"Gutierrez is still out there?" Harry shook his head, he didn't look surprised, but impressed.

"He is. He's also our most viable suspect in a murder investigation."

"This was a long time ago, when I knew him. But he was maybe the smartest convict I ever met. He got to several guards, had them doing his bidding, never found he had on them. Don't be taken in, and don't turn your back on Gutierrez, would be my advice." Harry fell back in time as he spoke. He told Madsen he had a good idea—unprovable—who had raped young Francisco Gutierrez. "Six full grown monsters, members of BGF. Not long after Gutierrez was released from the medical unit those men started dropping. Rat poison in one's oatmeal. Lighter fluid and dishwashing soap in another's light bulb. Homemade napalm burned him beyond recognition. I suspected Gutierrez, but looked the other way. Fuck the pedophiles right?" He looked at Madsen, not expecting an answer.

"Was there any retribution?"

"Payback? Hell no. La EME protected him. He killed their soldiers and they hired him as an enforcer. He was crazy, scared the hell out of the other inmates. But I swear he could turn it on and off, like some kind of psychopath spigot. Nine years into a twenty-five to life bit he changed. Complete one-eighty. Started working in the library, read law books like others read comics. Started helping the pastor with Sunday services. Crucifixes replaced the pin ups on his cell walls."

"You sure he didn't have a conversion?"

"Jailhouse epiphany?" Harry almost smiled. "I guess they happen, but not in Pelican Bay, and not to that crafty young man."

"You respected him."

"I did. I also respect rattlesnakes and coyotes." Harry drank more water, deciding how much to tell Madsen. "Screw it. Okay, the system fucked that young man, so he fucked back. Hard. Yes, I respected that. Hell, he convinced the priest, prison shrink, and ultimately the warden to petition for clemency. Got it, too. Just shy of his twenty-fifth birthday he was a free man."

"After that?"

"Don't know. Don't care. We took a kid, turned him into a stone

166

killer. He wasn't the only one, but he was the one that broke it for me. Day he was released I transferred out. Went to a minimum security forestry camp. Left gladiator school for a place I could actually do some good." Harry looked into Madsen's face, searching for a taint of judgement.

"I bet you did more than a little good."

"Maybe. You never know what ripples you start by bringing humanity to an inhumane system. At least that thought keeps me upright and enjoying my grandkids."

Driving away, Madsen thought about what he'd heard over and over. Harry Mapu wasn't lying, no motive. Was his decades-old assessment of Cisco valid? He called Kazim to fill him in. "He seemed to think Cisco was capable of faking his...brain thing."

"His intellectual disability? That the term you're searching for?"

"Sure, if that's still this week's term. How do you keep it straight?"

"Developmentally disabled vs. intellectually disabled?" Kazim paused to think. "Not easy to keep up with. Besides, who cares about the label; Cisco is Cisco is Cisco, right? Besides, culturally correct labels are a linguistic moving target."

"You arguing we should call them retarded?" Madsen half smiled at his partner having painted himself into a corner.

"No. I'm not. What I'm questioning is, are these evolving labels a good thing? If what we call a group of people keeps morphing, we have to keep reexamining them."

"You lost me, Kazim."

"The N-word was easy on racists, helped them keep black people in a box called 'other' or 'non-human.' Then 'colored' came along, sounded more genteel but it too was used to exclude. 'African-American,' damn, use that and you have to come to grips with the 'other' being American, with all the accompanying rights and privileges. 'People of color'? That

167

brought together a wide group of folks from around the world, joined them under one banner and scared the hell out of a lot of pale people. Labels shape how we view ourselves and each other."

"Thank you, Professor Heathen, that was a wonderful sociological civics lesson. Any chance in hell it has anything to do with our case?"

"It has everything to do with our case. Because of unexamined biases we have been running in a circle arguing over whether Cisco is or isn't intellectually disabled. It's a false binary: if he *is* intellectually disabled then he must be innocent. Why couldn't he be intellectually disabled *and* guilty of murder?"

Madsen both knew and hated that Kazim was right. When it came to other people's labels he always figured it wasn't his place to judge what they preferred. Neighborhood friends went from wanting to be called Hispanic to Latinos and Latinas to Latinx, no skin off him, so he rolled with it. Nat, Sergeant Booker, and the LAPD guidelines went for African-American. Lots of younger officers liked Black. LGBTQ? That alphabet soup seemed to continually be adding letters. Best move, when possible, was to avoid labels entirely. Don't use any, and no one would get mad at you for using the wrong one. The flaw Kazim had so kindly pointed out was if they didn't uncover and address their biases, the biases would affect their police work. Madsen believed in, if nothing else, that a detective's job was to discover the truth. Regardless of how they felt about it.

Chapter 20

"You LAPD thugs think jail has therapeutic value." Adair crackled in Madsen's ear as he drove home. "It doesn't. It will set her back *months*, maybe years. No room at County General? The Twin Towers can always find room for one more."

"First, the Sheriff's department handles jails, not LAPD. And second, this is dumped on me because…?"

"Because…" she had called to tell Madsen she was tied up, still trying to find her client a bed, and her anger got away. "Because you had the sad misfortune to pick up instead of letting it go to voicemail."

"I'm a big guy, I can handle a little verbal blow-back." He kept it light and easy. "When you get things settled, come on out to Hem's ranch. I have some steak marinating, I'm near genius with a barbecue."

"That actually sounds good. Mind if I bring my own whisky?"

"Only if you don't mind Hem laughing at your elitist Celtic firewater."

"Him I can handle." She started to relax at the thought. "How is Cisco?"

"He's fine." Madsen turned onto the gravel drive. This wasn't a lie, exactly. Odds were very good that it was true. Cisco was with Hem and Nat, had there been trouble they would have called. He promised to save Adair a plate and hung up.

The light was starting to soften into dusk. Rounding the curve, the ranch house sat silent and dark. The distant rumble of the freeway underlaid the sound of his boots scraping on dust as he moved across the yard. Front door was unlocked, and opened with a metallic creak. The living room was empty. He didn't turn on any lights and moved with stealth. Clearing room to room, corner to corner. Kitchen empty. Hem's room empty. His bedroom empty. Despite the air conditioned breeze, sweat dripped between his shoulder blades. Beds were made. Dishes clean and put away. There was no sign of a struggle. No dismembered bodies. Cisco hadn't killed Hem and Nat and headed south. Yet, that was the first place Madsen's mind went. It would be easy to write this off to the job coloring his world view darkly. But as long as he could remember, when frightened he jumped to the ugliest bleakest possible outcome.

The yard was silent, empty of horse snickers; the sweet sounds that always greeted his arrival. Those "did you bring me any oats" noises were absent. The barn was cast in shadows large enough to swallow a man. Madsen entered quietly. The stalls and tack room had dark corners where all manner of malevolent beings could be hiding. He fought the desire to pull his pistol. It would feel comfortable in his hand. It would be a talisman to ward off evil. That was how it would feel. But Madsen knew once a gun entered a situation it irrevocably changed the equation. So he sucked it up and kept moving through the darkness.

A silhouetted man leaned against the wall with a hay hook in his hand. He was deathly still. Moving closer Madsen discovered the man was made of a pitchfork, a straw hat, and an expectation fueled by imagination.

Methodically, he cleared the barn and found it empty of life.

Where the hell were they?

If Hem and Nat took Cisco to the Sagebrush for a beer he would skin the two of them. Tack their useless hides to the barn and let the coyotes gnaw on them.

How would they get to the bar?

They could take Nat's truck, but wouldn't. Nat would risk Aretha—yes, he'd named his truck—on a bar run. Hem was blacklisted by every taxi company in the area. His unpaid $400 bill to a cabby for helping him discover that the house in Lakewood he wanted to go to was demolished in the mid-fifties, insured that his business was unwelcome. A ride share app? Hem couldn't use one even if he had a cellphone. Forgetting all that, Nat had better sense than to take Cisco off the property.

Where were they?

Madsen stood outside the barn, turning slowly on his boot heel. Dusk slipped into night and dark consumed the land. The first sound was the light thudding of horse's hooves on packed earth. They were moving at a quick trot. Next came a whoop and cackle that could only be Hem. The hooves broke into a gallop. Three riders separated from the darkness, flying down the trail out of the hills. It wasn't until they were almost on Madsen that he could make out the men. Hem was in the lead with Cisco half a length behind him, Nat brought up the rear at only a slightly less insane pace.

"Whoa up." Hem pulled to a stop in front of the corral. "What took you so long?" He looked back at Cisco. "You ride like a girl."

"Is that bad, or good?" Cisco asked sincerely.

"Good question, Hem?" Nat said.

Hem thought it over before answering. "Damned if I know."

Madsen had a fifty foot walk to cool down. It wasn't enough. "What in the holy name of fuck are you doing?"

"Bad language, Tricky."

"I'm talking to these two idiots." He spun on Nat who was climbing down from his saddle. "This your idea or did you just co-sign Hem's bullsh-sh-shoot." Cisco smiled at Madsen's attempt to clean up his speech.

171

"Cisco's actually a hell of a rider. Should have seen him. Me and your grandfather had to work to keep up."

"What are you talking about. I outrode that pissant, pure and simple."

Madsen's blood pressure spiked. "I don't care who did what or when. Y'all were one gopher hole away from a broken neck. You think about that?"

"I don't think God kept me from getting killed in the line of duty just to squash me now." Hem swung his leg over the saddle horn, his leg slipped out of the stirrup, and he fell ass down in the dirt. "God damn mother fucking horse, he moved, did that on purpose."

Madsen looked from his grandfather to Cisco, "Why aren't you on *him* for his swearing?"

"He's from Texas, duh." Cisco said, as if everyone knew Texans swore.

"He got that right." Hem let out a good loud laugh.

Nat led the horses into the corral, Cisco running after him to help get them unsaddled. Madsen stood looking down at his grandfather. "You just gonna stand there soaking up moon light or you gonna help me up?"

"I'm deciding." Madsen gave it a few seconds before reaching down and pulling the old man to his feet. Hem took a step, his left knee locked up, and he had to drag his leg.

"There appears to be a hitch in my giddyup."

"Yep, and that is the least of your problems."

Madsen grilled steaks on an old-school Weber, mesquite and charcoal, no propane. *Might as well cook in the kitchen if you want that gas smell stinking up your meat.* Nat had gone home and Hem lay in the hammock, hat over face, snoring away. Cisco watched the embers, not meeting Madsen's eyes.

"Where did you learn to ride?"

"It's not hard. Horse does all the work."

"That's right, riding's easy, it's the not falling off part that takes practice. Where did you learn?"

"Are you angry at me Tricky?"

Madsen looked at Cisco, thought, then shook his head. "Guess I'm not. Just trying to figure you out."

"Me, too." Cisco scrunched up his face, blinked then looked at Madsen. "I rode a horse on a beach, I think. Do horses go on beaches?"

"Well, sure they do. When I was a kid I rode on a beach." Madsen thinks back, smiles. "Down in Mexico. Fell off because of a loose cinch."

"It hurt?"

"Not much. Sand protected everything but my pride. I was thirteen, figured the whole world was clocking my every move." Madsen turned the steaks and sent them sizzling. With a fork he tested ears of corn. Dusted them with chili-salt. "Few more minutes. Hope you brought your appetite."

"I'm always hungry."

"I noticed. I got no clue where you put all that food."

"My mouth. Then my stomach. Tricky, did you go to school?"

"Some, not enough clearly."

"That's okay. I know stuff and I'll help you out."

"Thanks, Bud."

In the house Madsen set two plates on the dining room table. He decided to let Hem keep sleeping. He brought Cisco a glass of milk and himself a Tecate. Cisco with steak knife in one hand and fork in other, pushed the meat around his plate, stabbing more than cutting it.

"Need some help there, Bud?"

"No." Cisco took several more unsuccessful attempts before giving up. "Yes."

Madsen sliced up bite sized chunks and slid the plate back. "Give that a try." Cisco chewed, a smile broke on his face. "Good?"

Cisco nodded, stuffing in a second piece. Madsen watched in amazement as Cisco plowed through the plate. He sat back and watched Madsen eating. He stared down at his fingers, picked at some dirt under his nail. Looked back at Madsen.

"You got something to say, Bud?"

"You won't get mad?"

"I can't promise that."

"Then no." Cisco focused back on his nails.

"Keeping things bottled up's no good. It'll feel better once you get it out."

"Like a burp?"

"Just like that."

"Okay…at the bad guy's house, I didn't tell you."

"Tell me what?"

"I…I remembered something…not good." Cisco searched for both the courage and the words to express what he felt. "I hurt someone, bad. I think. Maybe it was a dream…I can remember holding a gun. It was hot. Guns hurt people."

"David? Did you hurt him with that gun?"

Cisco looked confused, then shook his head. "No. A man with shiny hair. I don't know. I don't know. I don't know." He started to slap his own head, harder and harder. "I…I…I…bad…bad…" Madsen gently took Cisco's wrists and held them. Cisco strained to hit himself. "No…no…no…."

"Shh, Bud. It's gonna be alright."

"No." Cisco stopped struggling. "I think it won't." He slumped down, resting his forehead on the table. "Tricky, it wasn't a dream… was it?"

"I don't know, Bud. Truly I don't." He gently rubbed circles on Cisco's back. Outside Hem's snores mixed with a pack of coyote's yips and the nervous sound of horses stomping in their paddocks.

Chapter 21

It was after midnight when Adair finally got to the ranch. She looked in on Cisco, who was deep asleep and adding his snores to Hem's. Madsen offered to heat her up a plate, but she only wanted a tumbler with a splash of water in it. Taking a dented silver flask from her briefcase, she gave herself a healthy pour of Caol Ila. She sipped the whisky sitting on the front porch swing. Madsen toasted her with his mug of coffee, but said nothing. Slowly her shoulders dropped from her ears, and the tight skin around her eyes softened as the whisky and the silence did their job.

"This day was a hard-boiling kettle of crap." Adair said to no one in particular. "Finally found my client a bed in Sherman Oaks. A rehab facility, but they have a locked ward." She took a deeper drink of whisky. "Do yourself a favor, Detective Madsen."

"What would that be?"

"You decide to go mad, and you may, do it in a civilized nation. One with socialized healthcare."

"I'll remember that. If I decide to go that way." He tipped his mug up, draining it. "Can I get you anything? Another splash?"

"No thank you, sir. This is just enough to smooth the day's rough edges. Any more and I'm likely to trade today's agitation for tomorrow's pain."

Madsen appraised her, she was smart and passionate, good qualities. She also seemed ready to die on every hill. A trait that would grind a soul down. She looked too thin and too tired.

"When was the last time you ate?"

Adair had to think this over. "Hmm, that would be breakfast with you and Cisco."

Madsen checked his watch. "Fourteen hours ago?"

"No, wait, I had a granola bar somewhere in there."

"Oh, that makes it okay."

"Tasted like cardboard. Don't think it was actually part of any food group."

"That won't do." Madsen shook his head. "Grandpa Hem raised me with an iron clad rule, hospitality begins with a full belly. Please let me feed you or he will whup my ass come sun up."

"We can't have that." She followed him into the kitchen, leaning on the counter she watched him slice the grilled steak in to thin strips. He heated oil in a frying pan then chopped onions, bell peppers and a jalapeño.

"Who taught you to cook?"

"Nobody. Not that I recall. Hem, I guess. He worked cop's hours, I took care of the chores. Long as he remembered to buy it, I remembered to cook it. Worked out pretty alright I guess." He dropped the vegetables into the pan followed by the meat.

"Must have been hard losing your family so young."

"Can't miss what you don't remember having." He laid three corn tortillas over the steaming pan to soften. "You getting hungry?"

"Could eat a bear."

"Nah, too tough."

"You've eaten bear? No, really."

Madsen gave her an equivocal grin. He filled the tortillas, tearing up fresh cilantro over the top and set the plate on the table for her. "Give this a try." One bite in, she was smiling and moaning at near orgasmic levels.

"Good, right?"

Adair nodded enthusiastically, and chomped away. It wasn't until she had licked her fingers and the plate clean that she spoke. She asked how his and Cisco's day had gone. He told her bits and pieces, avoiding any mention of leaving him in the care two crazy old men or their night trail ride. "He told me tomorrow's Monday. He can't tell me where he was two days ago, but he sure knows what day of the week today is."

"And the time. Tracks it to the minute. Maybe it gives him a sense of order, a way to catalog, sort a day inside his chaotic mind. Daylight savings? Drives him bonkers."

"Hem bitches every time we adjust the clocks. Says that daylight savings was created by pen pushers with the sole purpose of driving him loco."

"Peas in a pod, those two." She took a long drink of the cool water Madsen poured for her. "Some days, I start to get dingy, only later realizing I forgot to hydrate."

"Maybe I should follow you around, taco in one hand water jug in the other."

"Handsome cowboy, nursemaid, how very American." She grinned at the thought.

"Handsome?"

"Gah, handsome-ish." She looked at him, appraising. "In an abstract, never-to-be-acted-upon way. Sure...what else did our Cisco say?"

Madsen paused just long enough to take note of her conversational left turn, smiled and moved on. "Apparently goes to his job Monday through Friday. He got slightly freaked when I told him tomorrow might not play out that way."

"See? Ritualistic. I'll talk to him. Can take time to process schedule changes."

"What's he do? His work?"

"He started at a job center. Piece work, counting out nuts, bolts, screws and putting them into polybags. Many clients find it peaceful, and there is the social aspect. Not Cisco. He told me he wasn't helping anyone, it was just about making money. Now he helps at Elysian Park Adaptive Rec Center. He works with the younger kids, he's a good rule-follower. It's a better fit."

"We all need our days to mean more than stacking up dollar bills. And if we don't, we should."

"Is that why you joined the police?"

Madsen thought about what version to tell her. He'd joined to serve and protect? Before discovering those were just words on a patrol car's door? Or maybe tell her he was a fouth-generation cop, it was what Madsen men did? He went with a vague, "Something like that." Then arced the conversation back to Cisco. "I took him to see his cousin."

"The criminal. Was that wise?"

"They wouldn't harm him with me there. Thing is, I think it stirred up some memories. Is that possible?"

"Yes and no. Memories don't show up on a scope or MRI. The effects head trauma causes can be impossible to prove one way or another. Doctors rely on tests and reports given by the person with the damage. Cisco might be having actual memories or situationally stimulated false memories. Make sense?"

"Sure. But he could be making this all up, right?"

"He's not. You can see that, can't you?" She searched his face for the truth.

"I don't know." Madsen said, honestly.

"Can't you feel the truth of Cisco? He's a good guy."

"Feelings aren't facts. I can't take a gut reaction or hunch to the DA. They need—hell, I need—real evidence. Without it, none of this means jack squat."

"That must be a sad way to live."

"It keeps things simple. My job is to divine and deliver the facts of

178

the matter. Emotional context, character, motivation, I leave all that to lawyers and judges."

"Cisco is a man, not a job."

"Except that he *is* part of my job." He respected Adair. Wanted her to understand. "If I met you and Cisco hanging out at a rodeo." She arched an eyebrow. "Okay, or eating a churro in a food court. Better?"

"A churro? No. A scone maybe." She was starting to soften to him.

"Right. And in this mythical scone-serving food court, my feelings, your feelings, Cisco's feelings would be all that mattered. I'd ask you to join me for a chimichanga and you would decide if that felt like a good idea."

"Sure, and even if I bought your trustworthy cowboy act, I might join you, but I'd keep one finger on 911 speed dial." She was half teasing him, enjoying the fantasy.

"Your job is to keep Cisco safe, right?"

"Yes." Her shoulders started to creep up as she sensed a trap coming.

"Much as you might want it to be, my job isn't looking out for Cisco." He simply stated the truth. "I'm not here for him."

"Who are you here for, then?"

"David. His family. His people."

"Fine. Why not arrest Cisco and be done with it?" Her nostrils flared and she looked like she might swing at him.

"I'm not convinced he did it. If he's not faking and we drop him in the joint, they will rip him apart."

"How can you care and be so callus at the same time? How do you reconcile that?"

"It's the job. Most days I get it right, that feels good."

"And when you don't?"

"I live with it, I guess." There was little else to be said. Madsen wished he had the eloquence to explain or convince Adair of the nobility of his job. That justice mattered, and if the system couldn't

179

bring it to a family, then they were left to find justice on their own. That seeking truth and not settling for anything less mattered. But she was a caregiver. Her job was to help make Cisco's life the best it could be. Her job demanded she have faith that he was a good man. Good until proven bad beyond a shadow of a doubt, and maybe beyond that.

Adair was too tired to argue the fine points of morality and ethical responsibility, and she said so. Madsen did what was left for him to do. He gave her a pillow, a blanket and a sofa, and moved onto the front porch to take up his night vigil.

In the soft pre dawn light Madsen woke to find Cisco hunched down staring at him. "Morning, Bud." Madsen spoke quietly, not wanting to wake the silent house behind them.

"Morning Tricky. You're out of O.J."

"Think we have grapefruit juice."

"I drank some. It's kind of sour."

"True. Wanna help me feed the horses?"

"Yes. Please." Cisco's eyes lit up at the prospect. He bounced all the way to the barn. "Do horses like pancakes?"

"They might, but it probably wouldn't sit well, so I think we'll give them alfalfa."

"Good. Can I feed Dancer?"

"Absolutely." Madsen broke off three leaves from a bale and handed one to Cisco. Dropping the hay into a wooden feeder, Cisco jumped back when Dancer trotted up to him. He crept slowly back to the eating horse and stroked his side. Dancer looked at him, huffed and continued chewing.

"Bud, catch." Madsen tossed Cisco an apple. Cisco watched it sail past him without attempting to catch it. "Oops." Madsen said.

With zero embarrassment Cisco picked up the apple. "Baseball's not my thing." He walked back to the horse. "How do I feed Dancer?"

180

"Hold your hand flat. Yeah like that."

Cisco laughed gleefully when Dancer took the apple from his hand. "Slimy." He said looking down at his slick hand.

"They can be messy alright." Madsen wiped Cisco's hand with his bandana.

"Tricky, did you know that horses poop and pee on the trail, while you are on them?"

"Yes, they do. Not much choice, we don't have a bathroom big enough for them."

Cisco laughed at that. He stroked Dancer's neck, leaning his face into his coat he breathed in. "He smells like sweat. Not in a bad way."

"Yes, he does. You like Dancer, don't you?"

"Of course, he's a great horse." His voice was muffled by Dancer's coat. "Tricky?"

"Yeah, Bud?"

"Can I ride him again?"

"Don't see why not."

"Now?"

"Not now, he needs some rest after your shenanigans last night."

"Shi-gana-whats?"

"It just means wild times. Like when you were racing Grandpa Hem."

"Oh. Okay, maybe I can ride him tomorrow?"

"He should be ready to ride by then." Climbing out of the paddock Madsen stopped and gave Cisco a serious look. "I don't think we need to tell Adair about the horse riding."

"She doesn't like shi-nana-thingies?"

"I don't think she does."

"Okay." Cisco agreed.

The house had the rich aroma of coffee. Adair was finishing

pouring hot water into actual factory-made coffee filters. "Did you know they sold filters at Trader Joe's?"

"Really?" Madsen said.

"And every other supermarket in the land." She batted her eyes playfully.

"Hi, Adair." Cisco was all happiness and joy. "I'm having fun. I didn't go on a ride with Grandpa Hem. Promise. We didn't race or anything."

Adair looked from Cisco to Madsen, shaking her head slowly. "You're an idiot."

"Guilty as charged." Madsen smiled. For a brief moment all was well and good, a truce reached. Coffee and breakfast lay ahead of them. Beyond lay trouble, but for this one silly moment they could pretend they met in a food court, that David wasn't dead, and that Cisco's life didn't rest in their collective hands.

Chapter 22

Adair was towel-drying her hair and almost out the door when Madsen and Cisco left the ranch. She needed to go into her office to let her supervisor see her and clear a piece of the avalanche of paper on her desk. They agreed to meet for lunch. Part of the bargain that involved Cisco not getting to go to the adaptive rec center was he got to choose their lunch restaurant. "Pat and Lorraine's." Cisco yelped. "They have Sofia, and huevos rancheros that make you want to slap your momma. Right Tricky?"

"Ab-sa-tively, Bud."

The air outside was already warm and smelled of wildfire. Ash drifted onto the windshield as Madsen drove out of the driveway. "You ever go to the snow?"

"Hmm…I don't think so. Is there snow in Mexico?"

"Sure there is. I got snowed in, in a cabin in Sierra de Juarez one time, down in Baja. Why, you remembering something?"

"Yes." Cisco nodded proudly.

"You gonna tell me, or whistle Dixie?"

"Can't whistle." Cisco put his lips together and blew. A spray of spit came out but no tone. "See?"

"I do. You cannot, in fact, whistle. What did you remember?"

"Right. Remember you rode a horse on the beach in Mexico."

"Yep. And you said you remembered riding a horse on a beach."

"So, maybe I saw snow in Mexico."

"Either did or didn't. Which is it, Bud?"

"I don't know. If I did, I don't want to tell you I didn't. Friends don't lie, mostly. Right, Tricky?"

Madsen started to answer when he came around a curve, his full attention grabbed by a sheriff's cruiser parked across the road. Two uniformed deputies stood waiting. One had a 12-gauge resting in the crook of his arm, the other had his right hand on his holstered pistol and his left held a microphone. Breaking hard, Madsen looked over his shoulder, shifting into reverse. Before he could hit the gas the murdered-out Dodge pulled quickly from a driveway and blocked their exit.

"Detective Madsen, step from the vehicle with your hands away from your side arm." The deputy's voice came through the patrol car's loudspeaker.

Madsen shook his head broadly enough for the deputies to get his noncompliance. He spoke quietly to Cisco. "Bud, do me a favor and don't make any sudden moves."

"Sudden moves?"

"Just keep still."

"I can do that. I think." Cisco clamped his hands on his legs, holding tight enough to whiten his knuckles. His lips moved but he kept any further words from coming out.

Madsen eased on the accelerator. The truck creeped towards the deputies.

"Stop the vehicle, now." The deputy said while his partner pointed the shotgun at Madsen.

Madsen kept rolling forward, leaning his head out the window he spoke, "Just getting close enough so we don't need to yell."

"Stop now, or we will be forced to shoot." The shotgunner said.

Madsen applied the brakes, ten feet from the men. "You want to shoot an LAPD detective? Really?"

"If I have to. Everyone knows you're in La Colina 13's pocket."

"You say so." Madsen said, flicking his eyes from one deputy to the other.

"Step out of the truck."

"Not gonna happen…" Madsen read the man's name bar, "Deputy Withers. Best move would be for you to drive away and we pretend this didn't happen."

The deputy held up a piece of paper. "We have a warrant for Francisco Gutierrez."

"You might. What you don't have is jurisdiction."

"Fuck jurisdiction." The other deputy said gripping the shotgun.

"Deputy Gallagher," Madsen read the other's name. "You may be ready to kill me. But are you ready have the full weight of the LAPD dropped on your asses?" Madsen held up his cellphone. It had no signal, but they didn't know that. "Smile." The phone took a picture.

"Get that phone." Deputy Withers yelled. Pulling his pistol, they both charged the truck.

In the rearview mirror Madsen saw a rifle barrel slide out the Dodge's window. "Hold on." Madsen told Cisco. Banging into reverse he stomped on the gas. The truck's tires chirped as they jerked backwards. A rifle shot punched several holes in the truck bed. By moving forward, Madsen had given himself enough space so that they were doing forty-five when the truck struck the Dodge. Metal on metal screamed as the truck's trailer hitch gouged a hole into the Dodge's door. The car rocked hard. Tires smoked and left six-foot long black marks from being pushed sideways.

"Ttttt…ttttrrrricky you crashed." Cisco was pale and trembling.

"Yes, I did. Get down." Shoving the truck into drive they jumped towards the deputies. Gallagher unloaded into the truck's front. Buckshot tore holes into hood and windshield. Feet before Madsen would have turned the deputies into stains on the asphalt, he cranked

185

the wheel left. The truck broke its way through a split-rail fence. Withers and Gallagher chased the truck firing as they ran. Slugs pinging and thudded into the cab. Madsen tore through a thicket of canyon oak and into an open field. Their escape seemed imminent when an irrigation ditch appeared. They bounced down hard, Madsen felt linkage in the steering column sheer off. He had no choice but to abandon the truck.

"Cisco, we have go." Madsen unbuckled his and then Cisco's seat belts.

"N-n-no. Tricky. Not safe."

The deputies were a couple hundred feet away and running towards them. "Bud, we have zero choices here. Come on." Madsen lead Cisco from the truck and, grabbing his wrist, he ran, half-dragging Cisco toward the relative safety of a barn across the field. The barn door was closed with a thick chain and lock. Madsen kept moving. In an unused corral he pulled Cisco down behind a wooden water trough.

"Tricky, you're bleeding." Cisco pointed to Madsen's face.

"Shh, we need to keep quiet." Madsen could hear the deputy's boots as they neared the barn. They were closing in. Taking his pistol in hand, he pulled a backup .25 automatic from his boot holster. He offered it to Cisco, eyebrow arched in silent question. Cisco look confused and afraid. He didn't reach for the offered gun.

"This has gone far enough." Gallagher called, racking the shotgun for emphasis. "Time to give up Gutierrez."

Madsen knew there was no way these motherfuckers would leave anyone alive to tell the tale of their attempting to kill a fellow cop. He slid the safety off his pistol. Ready. Wouldn't be long until they discovered him and turned his hopes and dreams into bloody pulp. Macho platitudes were fine right up until the moment the end became inevitable. That was when sinners and atheists took up praying.

God, I know we don't see eye to eye on a whole pile of things but this would be a hell of a time to show some mercy…. If you can't see clear to do that, maybe you could look after Grandpa Hem for me.

Madsen motioned for Cisco to lay belly-down. With a gun in each hand, he prepared to jump up. Blaze of glory time. Kill the deputies or die trying. He held his breath. And over the thumping of his heart he heard the distant wailing of sirens. It was the sweetest ugly sound he'd ever heard.

"You see him?" Withers asked.

"No. You?" Gallagher was starting to panic.

"We got to go."

"No shit we do." The voices stopped, and feet started running away. Madsen kept completely still, his hand resting on Cisco's back. They waited for minutes. Sirens got closer. The distinctive deep rumble of the Dodge faded as it drove away. On the street, sirens wound down and tires skidded to a stop. Madsen kept still.

"Tricky, you're squishing me."

"Shh." Madsen raised up enough to take his weight off Cisco but kept his body hovering to protect Cisco should it come to that. Sirens used to mean reinforcements had arrived, but not anymore. Madsen didn't know who to trust. Several cars came up the driveway, stopping by the barn. People ran, clearing the area. Madsen still didn't get up.

"You dead, praying, or just pooped your drawers?" Sergeant Booker looked over the wooden trough.

"Bit of all three." Madsen tried to smile, it played more like a grimace.

"That Gutierrez under you?"

Madsen rolled onto his back, freeing Cisco to flop onto his, so they both were looking up. "This is Sergeant Booker."

"He one of the good guys?" Cisco asked.

"Yes, he is."

"Good." Cisco smiled up. "Hi. Thanks for not letting those bad men kill us."

"Sure, no problem." Booker looked confused by the encounter. He turned to Madsen, all full of bluster. "You want to stand up and tell me who the hell had the nerve to shoot up one of my detectives?"

"A couple of Deputy Sheriffs."

"LA County?"

"None other."

"Those motherfuckers."

"That's bad language." Cisco said.

"No shit, kid." Booker was in no mood to be corrected.

"How'd you find us?" Madsen asked.

"Gutierrez' social worker called it in to your partner."

"Adair?"

"Guess that's her name. Short redhead, hates following orders?"

"That's her."

Cisco jumped up. "Adair! Adair!" Searching the faces of the officers he didn't see her. "Adair!"

Kazim came from the field. "Damn Madsen, someone messed up your truck."

"Yes, they did."

"Not that it was really cherry to start with." Kazim looked his partner over. "You're bleeding." He pointed to small cuts in Madsen's neck and a smattering of tears in his shirt starting to redden with blood.

Madsen looked down. "Forget it. I need you to get Cisco out of here. Quiet-like."

"You don't trust our guys?"

"I don't trust anyone." When Madsen introduced Cisco to Kazim, Cisco looked at him a long time.

"You. I remember you. You helped me."

"When you had a seizure?"

"Yeah."

"You remember that?"

"Yes." Cisco gave Kazim a look that said "obviously." "Are you Tricky's partner?"

"I am."

"Good, he needs looking after."

After they left, Madsen sat on the trough. He was suddenly exhausted. He took out his pad and wrote down "LA County deputies, Gallagher and Withers." Tore the page out and scribbled another note. Fellow officers who came by and tried to chat got a thousand-yard stare that backed them off.

Kazim sat next to Madsen, saying nothing.

"Cisco gone?" Madsen asked.

"He left with Ms. Hettrick."

"Good. Soon as the incident team arrives I'm going to be hobbled. You need to get gone, before they rope you in."

"Who did this?"

"Two deputies in a cruiser and the black Dodge, I didn't see the driver. But the driver's side door is tore up." He passed Kazim the names. "These are the deputies. Find out what you can about them. I have their picture." He clicked on his phone, scrolling to the picture he took, it was blown out by glare. "Or not."

Kazim looked at blurry picture. "Not. So, what'd they look like?"

"Khaki jar heads."

"Ok. Race?"

"Lily white."

"Noticeable scars or tattoos?"

"No."

"Get their unit number?"

"No. Sorry, I was kinda busy not dying."

"Wimp." Kazim closed his notebook.

"That's me." Madsen glanced around, an officer was studying the ground, trying not to look like he was listening in. Madsen lowered his voice. "I need you to be at Pat and Lorraine's at noon."

The officer drifted closer to them, looking away, but paying attention.

"Get me a burrito, okay?" Madsen handed Kazim a wad of bills.

"You almost die, and what you want is a burrito? You are an odd guy, Detective Madsen."

"Get on it. If Booker gives you any shit about leaving, tell him I told you to go."

"If Booker gives me any shit, I'll tell him to eat my chubby. It's halal."

"Kazim? Watch your back."

"I should be watching yours. You're the one people seem to hate."

"Fair point. Still." Madsen was serious. Kazim assured him he would keep one eye in his rearview mirror before splitting.

Uniforms spread out across the field and onto the street where they directed traffic, stringing out crime scene tape, starting their door to door. The circus was in town and Booker was its ringmaster, "Someone tried to kill one of ours. No one sleeps, eats, or pisses until we catch these sons of bitches."

The paramedics rolled up, lights spinning. Marta stepped down. "Who'd you irritate this time Madsen?"

"Marta, two times in one week. How'd I get so lucky?"

"Got in trouble near my rig, twice. You stalking me?"

"No ma'am." He bowed his head deferentially.

"Good." She looked over the cuts on his neck. A pair of forceps in her hand "Irritating the lady picking debris from your neck would be a big mistake." She dug into his flesh, Madsen flinched. "Does the big bad detective need a painkiller?"

"Yes, he does. But I've got a complicated day ahead, so it'll be a reluctant pass." He grimaced as she removed pieces of plastic and glass from his wounds.

"You want me to cut your shirt off?"

"No." Popping the snaps he exposed a constellation of bruises and abrasions.

Marta cleaned the blood away gingerly. "You need x-rays. Looks like only superficial injuries, but you never know. You're one lucky cop,

Madsen."

"Don't feel that way, but I guess you're right."

She spoke casually as she removed more foreign objects. "How's Cisco? He's a cool dude, you know."

"He's fine. What do you like about him?"

"Weird question."

"Humor me."

"He's sweet. Innocent. Life hasn't beaten him cynical like you and me."

"You got that from one meeting?"

"Sure. Anyone could see he's a good guy. It's like all those scars and the pain he must have been through didn't touch his heart." She stopped picking and stared Madsen down. "What is it you think Cisco did?"

"I don't know. Maybe nothing." Madsen made the decision to keep information on Cisco and the case to a need to know, and nobody needed to know much. The LA County Sheriff's Department had some very wrong deputies, that was common knowledge. In the late 1980s they formed their own gangs. Fight fire with fire, they'd said. More like fight criminality with criminality. The Bandidos, 3,000 Boys, Little Devils, Grim Reapers, Lynwood Vikings, all were deputy gangs. They threw secret hand signs. They spraypainted their tags over other gangs'. They had blood in blood out initiations. They operated out in the open in stations and jails. In 2014, a very public suit was filed against the Bandidos for making female recruits submit to sex with Bandido members as an initiation, that or survive the streets with no backup. The city paid the woman off, but didn't shut the Bandidos down.

That Sheriff's Deputies had shot at a LAPD detective didn't surprise Madsen as much as it should have. The *why* bothered him. Was it a failed hit, or a warning? They wanted Cisco under their control. But who? Who wanted him? A lot of deputies were stand-up. Others weren't bent but, because of fear or wanting get along, were willing to look the other way. And then there were the gangbanger thugs with badges. Madsen's only safe move was not to trust anyone flying a sheriff's star.

Marta finished taping up Madsen and—against her better judgement—she cleared him to return to work. He pulled his blazer over his bloody and torn shirt. "Sargent Booker, a moment?" Madsen called across the stable yard.

Booker moved quickly for a man of his age and size. "They didn't want you in the hospital?"

"I'm fine. Is Internal Affairs on the scene?"

"Five, ten minutes out."

"So, I'm locked down here. I need a uniform to go to my place. Take a note to my grandfather. If he's not there…" Madsen worried. "If he's not there, get back to me."

"You think they'll go after Hem?"

"Look at my truck. They weren't shooting blanks, so yeah, they might."

"On it." Booker took the note and called an officer over. He made it clear it was the officer's ass if he lagged or failed. The note was cryptic: "Hem, shit storm coming. You and Nat need to take a hike. Hide under a rock."

Chapter 23

"Detective Madsen, do you really want us to believe LA County deputies tried to kill you?" Hunt and Davis from Internal Affairs Bureau, Force Investigation Division, sat across the table from Madsen. Their office was deep inside the modern monolith that was LAPD command headquarters.

"Do you think I shot my own truck, crashed it, cut myself up, then ditched the guns and convinced a passing social worker to call this in? To what motherfucking end?"

"You seem angry, Detective." Hunt, the older of the two, spoke with an edge of skepticism. "Are you angry at us?"

"Three hours doing the bullshit two-step, bet your fat ass I'm angry at you."

"We're not your enemy." Davis was younger and had a naturally friendly demeanor.

"Really?" Madsen looked each of them in the eye. "Why the hell are you talking to *me* instead of Gallagher and Withers?"

"Them?" Hunt let out a short laugh. "Gallagher and Withers?"

"Yes. Bring those crooked bastards in and let's get this done."

"Slight problem." Hunt was enjoying dragging this out.

"What?"

"We checked the database, turns out deputies Gallagher and

Withers don't exist. That makes them, what? Phantoms? Hallucinations? Or fabrications of your overworked mind?"

Madsen took a breath to keep from leaping over the desk. He counted to ten before speaking. "Or—just spitballing here—they could have deputies wearing false names on their goddamn tags."

"Maybe. I don't think so." Hunt went hard, eyes emotionless. "Did you tangle with the wrong gangbangers? Gutierrez and La Colina 13 convince you to let him walk? Lay the blame on some mythical bad cops?"

"If that's how it went down, we get it." Davis was sincerity personified. "But you need to come clean."

"We know Gutierrez was at the scene, but not interviewed. He disappeared. That's on you."

"Did he threaten you?"

"Fuck you both. I'm done. I want to speak to my rep."

"Thought you didn't do anything. Huh, Madsen? Innocent cops don't whine and lawyer up."

Madsen's jaw muscles worked overtime to keep his mouth shut.

"Come on, Detective, help us help you. Okay?" Davis said. "We are all on the same side here."

Madsen put his boots on the desk, tilted his chair back onto its hind legs and pulled his Stetson down over his eyes. "Wake me when my rep gets here."

Hunt lost it. Jumping up, he sent his chair slamming into the back wall. "You think this a joke? I'll—" He was cut off by the door swinging open.

Bette Fong stepped into the room in all her badass administrative glory. "This is over. Detective Madsen, you're coming with me."

"We answer to the chief, not you, ma'am." Hunt said *ma'am* like it was an insult and the rest with pure contempt. "Close the door on your way out."

Fong gave Hunt a tight smile. Taking out her cellphone, she hit a number. It was picked up quickly. "Hunt is trying to obstruct our investigation. Yes, sir." She held the phone out for Hunt. "Chief wants to speak to you."

Hunt took the phone and started to speak but was cut off. As he listened his face grew an angry red. He didn't say a word. Handing Fong back her phone he stormed out of the room. Davis looked embarrassed by his partner and tried to apologize, but Fong smiled and told him he had nothing to apologize for. "Your partner, on the other hand, might want to consider finding another line of work."

Madsen rose silently, keeping his mouth shut until they were alone in the elevator. "That was a monumental pile of time-wasting horseshit."

"Detective Madsen, this here—you and me—is a momentary reprieve." Fong was all business. "We have found no proof to back up your version of events. The alternate theory being floated is—"

"That Cisco and La Colina 13 scared me shitless and forced me to make up a lie. Heard that one. It has more holes in it than my truck."

"Sell me, I'm all ears."

"One, if La Colina 13 wanted to scare me, why not do it when I was on their turf? Two, you know me. Even if I agreed to a deal, I'd flip it on them the minute the cavalry arrived. Three, Adair Hettrick, Cisco's social worker, and Cisco witnessed the shooting."

"I know who Ms. Hettrick is, she isn't picking up her supervisor's calls. She and Gutierrez are in the wind. We have a BOLO out for both of them. The deputies you saw don't exist. The picture you say you took is indiscernible. You see how it looks, right?"

"How it *looks*? Is that more important than how it actually is?"

"Don't go moral with me. You don't like politics, I get that, but you know how it works. Appearance is nine-tenths of everything."

Madsen's response was interrupted when the evaluator door opened. Neither of them spoke again until they were in Fong's office. It was decorated tastefully, not opulent, but expensive. Fong took a seat behind an oak desk. She called her secretary and asked that they not be disturbed.

Madsen looked out the window at downtown LA. "Damn Bette, if this view is meant to impress, it works."

"Minor perk for putting up with self-centered conniving macho cops all day long." Her smile had zero warmth.

"Speaking of conniving, interesting that you burst in to my rescue right when I called for my union rep…almost like you were listening in to a recording device that they forgot to tell me about."

"Moi? No. I run a clean shop."

"Wouldn't ever say you don't, even if tortured." He gave her a wink and leaned back on her credenza.

"Game's up, Niels. I need you to bring in Gutierrez."

"I don't know where he is. He and Hettrick booked from the crime scene."

"Where is he? I'm not asking, the chief is ordering. Bring him in."

"I really don't know." It was true, he had suspicions, could've guessed, but didn't *know*.

"Give me Fransisco Gutierrez—or your badge and gun." Fong's face went marble cool. "Time to decide who's side you're on."

"Bette, if I find Cisco and turn him over, you and I know odds are real good he'll go down with a Sheriff's Department bullet in him."

"I don't know, or even suspect, that. Bring him in. LAPD will keep him safe."

"LAPD? Right." Madsen looked away, afraid she'd see his distrust.

"What is that supposed to mean? You accusing fellow officers of something? Say it, Niels."

"Okay. I have no proof. But circumstantially, it's interesting that the sheriff's boys decided it was worth the risk to kill me just to get at Cisco, one day after I told you Cisco was starting to regain memories."

"Now you're accusing *me*? Who exactly do you think you are?"

"Not you, Bette. But those around you? All I know is those deputies

196

are afraid of something Cisco knows. And I don't think it's connected to the David Torres case."

"If you're right..." Bette picked up a paperweight, it was an award she received for valor in the line of duty. Turning it over, she didn't really see it. "If you are right, we need to take this to IAB."

"They'll act on my zero facts?"

"No. So what do you want?"

"A link into the Sheriff's Department's employee files. Let me identify the two who came after me."

"No." She slowed down to be really clear. "The chief ordered me to make sure you stayed away from the sheriff's people. He said we will look into your allegations. *You* won't. It's a political hornet's nest."

"Well damn if that won't make my corpse happy, knowing you'll look into it if they gun me down. I mean, unless it becomes politically inconvenient."

"Niels, I can't protect you if this goes south. You talk to the press, or go after the sheriff's people, the chief will bury you. They'll paint you as a mentally unstable rouge. You and I know that won't be hard to prove. Investigating corruption in the Sheriff's Department isn't your job. Finding out who killed Torres was."

"*Was?* Bette?"

"Please, Detective, find Gutierrez, bring him in and turn your case files over to Hertzog."

"Hertzog? Why him?"

"He's a good cop. And he has experience liaising with the Sheriff's Department without starting a war."

"Does Hertzog know he's taking over?"

"Only brass knows. Niels, what are you thinking?"

"Nothing. I mean if I brought Gutierrez in, and the case was already solved, you wouldn't mind, right?"

Fong stared at him in disbelief.

197

Chapter 24

It was late afternoon when Madsen walked out on to 6th Street. He called Kazim, who offered to come get him, but there were too many eyes looking down from the LAPD central offices. Keeping the brass from knowing how closely they worked together was the best way to protect his young partner.

"You pick up my burrito?" Madsen asked.

"I did. It's in the fridge, grease congealing as we speak."

Herzog yelled at the phone, "Tell Madsen if it's still here come dinner time, I'm claiming it."

"Herzog says—"

"I heard him." Madsen flicked his gaze around as he walked, making sure he wasn't being followed. "I'm gonna take the gold line. Meet me at the Highland Park Station in twenty minutes."

Pocketing his phone, he walked towards the subway stop. A block away from headquarters, the real downtown LA showed its face in all its multi-cultural multi-socioeconomic blended wonder. A drunk collapsed on the curb mumbling to a mannequin's head, while in a parking lot behind him bankers and stockbrokers bought carnitas and kimchi tacos from a transgender woman in a tube top and short-shorts. Madsen took it all in.

God damn I love this city.

He picked up his pace. In a few minutes, the workday whistles would blow and the buildings would disgorge a sea of suits, clogging the streets and Metro system.

Under the 7th Street subway sign, a pre-teen was banging on two overturned buckets. The kid had zero rhythm, but looked hungry. Madsen dropped a ten into his paper cup.

Madsen took the stairs down two at a time. Most people ride the escalator, leaving the staircase open. If he was being tailed, he would see them. After almost dying on his morning commute, Madsen felt good indulging his paranoia.

He hit the platform the moment the train's doors opened. Climbing aboard he wondered if his luck was changing. Three stops and he was at Union Station. No one was clocking him as he crossed to the Gold line. On the platform a large group of theater kids jostled, joked, and if Madsen's nose was correct, smoked some pot. A young man in a tux jacket over a Pan Bimbo tee was belting "Thank Heaven For Little Girls" until he eyed Madsen. He hissed in what he surely thought was a whisper to his friends to cheese it, 5.0 was on the scene. They all got real quiet. A young woman in a bowler with bee antennas swallowed the roach she was smoking. Madsen didn't have the heart to tell these young rebels that he didn't give two shakes of a bat's gonads about a little underage cannabis use.

When the train pulled in, the teens waited to see what car Madsen got on and then boarded one as far away as possible. No scary looking deputies, undercover cops, or gangbangers got on. The train pulled out. He stood holding the pole, there were plenty of empty seats, but he didn't want to be sitting if ugliness went down.

In Chinatown, three nuns with shopping bags got on. Madsen felt secure that no self-respecting Catholic would disguise themselves as a nun, so that ruled out La Colina 13. And nobody in the Sheriff's Department had that kind of creativity. There were three more clean stops.

Maybe lady luck is smiling on me for the first time since I caught this case.

At the Highland Park station Kazim sat leaning on a tan, unmarked cop car's hood. The train's doors opened. Madsen took a quick look around before stepping out.

Lady luck, that bitch. Fickle, fickle, fickle.

In the parking lot, tucked in beside a plumber's van was a Crown Victoria with two crew-cut meatheads in it. They weren't wearing uniforms. Didn't need to. Madsen sat down with his back to the platform. An eternity later the doors slid closed and the train rolled on.

Madsen rode three stops and got off in Pasadena. He walked to Memorial Park, and in the shadow of the bandshell he texted Kazim his GPS location and warned him he was being followed. He waited, hunkered down, hidden from most angles. The park was large enough that he could easily see anyone approaching. A hundred feet up a grassy hill, a mother lay on a blanket holding an infant in the air, both were laughing. Across a stretch of grass, three metrosexual lumberjacks in Bermuda shorts were playing pro-level Frisbee. Farther on, an Airedale was being chased over several park benches by a Boston Terrier while their owner took pictures. Madsen clocked it all, looking for danger— he only saw citizens enjoying the end of a summer day. This was no place for a confrontation. These people's trip to the park shouldn't carry the risk of getting run down or catching a stray bullet.

Two blocks over Madsen found a public parking structure. He had sweat through his suit by the time he climbed the stairs to the rooftop. It was mostly empty of cars. He texted Kazim his new coordinates and sat down behind an Oldsmobile to wait. Sunset was still hours away and the rooftop cement hadn't given up much of its heat. When this was over, Madsen made a promise to take Hem fishing in Alaska. It was something they'd always joked about—if Hem lost his job and later if Madsen did, they could always move to Alaska and live off the fat of the land. That sounded harder and harder with every passing year, but two weeks in a lodge with a guide might be as close to heaven as either of them could expect.

Ten minutes later, Kazim pulled onto the roof, parked, and got out. He turned a slow 360°, then leaned against the car and waited. Madsen listened and waited. When no one came up the ramp he stood.

"Madsen?" Kazim gave him a quizzical look. "What's with the mysterious super spy location switches?"

"Phone." Madsen held out his hand.

"Um, no." Kazim took a step back.

"Now. Or get the hell gone." Madsen snapped his fingers and flattened his palm.

"Fine, whatever. Here Detective Crazy-Man." Kazim relinquished his phone. Madsen powered it down and handed it back.

"Is that your only phone?"

"Yes. What happened?"

"Let's get out of the heat."

"That's a non-answer, but okay..." Kazim started to open the driver's door but Madsen grasped the handle first. "You driving?"

"Looks that way." Madsen dropped in behind the wheel not waiting for Kazim to acquiesce. Firing up the car he turned the air-con to arctic. As soon as Kazim was in, Madsen hit the gas. Tires squealed as they looped down three levels. He flashed the attendant his badge and when the gate went up he took a right turn the wrong way down a one-way street.

"What the f—" Kazim stopped talking and put his full attention on trying to not hit the window when Madsen took a high speed left down a too skinny alley—or an alley that *appeared* too skinny. Madsen blasted down it without scraping the paint. He stayed in the alley, crossing two streets he narrowly missed being broadsided by a beer delivery truck. He burned through a red light leaving a jam of slammed brakes and pounded horns. He jumped onto the 134 for a couple of miles and when he was damn sure they weren't being followed, he got

201

off at Figueroa in Eagle Rock and parked on a quiet residential street.

"What exactly is your motherfucking damage?" Kazim gasped for breath.

Madsen took his pistol out and set it on the dash, within easy reach. "Why were undercover cops waiting for me at the Highland Park Metro station?"

Kazim looked at him and sadly shook his head. "Man, you're a piece of work."

"How did they know I'd be there?"

"You want to accuse me of something? Do it. Come on, what is it you think I did?"

Madsen stared Kazim down, searching the younger man's eyes. After a full minute he exhaled slowly, closed his eyes and rested his forehead on the steering wheel. "I am a complete, total, asshole."

"That's a verifiable fact."

Madsen looked at him. "I'm sorry."

"Yes, you are. So I'm clear, you decided in that semi hillbilly brain of yours that I tipped off whoever it is that tried to shoot your stupid ass? That right, Madsen?"

"I guess." Madsen spoke, eyes down.

"They want you to get to Cisco, right? And I knew exactly where he would be at noon. If I told them where to grab him, they wouldn't need you. But I didn't. Why? Because I'm not working with them. Right? Right."

"When you put it that way I do seem dumb as a fence post."

"*Seem?*" Kazim's voice went up three steps. "And by the way, the folksy idioms are doing nothing but pissing me off. Okay?"

"Got it." Madsen leaned back. "You'd miss me if I was gone, wouldn't you?"

"No, I wouldn't."

"Maybe a little bit?"

"Fine a little. You're an ass, but…oh screw it."

"Partners?" Madsen held out his hand.

"Partners." Kazim shook it.

Madsen drove them to Cindy's, a diner serving good coffee and elevated Southern-tinged Americana cuisine. Madsen was buying. Kazim ordered the most expensive item on the menu, BBQ beef ribs, plus a side of sautéed broccoli. Madsen didn't flinch, he asked for the blackened catfish and a Mexican Coke.

While they waited for the food, Madsen laid out what went down with IA and Fong. Told Kazim he was sure he wasn't followed to the Metro. Kazim had taken enough loops and cutbacks to be sure no one tailed him from the cop shop, either.

"Anyone know you were picking me up?"

"I, um, told Hertzog."

"Told him where, what station?"

It was Kazim's turn to go sheepish. "Yes."

"Who else was in the bullpen?"

"Mauk and her partner."

"James."

"Right, I don't think they heard me."

"You don't think, well that's good enough for me. Any chance anyone else was, hanging around?"

"You think someone in Northeast division is dirty? Who? That's information you might want to share with your partner."

"Why, so you could do an interview with channel four? You didn't tell a reporter that I'd be at the Highland Park Station, did you?"

"Fuck you, okay, Madsen?" Kazim was saved from more ball-busting by the arrival of dinner. With the who-screwed-up-worse score tied, they slipped back into easy conversation. Clearly, there was no way short of a bright light and a rubber hose that they were going to discover who had leaked the location. They moved on. Kazim told

Madsen about seeing Adair and Cisco. He questioned Adair about what she saw during the shooting. If Madsen was looking for her to clear him with IA, he would need to look elsewhere. Adair saw the Dodge pull out blocking the truck's exit. She saw what she thought were police officers in front of them, but she couldn't swear to it. And Cisco had gone blank on the whole ordeal. "Both fear and adrenaline can scramble short-term memory like a magnet dragged over a hard drive."

"So, in laymen's terms, I'm screwed?"

"Pretty much."

Madsen took a sip from his coffee, looking inward, then up at Kazim. "When the deputies were closing in, I offered Cisco a gun."

"He didn't take it?"

"Nope. Looked at it like it was a copperhead. If he's pulling a con, he's one committed son of a bitch."

"Committed enough to die?" Kazim asked. Madsen shook his head.

Over apple pie and coffee Kazim asked Madsen what was in the note he sent Adair. "I told her where she should take Cisco. And that they should wait to hear from me."

"And where is that?" Kazim asked.

"Someplace safe... I hope."

Chapter 25

"A Chanel Five Action News exclusive. Sources tell us that a prime suspect has been named in the appalling murder of David Torres." The TV screen cut from Patricia Valencia to a photo of David: it looked like he was dressed for Easter, he had on a pale blue bowtie and a huge grin. "Torres, a young man with Down syndrome was shot and killed at an Eagle Rock bus stop on Sunday."

They cut to a video of Edward Torres looking seriously pious in front of the chapel at Saint Felicitas and Perpetua Church. "My grandson was a miracle. Sweet and caring. One of God's angels that walked among us, he was a beloved member of our congregation." Then he switched gears from loving grandfather to God's avenger. "The monster who took David from us must be brought to justice. To that end, I am personally offering a reward of fifty thousand dollars to the person who helps bring his killer to justice."

Patricia Valencia in the newsroom bobbed her head in a reverent nod of agreement. Exhaling, she appeared to be overtaken by her emotions, holding back tears. "A precious life cut short just blocks from the group home where David lived. The police are looking for this man," a mugshot of Cisco replaced the reporter's face. He looked battle-hard, tattoos showing and cold dead, eyes staring blankly out. A face it was easy to believe belonged to a killer.

"Chilling." The male anchor said.

"Yes, it is." Patricia Valencia's face hardened. "They are calling Francisco Gutierrez 'a person of extreme interest.' If you see him, call the tip line at the number below. Do not approach Gutierrez. Members of law enforcement consider him armed and very dangerous."

Madsen turned off the set. Adair and Cisco sat on the motel room's king bed. "What pure jobby." Adair had gone full Glaswegian. She flew to her feet and stomped around the room. "That daft cunt. Armed and dangerous, my arse." Cisco stared numbly down at his feet, too shellshocked to reprimand her for swearing.

The Rose Bowl Motor Court was an easy walk from Cindy's. Madsen hadn't told Kazim where he was going or how he would get there. "Still don't completely trust me?" Kazim asked.

"Not personal, Detective Kazim. Too many lives on the line to completely trust anyone."

The motel consisted of nine small cottages built in the 1930s. Adair paid cash, tipped an extra twenty-five and told the clerk her name was Mrs. Pink. No questions were asked, her expression made it clear no answers would be forthcoming. From the empty single-serving salad containers, peanut butter pretzels and juice bottles, Madsen knew Adair had brought in dinner from the Trader Joe's across the street.

"Yea dobber." Adair turned on Madsen. "Sold Cisco down the river, did you?"

"No." Madsen's arrival coincided almost exactly with the start of the news report. "This is the first I'm hearing of it. Swear."

"Awa' n bile your heed." Madsen couldn't help but grin, he caught Cisco's eye and soon both were smiling at her. "Screw ya both twice." She stomped out into the night, swinging the door hard behind herself.

"I think Adair has a super-sized bug up, um, bee in her bonnet."

"Not really, right?"

"No, just a way of saying she's angry."

"What was she talking? Not English."

"Got me, Bud. Whatever it was, it didn't sound good."

"I bet they were real bad words, right?"

"Sounded like it to me."

The smile fell from Cisco's face. "News lady thinks I killed David, right Tricky?"

"She's trying to paint that way. 'Extreme interest,' that's not even a thing."

"That picture, the mean man, that was me, right?"

"While ago. I don't think it's who you are now. People change, Cisco, you understand that?" Madsen struggled to verbalize thoughts he hadn't clearly worked out himself. "Like, when I met you, I thought you were a bad man, did bad things. But I changed. I, I think getting to know you, well, I think you're a good man."

"Do you think I killed David?"

"I don't."

"Someone did, right?"

"Right. I'm going to find out who."

"Why? David's not coming back. Finding who did something, won't change anything, right?"

"No. But whoever did this has to pay."

"How much?"

"I don't know, Bud. That's up to the courts."

"What if whoever killed David changed? They still have to pay?"

"Yeah. Maybe it will help David's mom and grandpa feel better."

"I don't think it will." Cisco puzzled it out. "Was that man David's grandpa?"

"On TV? Yeah, that was him. You never met him?"

"No. He didn't come to June's. David's mom did. But his grandpa always sent the big car to pick David up."

Madsen mulled this over, tagged it and filed it away under things to figure out in the morning. He asked Cisco if he needed a snack or a drink and was told he had already brushed his teeth. "No food after brushing teeth, Tricky." Cisco gave him the slightly sad smile that said, "Poor Tricky, he's nice but he doesn't know stuff."

Cisco was in bed and sleeping when Adair came back. Madsen drank coffee from a paper cup. He grinned at her.

"Shut up, you." She told him.

"Wouldn't say a word."

"Good."

"Might I ask you what a dobber is, or a jobby?"

"The night will go better if you don't."

"Nuff said, then." He tried to let it drop. But he couldn't help himself. "I'm thinking those weren't words you learned at finishing school…"

"You figured that, huh?" She checked to be sure Cisco was sleep. "Okay, dobber is an idjit, like you at this moment. Jobby is a stack of shite, also like you at this moment. Anything else you need to know, Detective Madsen?"

"No, I think you covered it perfectly, Ms. Hettrick." The words were much more formal than the looks moving between them. From her shoulder bag Adair produced her flask. Adding a shot of single malt to Madsen's coffee and serving herself in a plastic water cup, they touched cups and drank in silence.

"I really didn't know any of this was being leaked to the press." Madsen finally said.

"I believe you. But if not you, who?"

"Could have been LAPD, but then why not tell me? Could have been Edward Torres, he's got juice. My money is on someone at the Sheriff's Department." He put his hand over his cup when Adair offered to top it off. "When this clusterfuck is over, if I'm not in a cell or a grave, you and I are going to do some real drinking. Okay?"

"It's a date, barring the jail or dead thing, of course." She traced his jaw with her finger. Leaning down, she kissed him lightly on the lips. Then she looked at him, happy with what she saw.

"What was that?"

"A kiss."

"I know it was a kiss. I liked it, I did, might like more of them. But I guess I want to know *why* you kissed me?"

"In case." She shrugged and went into the bathroom. Moments later the shower came on. Madsen looked from the bathroom door, he hadn't heard her lock it, to the front door. Not locking a door wasn't an invitation. Hem had brought him up to believe if you are going to err, do it on the side of respect for others, not on the side that spoke to your own desires.

Stepping outside, Madsen called Bette Fong. Before he could ask, she said "No, we didn't alert the press."

"Come on, give it to me straight Bette. You owe me that."

"Don't insult me. Did some idiot begging to be fired maybe leak it? I can't say. Did it come through officially approved channels? No. Would I look you in the eye and not tell you our plans? Yes. Did I? No. I owe you nothing. That straight enough for you?"

"Yes, ma'am. Got it."

"Good. Now tell me you found Gutierrez."

"Wish I could. I'm running down a solid lead."

"Niels, I call B.S. Solid lead? Really. Bring him in before someone gets dead over this."

"You wound me, Bette, you do. I'll call you when I find him."

"I hope you do." A male voice called her name and she ended the connection. It didn't really matter, she had said all she was going to. Madsen was fairly sure the leak wasn't approved by upper command.

His next call was to Kazim, who answered in a sleepy voice and told Madsen to call back during normal business hours. Kazim's wife laughed in the background.

"Am I interrupting your marital congress?" Madsen asked.

"None of your business. Call tomorrow."

"I am." Madsen let out a laugh of his own. "Son, I'm just glad you're having some fun while I'm out here in the cold trying to save Cisco's life."

"Is he all right?" Kazim went serious.

"So far. Now zip your fly for thirty seconds and listen up."

Madsen could hear his wife complaining—not nagging, just letting her husband know she'd rather he hung up and get back in bed. "Okay, Madsen, thirty seconds starts now."

Madsen laid out what he needed from Kazim. "When you get in tomorrow, let everyone know you didn't see me yesterday. You went to Highland Park but I was a no-show. Got it?"

"It's not rocket science."

"That a yes?"

"Sure, why not. May I get back to my evening now?"

"One more thing, we need to know who besides Hertzog has contacts with the sheriffs."

"No, really?"

"Yes it's imp— You screwing with me?"

"Good night Madsen."

"Later, Detective Wise-Ass." Madsen's last call was to the leader of La Colina 13. It was going to be a long night.

Chapter 26

Madsen parked on a dirt road running down the spine of one of the brown hills that spread out from Montecito Heights. He and Rafael Ortiz had agreed on this spot because it had multiple exits leading to winding canyon streets that were easy to get lost in. That, and barring an air assault, it would be impossible to sneak up on them. Rafael was already there, waiting. He leaned against a fire-red metallic Suzuki Hayabusa. A low, stretched-out motorcycle built for insane speeds. At over a hundred and fifty, it still had the torque to lift the front tire. Madsen was driving Adair's Honda, with less than half the horsepower and four times the weight of the Hayabusa, there was no way Madsen could catch Rafael if he decided to run.

Rafael checked the Honda to make sure they were alone. Leaning over to look in the rear window, his leather jacket fell open and Madsen got a good glimpse of the revolver tucked into his belt.

"You have zero to fear from me." Madsen lifted his jacket and turned around.

"Got that right, Detective. My primo, appears you're still look to hang a murder rap on him. I deep-six you, maybe his problems go away." For Rafael, this wasn't a threat. He was mulling his options out loud.

"You could do that." Madsen nodded, helping Rafael with the

decision.

"I could. Why don't I?"

"Number one reason: I'm the only cop in LA county that thinks Cisco's innocent."

"Number two?"

"I don't have a number two. Figured number one was strong enough. If you don't care how it turns out for your cousin, I'm burnt toast no matter which way I sing this song."

"Verdad." Rafael looked out over the lights of downtown LA. The smoke and smog in the air sent it twinkling warmly. From a distance, it was a magical city.

"When Cisco went down, he was riding my fall." Rafael kept his back to Madsen, his voice soft enough Madsen needed to strain to hear him. "He didn't kill that maricón. They caught him with the gun, but Cisco was no killer. He was supposed to do a stretch in youth authority. Would have been strike three for me. Life, no plea deal, nothing. So I let him take it, no way I could have seen them sending a kid to Pelican Bay. I had no juice in there. They broke him bad. They didn't stop until he went cold inside and learned to be a life taker." Rafael turned to Madsen, "I owe Cisco my life. I owe Cisco *his* life. What do you need from me?"

"I need you to look at this." Madsen passed his phone to Rafael, on it were PDFs of the sheriff's files on Cisco. Rafael slipped on a pair of half frame readers. He flicked his finger to the left, scanning the files quick as any seasoned lawyer.

Getting to the last file he ground his teeth as rage built. "Carajo. Hijo de puta. This?" He stabs at the phone. "Bullshit. *We* beat down Cisco? No. Anyone touched him and—" he motioned slitting a throat. "Some anonymous OG says Cisco was drawing heat so…no. We go after a man, we don't hit the brakes until they stop breathing. But we didn't, not with Cisco."

"You say so. Don't make it a fact."

"Calling me a liar?" Rafael flared. He stepped up to Madsen's face. A move that backed most down. Madsen held his ground.

"I'm not calling you anything." Madsen stared the vetrano down. "Everyone lies to cops. I learned to not take it personal. I also don't believe most of what I hear."

Rafael gave a long, potentially violent, pause before stepping back. "We're like two old soldiers, too tough to die and too stupid not to know the war is over."

"Sounds right, only the war is far from over. I'm just getting wound up."

"Then let's get to the truth of it, what happened to mi primo favorito."

"I'm all ears."

"We found Cisco two blocks from my house. He was a bloody mess, more dead than alive. I took him to the E.R. Then I went looking for who done him. Wasted a lot of time and considerable threats, came up empty."

"Your ever hear of a detective named Wasson?"

"That pendejo worked East Los. Why? You think he hurt Cisco?"

"I honestly don't know. His name came up, that's all."

"If he did…" Rafael let his murderous thoughts hang unspoken.

"Don't fuck up my case. Only way I clear Cisco is by proving someone else shot Torres. If it was Wasson, or he knows who it was and you go after him, Cisco is screwed."

Half of what made Madsen a good detective was his ability to read people. He was sure Rafael was telling him the truth, he hadn't beaten Cisco. The other half was that Madsen didn't stop until he had the evidence to lock the perpetrator up. He was sure members of the Sheriff's Department were involved. And that Detective Wasson hid skeletons, but he didn't know which closet to search. Fong had told him to stay miles clear of the Sheriff's Department. That was looking less and less possible.

213

"I need one more thing." Madsen said.

"Never a 'please' with the LAPD."

"I need to get Cisco out of the county."

"Yes, you do."

"I need a clean car to pull it off."

"Detective, are you asking a known gangster to provide you with a vehicle?"

"Yes, sir, I am."

"Follow me."

Rafael gunned the Hayabusa and dropped the clutch kicking up a fan of dirt. It took all Madsen had to keep the bike's tail lights in sight. They went down into Lincoln Heights. Rafael unlocked a chain-link gate and they parked in front of what looked like an abandoned service station. Lifting one of the rolling doors revealed a pristine 1967 Lincoln Continental, two-door hardtop. Bagged and dropped. Two-tone bloody red on the bottom, whipped cream on top. Classy black pinstriping. It was killer. Madsen let out a low whistle.

Rafael tossed the keys, a proud grin sneaking across his face. "Paint job cost more than you make in a month, Detective. So be careful, or be ready to drain your 401k."

"It's nice. Subtle as a nun at a whore's convention. But, damn, no one will suspect a cop behind the wheel."

"My thinking exactly."

"Is it stolen?"

"Detective." Rafael mimes taking an arrow to the heart. "It's my mother's church car."

"Then I'll have it back by Sunday."

"You better."

After they moved the Honda into one of the bays, Madsen and Rafael hit the streets. When their paths diverged, Rafael shot a two fingered salute. Madsen returned the gesture but was sure it went unseen behind the tinted windows.

The Lincoln was a road beast. The V-8 462 came from the factory with 340 hp, but it felt like Rafael added more than one pony. Disc brakes at all four corners. It didn't handle like a modern sports car, but it also didn't handle like the flying brick it started out as. Cruising down the freeway Madsen turned on the stereo, and was greeted by Arron Neville singing What a Friend We Have In Jesus.

Fuck. What is the penalty for screwing up Rafael's mother's church car? Don't screw it up. Just don't.

On a hunch, Madsen pulled off at Highland Park and rolled past Holly Torres' bungalow. The house was lit up so he parked a few blocks down and backtracked. The fewer people able to link the lowrider to him, the better.

A rockabilly song drifted out Holly's open windows. She danced slowly around her living room, hugging herself. Out of reverence for the beauty of the moment, Madsen waited for the song to end before knocking.

"I'm sorry about the music, Mrs. Ableson I'll turn it—" Holly stopped when the door revealed Madsen. "You aren't Mrs. Ableson." She was tipsy enough to slow, but not slur, her speech.

"I'm not. How are you doing, Holly?"

"How?" She let out a harsh laugh. "That is the stupidest question. Unanswerable and yet everyone asks some version of it. Would you like to come in?" She walked back into the room without waiting to see if he followed. "You drink sangria?" She called, turning the vintage HiFI down.

"Sangria?"

"My specialty." She brought him a mason jar filled with ice, red wine and chunks of fruit. She looked into his eyes when handing him the drink. "You're not bad looking, in a Marlboro man, cowboyish way. You ever consider a mustache?"

"You've had more than one of these, haven't you?"

Holly threw a pout. "Don't you think I'm pretty?"

Madsen's smile was warm, in what he hoped she took as brotherly way. Turning from her, he clocked the record player. "Great music, classic. Carl Perkins edging into a Gene Vincent vibe. Who is it?"

"Not classic. Well, classic but part of the newer wave psychobilly. Tiger Army, local band. Years ago, before I was of legal age for, you know." She added a sexy curve to that line, but Madsen didn't seem to notice. "I saw them play at the All Star Lanes."

"The bowling alley. That must have been cool."

"It was that." She dropped onto the sofa, miraculously not spilling a drop of her drink. "Sit." She patted the seat beside her.

"Thanks." Madsen sat in a wing back chair, keeping a coffee table between them.

"You playing hard to get? Or…?"

"I don't have a lot of rules, but not taking advantage of beautiful grieving women is one of them."

"You think I'm beautiful? I'll take that." She smiled inwardly and let the coquettish come-on drop. "For just a moment, with some wine and music, I forget. No, not forget…but feel some distance from losing David. Does that make me a bad person?"

"Makes you a survivor. Some people are dragged under by loss and pain. Doesn't do anyone any good. You either come up for air from time to time or drown."

"Thank you for that. Even if it is a lie."

"It's not. Can I ask you a couple of questions?"

"Sure." She looked at his untouched sangria. "Would you like some coffee?"

"Yes, please."

While she boiled water and set up a French press Madsen asked questions. No, she hadn't seen the TV news report. No, she wouldn't believe Cisco had anything to do with David's death, they were real friends. No, she hadn't lied before when she said she had no contact with her father. Madsen watched her face for any tell. Best he could detect, she was being honest.

"Did you know David went to a Catholic Church in San Marino?" He asked.

"Saint Fricassee and Perpetual pain in the neck? No, my son didn't go there. He wasn't a Catholic."

"Your father tells a different story. Says he saw David, took him to church most Sundays."

"He what…? That sanctimonious son of a bitch. You know he's a homophobic asshat who believes in praying the gay out? He thinks same-sex love is an abomination." She disappears into her bedroom, coming back with a framed photo. "Is *that* an abomination?"

Madsen looks at the picture. Taken at a Valentine's Day dance, David and a pale haired young man are posed kissing in front of a string of red balloons forming a big heart. "Was this his boyfriend?"

"Jake was a boy who liked to dance with David. They never got serious. He wasn't the one." Thinking about this her face darkened. "If you talk to my father, could you ask him what kind of God made my son, and didn't send him someone to love?"

Madsen didn't answer, she didn't look like she was expecting him to. Before he left he asked if he could keep the Valentine picture for a little while.

"Of course." She pulled it from the frame and passed it to Madsen. "Detective?"

"Yes?"

"Thank you for being a good man."

"I'm not that good, trust me."

"I do, and you are."

Chapter 27

It was well after midnight when Madsen returned to the Rose Bowl Motor Court. Cisco was snoring softly, beside him, Adair had fallen asleep on top of the comforter. A case file rested on her chest. Her hair was rumpled and a small fleck of drool spotted the corner of her mouth. There was humanness and beauty in the moment that endeared her to Madsen. He gently moved the file onto the nightstand. Her eyes fluttered for a moment before she sunk back into deep sleep.

Madsen moved a chair against the door and leaned his head back. Hem and Nat had gotten his message, that much he knew. Had they made it to safety? That was another matter. There was no way to call them, but their lack of connectivity was a large part of their protection. He had to trust—admittedly not his strong suit. Hem and Nat had been badasses in their day, but the sun was long set on that day. Now, Hem forgot Niels' name, and to turn off the fire under a kettle. And Nat's street-fighting days had been replaced by arthritis and bad knees.

Madsen couldn't help feeling he had failed his grandfather. He'd placed Hem at risk to help a man he'd just met. On cue, Cisco coughed and mumbled something in Spanish. Madsen knew what Hem would have him do, regardless of the consequences. "We're put on earth to help our fellow travelers. If you can lighten another's load, you do. Remember that kid." Madsen was ten when Hem told him that. He never forgot it.

Sleep was elusive. Madsen had a million questions and not an answer in sight. Cisco had been living at the group home for a few years, why try and kill him *now*? If Rafael was telling the truth about deputies causing Cisco's brain injuries, and they wanted him dead, why not kill him with a hit and run? A person with special needs dying in a car accident wouldn't raise an eyebrow. Shooting him at a bus stop guarantees an investigation. If they had tried to shoot Cisco, missed and hit David by accident, how is it possible that Hill and Russo hadn't seen the shooters?

Don't overcomplicate it. Solve David's murder and the rest will follow.

Bette Fong was right about one thing, his job was to close the Torres case. And he sure as hell wasn't handing it over to Hertzog.

The smell of coffee woke Madsen. Adair said she was sorry. Looking at the bedside clock, he saw it was a few minutes after six. Cisco was gone. Before Madsen could panic he saw in the bathroom mirror that Cisco was in the tub, playfully skimming his hand over a tall stack of bubbles.

"He gets up early." Adair said passing Madsen a cup of coffee. "I would have picked up breakfast, but some great lummox was blocking the door."

"Sorry about that."

"Kidding, Niels. It made me feel safe."

"You are."

"Really?" She gave him a disbelieving smirk.

"Comparatively."

"Compared to what, Caracas?"

"Yes. Compared to that you are safe as—"

She looked at him, smile falling. "Cut the bullshit."

"Bad language, Adair." Cisco called from the bathroom.

"Sorry, Cisco." Her eyes told Madsen she hadn't known Cisco was listening.

"We really are safe as safe can be." Madsen spoke loud enough for Cisco to hear.

"Good. I feel much better." Adair sounded stilted, she was a poor liar.

"Can you help me get something out of the car?" Madsen headed out the door with Adair behind him.

"Tell me the truth, Niels…" Adair stopped speaking, looking around the parking area asked, "Where *is* my car?"

"It was too easy for anyone looking for you to spot." Madsen motioned to the Lincoln. Adair's jaw dropped.

"You, you traded my Honda for…this?" She did a Vanna White pose over the car.

"Best I could do in the middle of the night."

"When this is over do I get to keep it?" Her eyes sparkled.

"You *like* this car?"

"Who wouldn't, can I keep it?"

"Well, it belongs to a dangerous man, so I'm guessing no."

"Too bad. Really is amazing. So, no cool car, what other bad news do you bring?"

"I need you and Cisco to stay at the motel today."

"I need to go to work. I have other cases, you know."

"Will any of them die if you stay away a couple of days?"

"Tell me you're being a wee bit dramatic."

"Not. Whoever was following us stepped it up when they shot at us. Attempting to kill a cop is a whole 'nother level of bad craziness. Here's the score, I believe Cisco is being targeted by sheriff's deputies. And my boss wants Cisco arrested. If he's arrested, he will likely land in the hands of the same deputies who may have beaten him into his present condition. Dramatic? No. If anything I'm underplaying the trouble riding toward us. You want out? Want to go back to work and leave Cisco with me, go. I got this."

"No." She shook her head, resolute. "I'm in, until…until it's over."

"Good. While I'm gone I need you two to keep your heads down. Stay in the room. Tonight, I'll get you and Cisco to safety."

"If you don't make it back?"

"I will." He sounded more confident than he felt.

"Drop the bravado Niels, what do we do?"

"Call Kazim. You can trust him." Madsen hoped that was true.

On the way to pick up breakfast, Madsen called the Deputy Medical Examiner's Office. When Collins came on the line and heard Madsen's voice he sounded uncharacteristically shaken. "Did you give the receptionist your name?"

"No, told her I was a family friend."

"The phone you're calling from?"

"Burner. Untraceable. Clarence, what the hell?"

"Chief M.E. got word—from where, I don't know—that I met with you. I'm to stay clear of the Torres case. I was done examining the body, so normally I would be out of the case anyway. She knows that. So, why order me?"

"Sorry you got dragged into this mess. You following her orders?"

"Niels, my daughter just got accepted into Stanford."

"That's great. Congratulate Kayla."

"Thank you, I will. Point is, I'll do nothing, as in absolutely not one damn thing to jeopardize my paycheck. Got it?"

Madsen's phone pinged to tell him a text had arrived. "Got it."

Hanging up, Madsen checked the message. It was from an unknown number: "Followed up. Bullets found. Flattened. Rifling gone. No way to discern gun. Evidence tampered with."

Madsen deleted the text and silently thanked Collins. This was both good and bad news. They wouldn't be able to link the bullets to

221

the gun Cisco was holding. On the other hand, they wouldn't be able to prove who had really killed David.

Chapter 28

"Why aren't you in jail, or at the very least fired?" Edward Torres sat behind his desk.

"Want me to answer both those questions?" Madsen hadn't taken the offered seat. If Torres didn't like being looked down on, fuck him. "I'm not in jail because I haven't committed a crime. As to not being fired, I guess we'll chalk that up to a strong union."

"If I call the chief will he tell me that—against my wishes—you are still on my grandson's case?"

"Yep. Maybe your juice is weaker than you think." Madsen took out his phone and turned on the voice recording app. "You don't mind? Just to keep it straight."

"I mind. I want my lawyer here."

"Again with the lawyer and the chief? Let's get to it then." He took out his handcuffs.

"What the hell are you doing?"

"You know the drill. I'm going to charge you with obstructing a police investigation by leaking pertinent slash private facts regarding an open investigation to the media. And then you and I get to do the cuffed perp-walk dance."

"I didn't go to that reporter. She came to me."

"Sure. I bet you own enough television stations to get her to say whatever you want. Cool part is, I don't need to prove the case to book you. That's the D.A.'s business. But the press, damn their heartless scoop loving souls, they will run with it. The more degraded you look in cuffs, the more play it'll get. Hell, you might even wind up a meme." Madsen held up the phone, finger hovering over the record button.

"Fine. I have nothing to hide."

"Great." Madsen started the recording giving their names, the date and time. In his breast pocket he had his ace in the hole: the photo of David kissing a guy. If Torres stonewalled, he would threaten to go public with the picture and the knowledge that the champion and defender of traditional marriage had a gay grandson. Playing this card was morally wrong, but not as wrong as sending an innocent man to jail.

"Mr. Torres, have you ever met this man?" Madsen dropped a picture of Cisco on the desk. "Francisco Gutierrez?"

Torres looked for a blink before answering. "No, I haven't. But as I told you last time, many people work for me."

"Your point?"

"Simple math detective. More people know me than I know."

"Price of wealth. You're sure you haven't met this man?"

"Completely."

"But you know who he is."

"Yes. He is the thug who killed my grandson."

"Who told you that?" Madsen gave it a beat then struck again. "Who told you Gutierrez was suspected of murdering your grandson?"

"I don't, um, recall." Torres ran his thumb over his index finger, apparently feeling if he needed a manicure.

"You forgot? Is that really your answer?"

"Yes. It's the truth."

"No. That's not the truth. You're a liar." Torres looked shocked at being called out. Madsen didn't give him time to object. "How did your grandson get gunpowder residue matching *your* revolver on his

224

hand?" It wasn't true, but most of the public watched *CSI* on TV and they'd believe anything was possible.

"I..." This time Torres' thumb moved over his middle finger. "I haven't any idea."

"Really?" Madsen smiled and kept dropping bombs. "How did Francisco Gutierrez get hold of your .38?"

"I don't—"

"Did you hire him to kill your grandson?"

"Why would—"

"You tell me." Madsen sat down, losing a tactical advantage, but giving Torres a feeling of security. "Mr. Torres, if you gave the gun to someone by accident, tell me and we can figure this whole deal out. I know you loved your grandson."

"I did." Torres' facade started to crack. "I did. I loved David."

"Who did you give the revolver to? Please."

Torres ran his thumb over the next finger before speaking. "Gutierrez. I gave it to Francisco Gutierrez. He threatened to hurt David if I didn't give him the gun. I thought he was going to sell it. If I..."

Madsen slowly exhaled, whistling. He let the silence stretch past uncomfortable.

Torres filled the silence. "I didn't tell you before because Sheriff White assured me there was already enough evidence to convict Gutierrez." Torres ran out of fingernails to feel so he started back on the index finger. Madsen kept quiet, his face emotionless. "If they knew it was my gun there would be liability. And...maybe Gutierrez let David feel the gun, or...I know I should have told you. I screwed up."

Madsen leaned forward and turned the recording off. "You need to stop right now. Cisco didn't kill David. They were friends. How do I know this? I've spent time with him. I know the sheriff told you about his record. But believe me, the man in that file and the man I know are as different as Cain and Abel."

"They told me he has you fooled. He's a con artist, and you're buying his line."

"Look at me, Mr. Torres. Do I look like a guy who believes in fairy tales? Hell, if God himself sent me a message in a burning bush I'd want to see hard evidence before repeating it to anyone." Madsen knew pushing religious angles might hit home.

"You're a cynic, Detective."

"That's not a bad thing. And I'm telling you objectively, Gutierrez is innocent."

Torres swiveled his chair so that he faced the window.

Madsen spoke to the older man's back. "We've established I don't know scripture like I'm sure you do. But I'd bet that if Jesus were asked, he'd tell us he believed in redemption, in the power of God's love to help people to change. I can't explain how, but Cisco is changed. No recording, just you and me in the room, I need to know what happened. Come on, you know it's what David would have wanted."

Torres turned back, his eyes full of tears. "He would."

"I'm listening."

"Turn that on." Torres pointed at the phone. His back grew stiffer as he set his hands palms down on his desk. "David wasn't perfect, I loved that kid, maybe too much... He loved shiny things. I called him my little magpie. He thought that was funny. He'd run around my vault cawing and touching anything gold." He drifted into the memory.

Madsen waited until he was sure nothing more was forthcoming before speaking. "Did David steal a binder of coins from you?" Torres nodded, his lower lip trembled. "And the Bijan Colt, *he* took that, not Cisco?"

"Yes." Torres' momentary strength flowed away.

"Why did you lie to us?"

"They told me Francisco did it, and that my gun would only confuse the case."

"That's the rationalization, but not the 'why,' is it? Come on, Mr.

226

Torres, come clean."

"Clean?" Torres felt the word like it was a foreign concept. "Come clean, Okay. I didn't want people to find out David was a thief. Didn't want them judging him. Where is the harm in that? He took things I would have freely given him if he'd asked."

And there it was, the truth laid out. No gun for hire, no massive conspiracy, just a grandfather's love and misguided desire to save his grandson's reputation.

Madsen asked when the gun was last fired. Torres told him he had shot it with David the Sunday of his death. He had a range in his basement. David liked target practice. "He almost never hit the target, but the noise made him laugh." His face got very serious. "Was it my gun that killed David?"

"I don't know." Madsen could have lied and said no it wasn't, but instead he told him, "Someone, I suspect from the Sheriff's Department, destroyed the bullets that killed your grandson. Did you ask them to do that?"

"No." Torres stared down, lost again. Madsen poured and brought him a tumbler of scotch. He told himself he wasn't acting out of kindness to the old man. He was doing what was needed to get the interview back on track. He waited until Torres finished his drink and poured another before asking him if he had any idea who might have killed David.

"I…can't think…"

"Who had a reason to harm David? The two big motives are love or money. Anything like that?"

Torres looked up. "I keep track of David's trust fund. Holly controls it, but I have passive oversight. I noticed in the last couple of months more than forty-thousand dollars has gone out. I figured they needed something medical for David. But I don't…. Ask that lady who runs Bridge-Way. That's who withdrew the money."

Chapter 29

Madsen parked behind Bridge-Way group home and saw an incoming text from Kazim. "HORNET'S NEST BUZZING. Queen has me in her sights. So far Hertzog is the only D with SD connect. Widening search."

"Booker?" Madsen typed.

"Not connected. Reach out?" Kazim sent back.

"Yes. Step carefully." Madsen pocketed the phone and headed up the back walkway.

Rashona wasn't happy to find Madsen knocking at Bridge-Way's backdoor. "Yes?"

"I'm Detective Madsen."

She recognized him. "June isn't here."

"Will she be gone long?"

"Hard to say."

"I'll wait, if that's okay."

"I won't stop you." She stood back, allowing him to pass through the kitchen. Madsen took notice of the brand-new high-end stove and fridge. The tiles on the floor shined and the walls gleamed with fresh paint.

Rashona left him sitting in the living room. The room was clean but, like most underfunded facilities, it needed a plaster patch here, a paint touch-up there, threadbare carpet replaced. Donald sat in his wheelchair staring at a TV situated in front of a nonfunctional fireplace. On the screen The Mandalorian was running silently from an alien monster.

"Hey, partner, you want me to turn up the sound?"

Donald mumbled at the screen. "Mandi, run…Oh no, no, no, no…."

"He can't hear you." A blur in a pixie cut dropped down beside Madsen. "Donald? He wears headphones." Lilly tapped her ear in case Madsen was weak on the concept.

"Is Donald hearing impaired?"

"What?" She tilted her head, like that might help her understand him.

"Does he have a hard time hearing?"

"I know what impaired means. If he didn't use headphones we'd be impaired."

"Donald likes his shows loud, huh?"

"Right." That settled she dropped the smile. "I know you." She pointed a finger at Madsen. "You're police. You took Cisco away."

"To protect him."

"Really?"

"Promise."

"Maybe that's okay."

"You're Lilly, his girlfriend."

"That's right." Lilly smiled proudly. "Did he tell you about us?"

"You did, last time I was here. Told me he was innocent."

"He is."

"I know. I could have saved some time if I'd just listened to you."

"See?" She was well pleased with herself. "Where is Cisco now?"

"Safe, he's somewhere safe. Want me to take a message to him?"

"Yes." She said quickly, and then paused to think what that message should be. "Okay, I got it. Tell Cisco I miss him. And…" She forgot what came next.

"He'll be home soon, maybe you want to tell him yourself."

"Can I see him today?" Her smile was all crooked teeth and joy. "Please?"

"Sorry, no. Not until he's out of danger."

"You are…" Fear crowded out her smile. "Danger? He needs me."

"Cisco will be fine. I'll protect him."

"No." Lilly stared Madsen down, but before she could say more Rashona called her to come help in the kitchen. At the doorway Lilly turned back to Madsen. She had something to say, but couldn't find the words. Instead she shook her head and left.

While Madsen waited, he had enough time to watch most of *The Mandalorian* episode. He found himself enjoying it. Reminded him of the Sergio Leone man with no-name westerns Hem liked to show him when he was a kid. He forgot how cool Eastwood was back then. He was thinking about growing a mustache when Lilly dropped back down on the couch.

"Why are you still here?" She asked, then answered herself before he could. "You're waiting for June. She went to Ralphs for watermelon. Pris will freak if she can't get her melon. Did you meet Pris? She screams sometimes."

"How far is Ralphs?"

"Twenty minutes by bus. But June doesn't take a bus, she has a car."

"So how far by car?"

"Less. Watermelon's on special."

"Good to know."

Entering the kitchen Madsen found Rashona chopping vegetables and dropping the chunks into an industrial sized soup pot. "You haven't left yet?" She asked, clearly irritated that he hadn't.

"No. Is it something I did, or just that I'm a cop that you don't like?"

She mulled this for a moment. "Both. We saw the news. Why're you making Cisco look like he murdered our David?"

"I'm not."

"Looked that way." She was rhythmically chopping a bunch of celery stalks while she spoke. "That picture of Cisco? Not the Cisco I know."

"A mugshot from the last time he was arrested. Again, not my doing." Madsen snapped his fingers to get her to look up from the vegetables to him. "I know Cisco didn't kill David."

"Then why's he not home."

"The problem is…I should be having this conversation with June."

"Because some immigrant cook could never follow your thought train?"

"It's not that."

"Oh, yes, it's that. I see you, Detective. You pretend to be open to all kinds of people, like we all the same to you. First day you came I saw you pretending that our clients don't bother you. I see you recoiling on the inside."

"You got me wrong."

"No, I don't. I'm an RN, worked psychiatric hospitals. I can see below the face you show."

"Maybe you *were* right about me." Madsen leaned in the doorway, closed his eyes before continuing to speak. "But, I get it now. Cisco isn't the man in that mugshot anymore. Problem is, I can't convince my colleagues. There is enough circumstantial evidence to arrest him. With his jacket and a vehement enough D.A. they might get a conviction. Neither of us want that."

"Have a seat, Detective." She motioned to a chair at the table, waited until he sat and had placed a tall glass of herbal ice tea in front of him before she continued. "Now I can see your heart. What do you need to keep Cisco safe?"

"I have to find out who killed David." He unfolded a printout, laying it on the table.

Rashona leaned over his shoulder. "A spread sheet from the David Torres Trust."

"Yeah, that's right."

"You're surprised I know what it is? Or that I can read?"

"No, it's not…."

Rashona let out a low chuckle. "You fluster easy for a cop."

"Not always."

"Why do you have this?" She pointed a finger at the paper.

"Edward Torres gave it to me. He thinks June stole over thirty-thousand dollars from David's trust." Madsen said without judgment. "Is he right?"

"No." She stood erect, proud and looked down on Madsen. "June is the finest woman I've ever known. She didn't kill David."

"Didn't say that." Madsen kept it cool.

"You implied it. This place, these people? She gives her life to them. She would die for them."

Madsen points at the printout. "I hear you. But, June withdrew the money. No explanation."

Rashona's shoulders slumped and her head dropped into her fingers. "This, it's not how it looks."

"Time we got in front of this. You want to help June? Tell me what's what."

"Last May a new health inspector told us to bring our kitchen up to code or he would shut us down. Old inspector turned a blind eye. I know food safety, I'd never endanger our people. Still, laws are laws."

"So June embezzled from David Torres to pay for the new kitchen?"

"No. Not like that. She…"

"Anyone found out, the house would lose accreditation, right?" Madsen was starting to push.

"Yes, but—"

"And June would kill to keep Bridge-Way open. Right? Right?"

"No. Yes, but no. She'd never hurt David."

"How did it happen? He found out, they argued and the gun went off?"

"No." Rashona's face flushed with anger. "That is *not* what happened."

"Okay. Did you shoot him to protect June?" Madsen showed only compassion.

She looked at him, shook her head. "She was paying the money back."

"Really?" Madsen wasn't buying.

"Two hundred dollars every month."

"You sure about that?"

"Yes. Check the account. But you know I'm telling the truth."

Madsen took his time before answering her. She was right. He could subpoena bank records, but he was certain they would show that June had been repaying the trust a piece at a time.

"June had half a brain, she'd let them take the home and go back to private practice."

"She's a shrink?"

"Yes. She got tired of listening to healthy rich people whine about their mommies and daddies. She wanted to do *good.*"

Madsen respected these women more than he could say. More than either of them would want to hear.

Lilly burst into the kitchen and without looking around she started to speak to Rashona. "June was going to give me a ride. She's gone too long. Too long. I checked my watch."

"Lilly, when does your shift start?"

Lilly looked at her watch. "Too soon. I'm late. I can't be."

"I can give you a ride." Madsen said. "I need to talk to June if she's there."

"Can he?" She asked Rashona.

233

"Go on. Get your smock."

"It's a uniform." Lilly corrected.

"Get it and go."

Entering the Ralphs parking lot Lilly excitedly started pointing. "The blue one. That's June's." It was a ten year-old minivan. Pulling alongside it, they both saw the driver's door open, and a shopping cart on its side, contents spilled. "Oh, no. That's not good. Where is June?"

"She just went to get help cleaning this up."

"You sure?"

"Sure. Run on now, don't want to be late."

"No. Not late." Lilly was out of the car, then stopped. "You will make sure June is okay?"

"Won't leave until I do."

"Okay." Lilly hurried toward the store.

Madsen hid the Lincoln on a side street before walking back to the minivan. Smashed watermelon carnage littered the area by June's car door. Her purse and keys lay on the driver's seat where she probably tossed them before unloading the cart. Theft wasn't likely. He scanned the lot, nothing seemed off. Circling the store, he searched for any sign. Back by a row of dumpsters he was about give up when he heard a groan. June struggled to pull herself upright. Her face was bleeding and bruised, her left arm hung uselessly at her side. Madsen ran and caught her. "Can you stand?"

She shook her head. When he reached an arm around her waist her eyes popped wide with pain. Using her good arm he supported her best he could. He helped her to a half wall that she could lean against while he inspected her wounds. "Who did this to you?"

June tried to speak, came out a whisper. "Two…men…wanted Cisco."

"To know where Cisco was?" She nodded for an answer, speaking

234

was clearly painful. "Cops?"

"Maybe...."

"White guys?" Again, she nodded.

A young stocker stepped onto the loading dock. He yelled at Madsen to leave that woman alone. Madsen held his badge over his head. "Call 911, she needs an ambulance. Now." He stayed with her until the paramedics arrived. Through gasps and rattling breaths she told him two men tried to drag her into their SUV. She kicked one behind his knee and punched the other in the face. It hurt too much to laugh, but she smiled telling Madsen she broke the man's nose. They chased her to the dumpsters. Both men had ball caps, sunglasses and wore leather gloves.

After June left for the hospital, Madsen called Adair. "Boredom central, how can we help you?"

"June was attacked."

"No. Is she okay?"

"She will be. They were trying to find out where Cisco was."

"Oh." Adair went quiet.

"Stay away from the windows."

"You're leaving us here?"

"You're safer there than with me. I'll be there soon as I can."

Madsen's phone pinged just after he hung up. It was a text from Kazim. "We need to talk. Urgent. Call in ten."

No shit we need to talk. Attacking a civilian in a public place was bold and stupid. They are scared and that makes them dangerous.

Chapter 30

"Boy, you go to Simi Valley, you better walk right." Nat had told Madsen when he was a teenager. "I was dating this white nurse, pretty woman with a good heart. She invited me to dinner at her place in Simi Valley. The place where they let Koon and his crew off and lit the fuse for the LA uprising, no thank you. She batted her eyes and wiggled her tail, and well... Night I went to visit her, I was stopped a block from the freeway exit. Slammed on a hood, frisked and asked what I was doing there. It was a damn border crossing and I apparently didn't have a visa. They told me to get on the road and not stop 'til I got back to Compton. I never lived in Compton my whole life, but I didn't argue the fact. Never found a reason to return to Simi Valley." Hearing this Madsen decided to give Simi a wide berth. He would never go that deep into the Valley.

And yet, here he was, headed down the 118 toward Simi, rolling with a Muslim-American and no jurisdiction into the center of the beast. Simi Valley sits thirty miles from downtown LA and decades away in racial relations. Its population is seventy-five percent white, and a lot of those are cops.

Reason for the run was Kazim's urgent call. He'd discovered that Detective Wasson of the sheriff's Anti-Gang Squad was the proud registered owner of a black Dodge Challenger. That made Wasson the only person involved in this violent mess that they had both a name and address for. Madsen wasn't about to turn Wasson over to Fong so she would either give it to Internal Affairs or sit on it. Fronting Wasson at his station was out. It would be Madsen and Kazim against a whole posse of deputies, even the clean ones would back Wasson if it was him or two LAPD detectives. The only choice was to hit Wasson at his house. And that was in... Simi Valley.

From the road Madsen called Bridge-Way. Rashona told him she had heard from June, "She said they wanted to keep her in the hospital, so she told them to tape her ribs, give her an aspirin and sign her out, she has work to do."

"Does she ever rest?"

"Not that I've seen."

"I'm sorry." Madsen said.

"What for, for being a cop, or for being you?"

"Both. Never should have doubted either of you." Rashona laughed and told him to clear Cisco and they would be even.

Wasson lived in an older planned community, five suburban blocks of look-a-like single-story ranch style homes. If Madsen didn't know the local history it would be easy to find it pleasant and safe-looking, and he guessed that was true, as long and your skin was pale and your politics slightly right of Sean Hannity.

Kazim parked his Kia Soul a block past Wasson's house. He adjusted the mirrors so they could surveil the house without facing it. From the back hatch he brought out two Kevlar vests and a Benelli M4 shotgun. Madsen balked at the vest, thinking it sent the wrong message.

"Is, 'shoot at me again I'm right here, unprotected' a better message?"

"Yes, but—"

"Nothing. Vest up or I drive us home now."

"Okay, Mom, I'll wear it." Madsen said, but smiled at the kid's growing self-confidence. He looked around the strangely boxy cute-ute. "You're a full-grown detective, right?" Kazim nodded but didn't take the bait and answer. "I'm asking 'cause you drive a kid's car."

"Really, Madsen, you want to have a 'what you drive reflects on your masculinity,' debate?"

"Please no, not that." Madsen held his palms out in surrender. "I admit, it rides a hell of a lot better than my shot-up Ford."

"Yes, it does. And it gets thirty-one miles per gallon. Your truck?"

"Fifteen…downhill…with a tail wind."

"Does it have an infotainment center? Bluetooth? USB player? No? How about ice-cold air?" Kazim put his face near the vent, cold air blowing his hair back.

"This box on wheels is brand-new, right?"

Kazim hesitated, knowing there was a trap here that he couldn't see. "It's a year old."

"Then my truck has one thing your Kia doesn't. Know what that is?"

"You'll say style."

Madsen shook his head.

"Character."

Another shake.

"Heritage?"

"None of the above. My Ford has a…paid off pink slip. Zero payments per month."

Kazim laughed, letting loose an appreciative whistle. "That is a luxury feature I wish I had."

On the drive to Simi Valley they discussed Kazim's progress in discovering the leak. Other LAPD officer's employment records were near impossible to get a look at. When he'd asked Sergeant Booker, the man almost had an aneurism. "I told him it was for you, he said he didn't care if it was for Daryl Gates' ghost. His men were clean, end of story. Oh, and if he heard I was sniffing around them again I would get a 'night stick enema.' Nice guy. Good friend?"

"Booker is old school, but a solid cop. Not a chance in hell he's bent."

"Sure about that? Really?"

Madsen mulled it over before answering. "Anyone can be bent for the right reason or price."

"Then I keep digging."

"Yes." Madsen reluctantly agreed. Hem told him stories of corrupt cops burglarizing stores then taking the call, so they could investigate their own robbery. Told him of Chief Gates' secret unit whose sole job was collecting dirt on city leaders and private power brokers. Dirt he used for blackmail, to ensure no one fucked with his job or his beloved LAPD. Fact was, when the 1992 riots broke out, command couldn't reach Chief Gates because he was in Beverly Hills at a fundraising event to fight a city charter amendment that would limit his power and terms of office as chief. As Hem had put it, "I'm sure he thought he was doing the right thing. Sanctimonious son of a bitch. But he wasn't."

Madsen kept his eyes on his job and tried not to focus on the bigger picture. He did the best he could to do the right thing every day. Let IA handle any bent cops, he would handle solving murders. A solid strategy that he seemed hell bent on screwing up.

"You know how you make God chuckle?" Madsen asked Kazim.

"Tell him your plans?"

"Bingo buffalo chip. You win a—" In the mirror he saw a minivan pull into Wasson's driveway. The door opened turning on the interior light and illuminating the back of a man's head. He stayed in his seat. It appeared he was talking heatedly on his cell phone.

"That him?" Kazim asked.

"Hope so." Madsen slipped the leather sap that his grandfather used to carry from his boot into his blazer pocket. Kazim's face was a question waiting to be answered. "What?"

"That's not regulation."

"No, it's not. Neither is trying to kill me, so I guess he and I are even." Madsen stepped out onto the sidewalk. "Stay put, unless it looks like I might be about to experience loss of life."

"Then?"

"If he kills me, send that son of a bitch to hell, where *I* can deal with him."

"You got it, partner."

Madsen crossed the street. Staying watchful that the man didn't turn around, he ran on lawns, keeping hedges between him and the mini-van. Hitting Wasson's driveway, he crouched down behind the minivan and waited. He could hear a mumble that sounded like the guy with clenched teeth was having an angry conversation. The talk ended and the man got out. Madsen waited until he heard the minivan's door close before revealing himself. He hoped the man would be turned away. He also hoped the guy wasn't big and muscular. He was wrong in both cases. Upside? It was Wasson. Madsen remembered him from the night he staked out the ranch. Downside, the beefy bastard saw Madsen charging. He stepped back and grabbed Madsen, using his momentum to slam him into the minivan's side. Air exploded from Madsen's chest. He grabbed for anything to stop his fall, found nothing. He hit the pavement on his side. A boot sailed at him. He rolled away an instant before Wasson stomped his head in.

Wasson cleared his holster and aimed at Madsen. "Freeze, asshole."

Madsen looked up at the .45 caliber barrel. It looked like a tunnel ready to take him out. "LAPD." Madsen said, reaching into his pocket.

"I don't need to see a badge. I know you. You're Madsen. And one dead—"

Madsen brought the sap down on Wasson's arch. If it broke bone, the sound was drowned out by Wasson's howl. The pistol fell. Wasson tried to hop away. Madsen struck the man's good foot. Wasson crumpled down, rolling onto his back. The howl became a barely controlled moan.

"Stop moving." Madsen kneeled next to Wasson, sap raised over his head. "I *will* pop your skull. Try me." Wasson stopped moving. "You have a backup?"

Wasson looked down. His legs and feet were trembling when Madsen pulled a snub-nose from his ankle holster.

"Anything else?" Wasson shook his head. "Good." Madsen grabbed the back of Wasson's jacket collar and dragged him into the garage. He dropped Wasson and sent him groaning louder. Madsen put a finger to his lips. "Shh, wifey comes through that door you're both dead."

"Divorced." Wasson mumbled.

"No surprise there. Anyone in the house?"

"No, swear."

"All right, then," Madsen plucked a hammer off a peg board. "We have some time. Good." He opened a fridge in the corner. "Look here." Madsen pulled a bottle of domestic beer. He popped the cap and flipped it at the man on the ground. "Time we had a chat, Detective Wasson."

"I did nothing."

"Really? Minivan is a real come down from your Challenger. Is it in the shop?"

"No. I-I-I loaned it to a guy." Wasson was getting the pain under control.

"Really? So this friend of yours is who's been tailing me, not you?" Madsen slapped the head of the hammer into his palm. "You sure that's the horse you want to ride down this trail."

"It's the truth. Madsen you have to believe me."

"And I do. Except one little thing…" another hammer palm slap. "I saw you outside my place. Taking a piss. Ring any bells?"

"That was you?"

"That was me. You have a decision to make, we have an honest talk, or you get ready to train for the Paralympics."

"You got me fair and square." Wasson pulled himself up until he was sitting against a cabinet. "Any chance you could grab me some ice out of the freezer?"

"Anything for a fellow peace officer." Madsen tossed Wasson a bag of ice.

Tearing the bag open with his teeth, Wasson poured ice cubes over his ankles. "You don't happen to have any morphine on you?"

"That stuff will kill you."

"Had to ask." Wasson grimaced, but was able to deliver a conversational tone.

"Withers and Gallagher? Those aliases? They part of your crew?"

"Aliases? No, that's their names. And they're not mine. They're jail clique boneheads."

"And yet, you joined them to try and take me off the board. Slick move, pal."

"No. Madsen, listen, we weren't supposed to shoot. Talk, that was it. Those knuckleheads changed the play on me."

Madsen turned away and started rummaging through cabinets. "You don't have a skill saw, or a sawzall?"

"Wait. Stop."

"Your boys didn't stop before beating the hell out of a good woman." Madsen fought to keep his anger in check. "You in on that, too?"

"What? No."

"Someone beat on June Cleaver, wanted to know where Cisco was."

"All of this, the pain and damage, it's on *you* Madsen. Bull-headed bastard, all you had to do was drop one murdering gangbanger and this would've ended."

"It's on *me*, huh?" Madsen lifted up a hacksaw. "Ah, here we go."

"No, Madsen. You really gonna choose some Mex gangbanger over me?"

"Yes, I am. See, Cisco never lied to me, and that's all you've done." Madsen felt the hacksaw's blade. "Bit dull. You really should keep your tools in better shape, I'm afraid this is gonna hurt."

"You're getting played. Gutierrez is the dirty liar. Not me."

"Where to start..." Madsen looked from Wasson's feet to his

hands. "Stupid me." He smacks his forehead with the hand holding the hacksaw. "Toes, right? I mean your feet are already screwed."

"No, no, no, no... You do this you'll have to kill me."

"Oh yeah, that's the plan. But this?" Madsen raised the saw. "It's on you. Choose a couple of low-life prison hacks over your own body parts. Okay." Madsen turned a slow circle, searching. "You don't have a tarp, drop cloth? No?"

Wasson studied Madsen's face. "You aren't screwing with me, are you?"

"No. You and those motherfuckers pushed me way past screwing around. Give up your buddies or say your prayers. You Christian?"

"What?"

"If you are, maybe you'll be redeemed. Kinda doubt it though." Kneeling, Madsen grabbed Wasson's ankle and yanked up. The motion caused him to yelp. The hacksaw blade moved across his big toe drawing a smear of blood. He stuffed his pain and start talking. He gave up the prison guards' names. They were members of the deputy's clique called CB Killaz. He gave them up for taking down June. "Wasn't one of my boys, citizens are off limits."

"Cisco's not a citizen?"

"He's a combatant. He knows the rules. He broke 'em. Don't do the crime if...aah, fuck!" Madsen was kneeling, his full weight on Wasson's ankle.

"Damn, that hurt, huh?" Madsen took the pressure off. "Want to make sure I got your story. A gang of jailers want to get to Cisco so badly, they to try and kill a cop, and failing that they beat a woman in broad daylight."

"Yes. That's it."

"Why Cisco? Jails are full of bangers. Be like shooting fish in barrel."

"No. Like I said, this guy is a murdering skid mark of human waste."

"You were doing so good. Why start lying now?"

Wasson kept his eyes focused on the floor. "I'm not."

243

"What're you all afraid Cisco will remember?" Madsen knew this landed by the shock on Wasson's face. "Oh, you didn't think I'd figured that out?" Madsen set down the hacksaw and picked up a box cutter. "Time to spill your guts or um, I'll spill 'em for you."

Wasson's courage got up and left the room. Maybe he figured the truth would save him, or maybe he thought it would buy him a quicker death. Regardless he started talking, he told Madsen how he finally had a solid case against Cisco, a third strike. But as he was buttoning up the last details he'd heard from a snitch that Cisco was getting ready to split to Mexico. "Man, I was out of options. This motherfucker is a baby-killer. I asked the jail crew to hold him, off the books, until I had the evidence for a warrant."

"So that's where you beat him, in a jail cell?"

"No. Not me. CB Killaz, they were just tuning him up and went a little too far.

"These boneheads were tuning him up?" Madsen's blood pressure spiked. The veins in his forehead throbbed.

"That's what I said. You okay?"

"Oh yeah, I'm fine." Madsen was gripping the box cutter, staring at Wasson's gut. "You think when a Taliban fighter tortures one of our soldiers, cuts off his head, his buddies use euphemisms like, 'bonehead' and 'tuning the guy up.' Do you?"

"Why are you yelling at me? All I did was dump the banger where his homies could find him."

"You left him to die?"

"Hell Madsen, he was nothing but a ball of blood. I thought he *was* dead."

Madsen could feel Wasson was finally telling the truth. Her then gave him all the CB Killaz names that he knew. "We're almost done, and you still have all your body parts. You're on a hot streak, let's keep it that way. Okay?"

"Ask what you wanna ask."

"Did you shoot David Torres by accident?"

"What?"

"Only way I can see it. Aiming at Cisco, missed. Accidental. Manslaughter, worst case."

"What are you talking…I didn't shoot at anyone." He was sincerely trying to convince Madsen.

"Well, if we're being strictly honest. You shot at Cisco and me. Killed my truck."

"No, I aimed high. Scaring you. And Torres? I couldn't have done him. I didn't even know where Gutierrez was hiding until I got word you'd taken him in."

"If not you, who shot Torres?"

"Francisco Gutierrez."

"Nope. Wasn't him."

"Then I'm out of answers. Kill me. Don't. Whatever."

Madsen looked down on the battered cop. If he was telling the whole story, he was—at worst—a guy who made the mistake of turning over his suspect to the wrong guys. Then he had panicked when he heard Cisco had killed again. "I'm almost out of here. Couple of loose ends bugging me. The deputies could have found Cisco earlier, why wait until now?"

"Those dumbasses believed he had complete memory loss, then they heard you were helping him remember things. So that's also on you, a bit."

"Guess it could be. Who's your plant in my department?"

"Plant?"

"Who has been tipping you off about my case."

Wasson looked confused. "Wait, Okay. Hertzog, he remembered Gutierrez, called me to ask about him. I sent over my file on him and asked Hertzog to keep me in the loop."

"That's it?"

"What else would it be?"

Madsen set the boxcutter on a work bench. "You want me to call you an ambulance?"

"Hell no. Nothing broken. You going to rat me out?"

Madsen thought about it, then hunched up his shoulders. "I don't know. I really don't."

Chapter 31

"We have a rattlesnake nest to clear out." Madsen said to Kazim as they drove from Wasson's neighborhood. He gave him the rundown of what happened in the garage.

"You broke his feet?"

"Just the arches. Think massive bruising, not fracture. And, maybe a slight hacksaw burn on his big toe."

"Fine, so we have a limping angry armed man who may be coming after us."

"After *me*."

"Right, cool. So, what's the plan?"

"Tonight, I get Cisco and Adair out of town. Tomorrow you and me tear central jail apart. We take scalps and put heads on pikes. You up for that?"

"Metaphorically, yes. What am I saying, you want to take actual deputy scalps, I'm in."

When Kazim stopped a block from the Rose Court, Madsen gave him the address where he was taking Cisco. "This mean you trust me?"

"Don't make it more than it is."

"You *do* trust me. You getting soft, Madsen?"

"Don't you have a wife to bother?" Madsen slammed the door. Stepping into the shadow cast by a beauty parlor awning he watched Kazim's Kia drive off. He waited, searching the street for anything that looked like a cop. After ten minutes with no sign of danger, he slipped into the motel's parking lot. He knelt down by an unruly hedge and gave it another ten. When all was clear he knocked. An eye darkened the peephole. Madsen heard Cisco's muffled voice call to Adair, "It's Tricky."

"Let him in." She answered.

"Okey-dokey." Cisco smiled, happy to see Madsen.

"How you doin', Bud?"

"Good. We had pizza. Ate it all, sorry."

Madsen clocked the greasy box on the bed. "Where did it come from?"

"Niels, relax, I had it delivered." Adair said. "We haven't left this room all day."

"Yeah, Tricky, it was boring. You can't just watch TV all day."

Madsen kept focused on Adair. "Did the delivery guy see Cisco?"

"What? No."

"She made me hide in the bathroom. I didn't have to go or anything."

"Good. Collect your stuff, we're blowing this pop stand."

"Are we going to June's? I miss my room."

"Not June's, Bud. Come on, let's go, let's go, let's go."

Getting in the Lincoln, Cisco's eyes popped. He crawled into the back seat. "Tricky, where are the seatbelts?"

"It's a classic, Bud. They didn't have seatbelts when it was made."

"Is it safe?"

"Yes. But only in a classic."

Cisco relaxed feeling the velour upholstery. They hadn't gone a

248

mile before he leaned over the front seat. "Where are we going?"

"It's a surprise, okay, Bud?"

"No. Not okay. I don't like surprises, remember?"

"He doesn't." Adair mouthed.

"Right. But this is a good one. They have horses. You like horses."

"Is Hem and…um?"

"Nat. And yes they are both where we're going."

"Is it Mexico?"

"Not quite that far. Now sit back and relax, Bud, it's a ways."

"Okey-dokey." Cisco leaned back.

"He's starting to sound like you." Adair said.

"Say that like it's a bad thing."

"Tricky?" Cisco popped back up. "How far is a ways?"

"Hundred miles."

"That *is* far." Cisco sat back. He put his back against the door and stretched out his legs. "I'm glad this is a classic."

They floated east down the 210. Madsen kept a watchful eye in the mirrors. Adair kicked her shoes off and put her feet on the dash. "You want to tell me what's up?"

"Maybe later." Madsen could see Cisco's eyes were still open. "Y'all are going to be safe. Then I'm coming back here to clean this mess up. I'll be raisin' Cain, and takin' names."

"You're a cocky man. And at this moment, that's a good thing." She closed her eyes. "I got an email. If I don't show up tomorrow I think I'm fired."

"You don't sound upset."

"I think I'm too tired at this point to care. It will sort itself one way or the other."

"Yes, it will." He drove while she rested. After about fifteen minutes, he noticed Cisco watching his eyes in the mirror.

"You looking for followers, Tricky?"

"I guess I am."

"Me, too." Cisco kneeled on the seat and looked out the back window. "Tricky?"

"Yeah?"

"I see lots of lights following us."

"They're just going… Wait, are you messing with me, Bud?"

"Yes." Cisco beamed.

An hour later, Madsen left the freeway. He pulled to the side of the road and waited to see if anyone followed. Cisco was snoring away peacefully. Adair woke at the sound of the car's tires on gravel. "We there?"

"Not yet. This is Hemet. Still a while to go."

"Okay." She closed her eyes and was stone cold out in seconds.

Driving up the curvy two-lane road into the San Jacinto Mountains it became easy to tell they weren't being followed. Looking down any of the switch backs you would see another car's headlights. If they got slick and drove with their lights off, the fall and inevitable fireball would stop them. Madsen relaxed. For the first time in days he felt, even if momentarily, safe. Odd that piloting a massive boat up a mountain road could be relaxing, but compared to what LA held, it was.

Dropping down into Garner Valley, the terrain opened wide. It was a mix of cattle ranches, inexpensive homes and million dollar haciendas. Passing Lake Hemet recreation area Madsen turned left down a gravel single track road. After the first drop in the road all signs of civilization were lost.

Adair sat up and looked around at miles of grassland broken up by tall trees. "You aren't a serial killer, are you?"

"Hell of a long drive if that was my plan."

"True, but serial killers aren't known for their keen logic."

"Adair?" Cisco popped up over the seat-back. "Why do people kill cereal?"

"I don't—"

"'Cause they like pancakes and waffles better." Madsen bailed her out.

"Yeah, I hate cereal. Except Corn Flakes, and Cheerios."

"Lucky Charms?"

"No, Tricky. Too much sugar, and food coloring. Makes me—" Cisco made his eyes go crazy while he held his hands out trembling wildly. Madsen and Adair fell into a laughing jag that made him run off the road. "Tricky."

Madsen yanked the wheel and pulled the left tires back onto the road. "No harm, no foul."

Several miles of gravel led to a tall iron gate. Madsen unlocked it. Before them lay a large ranch house with a barn, paddock, and a kidney shaped swimming pool.

"Nice place." Adair's eyes lit up. "It's a masseuse away from a real vacation."

"Adair, wait, it's—"

"Tricky…" Cisco sounded panicked.

"What?"

"I don't have a swimming suit."

"Then I guess it's good we're not stopping here." Rounding the barn, he took a rutted dirt road up towards the mountain peaks. Adair looked wistfully out the window as her dream of a spa retreat disappeared into the distance. The Lincoln bounced and jutted left and right like a bucking bronco. Over the car's racket Madsen told them how Hem had helped the ranch owner's son out of a jam years back. To repay him, they'd given him the keys to the gate and a hunting cabin they never used. They were an older couple ,and only came up the hill a couple times a year. So, mostly, Hem and Nat had it to themselves.

As the road gained elevation the grass was replaced by pines, oaks, and cedars creating a forest that was tall enough to steal what light the quarter moon supplied. The cabin sat in a small clearing, backed up against a hundred foot granite incline. Above that was a wilderness that belonged to the national forest. Warm golden light spilled from the windows of the rough-hewn log cabin. Madsen parked beside Hem's horse trailer and killed the engine. Cisco started to climb over the seat.

"Ease up, Bud." Madsen whispered. "Let me check it out first."

Cisco could see Madsen was nervous. He sat back down without a word.

Madsen slipped from the car, closing the door quietly. He worked his way past a corral, Dancer snickered as he passed. No one moved in the house. Nat's pickup was parked behind a stack of hay bales. Madsen stepped past the hood. The distinctive sound of a hammer cocking froze him. Madsen slowly raised up his hands.

"Damn you, kid." Nat stepped into the light holding a short-barreled lever-action saddle gun. "Why didn't you warn me you were driving up in a gangster low rider?"

"How? Smoke signals?"

"Something. Driving up like that is an easy way to get shot."

"Hell, Nat, seems like breathing is an easy way for me to get shot lately."

"That bad, huh?"

"Worse."

Chapter 32

The cabin was one big room with a wood stove for cooking, or warmth in the winter. Bunkbeds were built into one wall, two cots leaned against one another. A rag rug. Two recliners covered in cracked leather and several folding camp chairs. Two rifles hung in deer antler racks by the door. Kerosene lamps were the only source of light.

Nat cooked up a midnight snack of franks and beans. Cisco cleaned his bowl. "I like second dinner."

"Don't get used to it." Adair said. "When you are back at June's there will be no late-night meals."

"Only lights out and sleeping at night." Cisco yawned.

"You tired, Bud?"

"Yes, but…" Cisco squirmed in his chair. "I have to, you know."

"Play chess?" Madsen said.

"No. Go to the…"

"The roof?"

"No."

"Niels, give the man a break." Hem said. "Before he pisses himself."

"Fine, come on, Bud. I'll show you where."

"Here." Nat handed Madsen a flashlight. "Check for barking outhouse spiders."

Cisco stopped walking. "Spiders?"

"It's okay." Madsen tried to move him, but Cisco had gone statue.

"No, Tricky. I can hold it."

"For the next couple of days?"

"Yes."

Adair shot Nat a dirty look. "Cisco, they're joking."

"No spiders?"

"Only teeny-weeny ones."

They survived the outhouse—or as Cisco named it, the stinky bug motel. Madsen pumped water into a bucket, pouring it in a bowl so Cisco could wash up. After his prayers, Cisco curled up on the lower bunk. Adair pulled the quilt up to his neck. "Adair?"

"Cisco?"

"You're staying." He looked around the room with drooping eyes.

"We all are."

"Tricky too, right?

"Right. Now off to sleep you go."

Cisco nodded. His eyelids closed. Adair sat beside him until his breath slowed and he drifted off. Hem and Nat lay in the cots, snoring and farting like old men do. In the yard, just beyond the cabin, Madsen sat under a two hundred year-old black oak. He convinced Nat he was too wired to sleep, so he should take the first watch.

"You better wake me in four hours."

"Or?"

"Or I'll tell Hem and he'll tar your ass."

"Yes, he will."

Madsen loved the feel of the oak's bark against his back, it gave him a sense of place in history. He would live his life, end it today or in fifty years and this tree would keep growing. It would hold the history of the world in its rings even after it had ceased to grow. He tuned his ears in to the night, searching for but not finding anything out of place.

Adair stepped quietly from the cabin. She had brought Madsen a cup of coffee. He thanked her, and she sat on the earth. Laying back she looked up at the blanket of stars twinkling above the oak branches.

"Beautiful, ain't it?"

"It's as if they have a billion extra stars up here." For a bit they were silent. When Adair spoke she kept her eyes on the sky. "Things are out of control, I know that. What I need to know, honestly, how out of control is it?"

"Not very. Scale of one to ten, a solid six."

"That's not true is it?"

"Okay, seven. Maybe eight."

Adair sat up so she could see Madsen's face. "Please don't be flippant. I understand keeping calm and funny with Cisco. I'm fully grown."

"I know that."

"Then tell me, who you are staying up all night watching for?"

"You're right, you deserve to know everything." Madsen told her the completely true unvarnished version of what he had been through, what he suspected, and what he knew.

"You see that Cisco is innocent now?"

"I believe he is." He didn't tell her that the way the system worked in the face of "no alternative shooter" was they would go with the easy answer and arrest the gangbanger found holding the gun. Odds were the jury would convict him and throw him in a hole for the rest of his life. Being intellectually disabled bought no mercy. Ten out of every hundred inmates could attest to that fact. Unless Madsen could find the real killer, Cisco would go down, never to rise.

"Kazim and me, we will clear Cisco."

"Or die trying?"

"Hope it doesn't come to that. Maybe you should get some sleep."

"I think I'll stay here." She sat against the trunk, near enough for Madsen to feel the warmth coming off her. He once again wished like hell he had met her in that food court, before all this insanity. A quiet date, maybe a movie and a kiss at the door when he dropped her off. She was a road not taken. A land yet to be discovered. She made him yearn for a future that might never come. He had to actively push her from his thoughts and concentrate on what lay ahead.

The sky was starting to pale when Madsen heard the engines. Adair had fallen asleep leaning on him. She woke quickly when he gently shook her. While she ran to the cabin, he got in Nat's Dodge. The keys were under the visor where Nat always kept them.

Madsen was going to take the fight to whoever was coming. He took the dirt road faster than was smart. The steering box was loose with a couple of inches of play. The drum breaks were not much better than tossing out an anchor. Hitting a hump, the truck flew up then slammed down, bottoming out its suspension. Madsen stopped at the mouth of a thin stretch of road. Trees pressed in on both sides, making it impossible for anything bigger than a motorcycle to get past him. He stepped onto the running board, keeping the truck's open door between him and the road ahead. Best he could discern it was a couple of vehicles. Judging by their speed on a dirt road, they were four wheel drive.

Knowing it was hopeless, Madsen checked his cell. It had no bars. His pistol was holstered in the small of his back. Not that it would do him much good. Best he could hope to pull off was maybe buy the others time to prepare for the onslaught.

Won't I feel the fool if it's a local rancher looking for a lost cow or an adventure tourist on the wrong road.

At the end of the tunnel of trees a SUV bounced into view. Even at over four hundred feet Madsen could see the black body and white top that identified it as a police vehicle. A second SUV pulled up behind the first. A voice boomed over the grill mounted speaker. "In the truck.

This is the Los Angeles Sheriff's Department. Toss out your weapons. Raise your hands and step clear of the pickup."

Madsen didn't move, or speak, or breathe.

He waited.

After a long moment, a man got out of the lead SUV. He shouldered a scoped bolt-action rifle toward the truck. Madsen dropped out of sight. The door wouldn't stop a high-powered round but why make it any easier for them to hit him. Looking through the crack between the door and truck body Madsen saw the man move off the truck and scan the forest around them. They knew now that they had lost the element of surprise. The man was looking for an ambush. Madsen wished he had been smart enough to plan one. Then again, with a tac-team that consisted of Cisco, two old men and a social worker, bluff and stall was the smart play.

"In the truck, step out now or we will be forced to fire on you."

Madsen kept his eyes forward while he reached under the truck's seat, feeling for something with heft.

Deputies fanned out from the SUVs, guns in hand.

Madsen pulled a tool box from under the seat and sat it on the gas pedal. The old flathead six roared as the RPMs climbed.

"Turn off your engine." The voice was starting to sound unsettled.

Madsen pulled the shift down and the pickup leapt forward. He held the wheel as straight as possible, given he was on the running boards with the door banging against his side.

"Kill that motherfucker." Someone screamed, and a cacophony of gunfire rocked the forest. Lead pinged, thudded, and smashed its way into the Dodge. A round punched through the door, whizzing past Madsen. He leapt from the truck, tucked and rolled over the ground and into the brush. Whatever he hit had thorns that tore at his flesh. He heard the truck slam into something heavy. Most likely at tree, not enough metal on metal ripping for it to be one of the SUVs.

One more volley was fired into the Dodge. Then it stopped, replaced by a moment of silence. Woodland creatures large and small froze. Madsen pulled himself deeper into the bramble. The deputy's boots crunched the earth as they advanced up the road. Finding the Dodge empty, they started yelling all the mean ugly things they planned to do to the driver once they found him.

Chapter 33

"Where the hell is Aretha?" The first thing Nat said when he saw Madsen returning on foot.

"Call me the truck killer." Madsen shrugged.

"Heard the gunfire." Hem said. "You irritate a platoon of Rangers?"

"Close, a couple carloads of angry deputies. They're ten minutes behind me."

Hem tried to connect these words to any reality. "Lawmen shooting at you? Why?"

"They're bad cops, Grandpa."

"But you're not?"

"No, sir."

"Good." Hem's face relaxed. "Real good. Hate to have to arrest my own flesh and blood."

"I'd hate that too." Madsen put his hand on Hem's shoulder, squeezing gently. "Where's Cisco?"

"Cisco? Oh yeah, good fella. He's in the cabin with that pretty lady. She a friend of yours?"

"We need to get them out of here, pronto."

"There's no way out of here." Hem cackled. "Unless you're part mountain goat."

"Horseback?"

Nat shook his head. "Winter storms washed out the old trail. We're bottled up tight." The deputies stood between them and the only other trail up to the mountains.

"Neither of you are hiding a helicopter, are you?"

Hem shook his head. "Time to go Alamo."

"Alamo?" Madsen looked to his grandpa.

"Hunker down. Hold 'em off 'till we're all dead." Hem shot Nat a tight grin. "You up for one last stand, you black bastard?"

"I am, if you are, you pale-assed honkey." Nat ran toward the corral, saddle gun in hand.

Hem turned back to Madsen, serious. "I did everything I knew how to raise you up right."

"No. We're not saying goodbye, Hem, *not*."

"Kinda have to, kid. You need to serve and protect the civilians. Took an oath."

"No."

"Remember, Neils," Hem took his grandson's face in his hands and stared into his eyes. After a moment it was clear Hem had lost the thread.

"Remember what?"

"I'm sure I had something important…"

"Tell me when you remember."

"I'll do that." Hem picked up a hunting rifle leaning against the oak and moved behind the outhouse, putting himself and Nat on either side of the cabin, facing the road.

"Tricky, you're bloody." Cisco said when Madsen entered the cabin.

"It's nothing, Bud. I ran into a thorn bush."

"You need to be more careful."

"Yes, I do." Madsen pulled a mattress off the top bunk bed. Adair looked at him like he had lost his mind.

"Whatcha doing, Niels?"

"I'm making a fort for you and Cisco."

"Cool." Cisco said. "Can I help?"

"Grab all the blankets and pillows and pile them up." Madsen dragged the chairs for a front wall and the mattresses for a ceiling. When done they had created a bullet-resistant cave in the rear corner of the cabin. Cisco crawled in without needing any encouragement. Adair paused, about to say something.

"Don't." Madsen told her. "Nothing noble here, I'm just doing my job."

"It's a wee bit noble."

"Maybe. Now get in there and don't come out until I say."

"Yes, sir, detective." She almost kissed him, but he turned to the window. Climbing in she told Cisco they were going to play a game. "Do you know tic-tac-toe?"

"Everyone knows that. Middle first, always."

Middle first.

Madsen tuned out their happy chatter and stepped from the cabin. He pulled the door closed and walked toward the road. The deputies must have cleared Nat's truck because the SUVs were on the move again. Madsen stood at the spear point between Hem and Nat. He pulled his Stetson down tight and waited.

A polar airflow moved down the coast and inland overnight. The cool wind blew heavily laden rain clouds over the mountain peaks to the west and down into Garner Valley. Dry lightning and thunder boomed. Madsen looked up and smiled.

At least if I die to today, I won't be sweating.

The first of the SUVs rolled to a stop forty feet from the cabin. The sharpshooter was out first, aiming at Madsen. Deputy Withers came next. "Reach for your—hell, you even twitch, you're dead."

"What?" Madsen cupped a hand to his ear. "I can't hear shit since some ass-wipe shot up my truck."

Withers nodded to the sharpshooter and walked half way to Madsen. "You hear me now?"

"That you, Withers?"

"Sure is."

"Wasson sends his regards."

Withers stiffened. "Where's Gutierrez?"

"Couldn't say." Madsen looked past Withers to the SUVs. "Gallagher in one of those baby haulers?"

"Fuck you, Madsen." He turned back to the sharpshooter.

"I wouldn't do that." Madsen shook his head. "No, I wouldn't."

"Why not?"

Madsen motioned with his left thumb over his shoulder. From inside the horse trailer a rifle barrel protruded. His right thumb led the deputy's eyes to where a barrel poked from behind the outhouse. "You want to light this cherry bomb, do it. But I goddamn guarantee you won't walk away."

Withers looked right and left again. "That raghead partner of yours out there?"

"Yes, he is. Locked and ready."

"No, he's not. I know because he's the one told us how to find you."

"No. He didn't."

"Did." Withers turned around and yelled. "Bring him out."

Two brawny crew-cut Neanderthals opened the rear hatch and dragged out a broken form. Grabbing the man by the hair, they pulled his head up—showing Madsen it was Kazim. His face was a mess of cuts and lumps. His eyes swollen near closed. Split lips exposed broken teeth. He tried to speak, but only managed a gurgle.

Lightning cracked and deep thunder shook the ground. The storm was almost upon them. The sky matched Madsen's rage. His partner had been broken by smug heartless little men. Men not good enough to shine Kazim's shoes. Madsen felt a deep kinship to his berserker forebears, understood the need for blood. He locked on Withers' neck and bent his knees, ready to charge.

"Ease up, Madsen," Withers sensed the danger coming for him. "You move, he dies." Withers pointed to a deputy, who pulled his .9mm and pressed it into Kazim's temple.

Madsen forced his body to relax its stance. He raised his hands "No. Come on. Please, he wasn't part of this."

It took heroic effort for Kazim to yell, "Fuck them!"

The man holding his hair shook his head violently and Kazim went silent, save his ragged wet breathing.

"Let me take him in the cabin, and I swear on my mother's grave I'll bring you Cisco."

"I don't think so." Withers spat on the ground between them. "How 'bout I kill the raghead, then I kill you, then whoever you got hiding in the wood pile?"

The lightning struck, and thunder forced Madsen to yell to be heard over the storm. "No. Don't be stupid. You kill LAPD, you'll fry."

"I'm not gonna kill you." Withers yelled though cupped hands. "The banger's gonna do it. Don't worry, you get to kill him before you die."

Rain exploded from the clouds pounding down as the other officers started to move in on Madsen. Six men in armored tac gear, two more holding Kazim, eight armed men stood between Madsen and everyone he cared about.

Instead of a battlefield religious conversion, Madsen was struck with the knowledge that this life, these people, this moment were all he had. He could do with it what he wanted, but it would not come again. He had no family beyond Hem, no one to mourn or memorialize him.

This was it.

He would shoot until he had no blood or bullets left. Make them explain their dead and wounded deputies to the LAPD.

Rain sheeted across Madsen's face. He reached back for his pistol.

Two large caliber shots rang out.

Through the rain, Madsen saw the deputies holding Kazim drop.

Kazim staggered forward. Knees buckling, he went down.

The deputies turned away from Madsen. Searching for the shooter behind them.

Madsen exploded. His calm replaced by pure clean rage. He charged Withers, grabbing him around the waist he lifted him into the air before throwing him down.

Withers struggled to his knees.

Madsen attacked, leaping onto the man. They rolled in the mud, mixing dirt with blood as they traded blows. Madsen struck Withers in the kidney, and laughed, spraying a pink mist.

Crawling on top of Withers, Madsen pounded his face. After three blows, Withers stopped struggling. His face was a pulpy mess.

End this now.

Madsen raised his fist, but didn't strike. Withers was moving his lips but making no sound, like a trout when you pulled it off the hook.

Catch and release.

Madsen rolled off of Withers. He lay on his back laughing up at the rain as it fell.

"You done playing with this deputy?" Sergeant Booker looked down at Madsen. "If you are, I'd like to cuff him."

Madsen tried to speak, but only laughter came out.

Booker shook his head, rolled Withers over and snapped a pair of flex cuffs on him.

A small sea of LAPD blue uniforms mobbed the deputies. Cuffing them, giving first aid to the ones still breathing. Hertzog stood up with Kazim held gently in his arms, he was carrying him away from the danger. Just before they disappeared into the storm Kazim's head bobbed up, as if he were searching for Madsen.

Chapter 34

Cisco's face lit up when Madsen pulled the mattress up. "Tricky. You didn't get dead."

"No, Bud, not yet. You okay?"

"Yeah, but I have to pee."

"Want me to take him?" Mauk asked from the doorway. Cisco looked unsure.

"Bud, this is Detective Mauk. A friend. She's good people."

"Good people. Good people." Cisco rolled the phrase around his mouth.

"I am. Come on." Mauk gave him an easy open smile.

"They have killer spiders in the bathroom."

Mauk looked nervous. "What?"

"It's a joke. Not real."

"Good 'cause I hate killer spiders." Mauk led Cisco out into the building chaos of the LAPD and the newly arrived Riverside County Sheriff's deputies.

"What a mess." Madsen felt more at ease than he had in a long time.

Adair looked Madsen up and down. "You look fantastic."

"Bloody mud is my best color. Brings out the red in my eyes."

"It does that." She took his hand the knuckles torn and raw, she kissed it gently. He winced but didn't pull back. "Hurt?"

"Not much." Through the window Madsen could see an argument building. Booker was jabbing his finger at a Riverside County deputy.

"Any chance we get to go home tonight? Cisco needs normalcy."

"That cluster fuck is a jurisdictional Rubik's cube. But I'll do the best I can."

An hour after the storm began it was gone, blown out over the desert leaving blue skies and the fresh smell of the rain-washed forest. Deputy Withers was alive, mumbling dire threats against Madsen when they loaded him into an ambulance. The big honcho, Riverside County Sheriff Duffy rolled up. He outranked them all. Booker tried to explain what went down, but Duffy wasn't listening. "Here is how this is going to go." Duffy said in a voice that needed no amplification to be heard. "The injured will be treated. The rest of you will be transported for questioning. Deputies please relieve these officers of their weapons."

"This is some serious bullshit, and you know it." Booker told Duffy, then turned to his own officers. "Do not relinquish your firearms." The LAPD men and women formed a unified line, ready for a fight.

"You want to play it this way?" Duffy tried to keep control of a situation that was starting to spin.

"Johnny Duffy?" Hem stepped up to the Sheriff, grinning. His hunting rifle rested in the crook of his arm. "How the hell's your daddy?"

Duffy took a moment to recognize Hem. "Mr. Madsen?"

"Righty-oh. Now what is this horse crap you're dealing? You a few pickles short of a barrel?" Hem sounded entirely coherent, but Madsen knew it was likely only moments before Hem went off the rails.

"It's protocol, Mr. Madsen."

"Comes down to us." Hem nodded to the LAPD. "Or protocol.

Pick your switch." Hem tightened his grip on the hunting rifle. Duffy looked from the old man to the resolve of the LAPD officers and tried to find a place to back pedal into.

Booker stepped next to Hem. "Why don't you let me hold that?" He reached for the rifle, but Hem wasn't giving it up.

"Booker?" Hem saw him for the first time. "You grew up. You know Johnny Duffy?"

"We just met."

"He's a good kid."

"You say so. Can I have the rifle?"

"Not on your life. Some bad men coming. Need to be ready."

Madsen walked to Hem and lifted the gun from his hands. "I'll take that. Why don't you and Sergeant Booker go in the cabin and brew a gallon or two of coffee. That sound okay?"

"Coffee?"

"Yeah, Hem, we're gonna be here a while." Madsen waited until Booker led Hem into the cabin before speaking quietly, for Duffy's ears only. "Sir, me and my family were just about killed by some deputies—"

"Not Riverside's."

"No, but you will understand our reluctance to trust anyone wearing a star. An LAPD Force Investigation team is on its way, how about we hang until they get here? That work for you?" Duffy looked at the standoff between his men and those in blue. He nodded assent, then called to his men to stand down. He let everyone know that they would wait for LAPD investigators to join them before taking any further action. The Los Angeles Sheriff's deputies were to remain cuffed and separated.

While they waited, Booker told Madsen that Kazim's wife had alerted him to the trouble. She'd called Booker's cell after midnight, "Kazim hadn't come home. Guess he always calls if he's going to be late. He was nervous enough to leave her with both our numbers."

"He gave his wife your number?" Madsen asked.

"Yeah, apparently you told him I was one of the good guys."

"Never said that."

"Lucky for you I am. I've been looking for connections between my men and the Sheriff's Department."

"You listened to Kazim?"

"Busted his balls for asking, and then I went digging."

"And? You gonna make me beg?"

"Reason we hadn't made the connection before is the Sheriff's department keeps a separate database for jail employees. Turns out our rookie Officer Russo did two years as a deputy at the downtown jail before he joined us. He served with deputies Withers and Gallagher."

"Well, fuck me running." Madsen let out a long breath.

"Course Russo's not admitting anything. He was kind enough to loan us his thumb to unlock his phone."

"Willingly?"

"Sure, we'll say that. We found a text from Deputy Withers asking if he wanted to join them on a hunting party up in the San Jacinto mountains."

"This is big mountain, how'd you find us?"

"When I was new on the job my lieutenant took me to one of Hem's BBQs up here. I took a chance."

The Force Investigation team was led by Madsen's old friends Hunt and Davis. "Madsen, get in the car," was Hunt's only greeting.

"Fong let you keep your badge?"

"In." Hunt held the back door of their unmarked sedan, slamming it behind Madsen.

Madsen tried the door, the internal locks were set. Mesh blocked the front. He was stuck, forced to watch as IA detectives interview LAPD and Sheriff's Deputies.

"Where's Francisco Gutierrez?" Hunt yelled loud enough for Madsen to hear through the glass. Madsen worried watching Hunt stomp toward the cabin. Then it got worse. Hem blocked the doorway, rifle in hand.

"Put the gun down, now." Hunt rested his hand on his pistol.

"Reach for it. I'll drop you quicker than a bad habit." Hem was not backing down.

Davis pulled open the sedan's door. "We need your help."

Madsen ran to the cabin shouting cheerfully, "Gentlemen? Please, we're all cops here."

"Niels?" Hem seemed surprised. "Thought you were sleeping."

"No, I'm awake. What's going on here?"

"This fella's trying to…" Hem looked lost. "He was doing something bad."

"No. Hunt, you weren't doing anything bad were you?"

"No sir." Hunt spoke to Hem with reverence.

"He's LAPD. Show him your badge."

Hunt pulled back his jacket revealing a gold shield hanging from a lanyard.

Hem squinted, recognition of the badge relaxed his stance. "On the job huh? Want some coffee? I think Grace just made a pot."

"That'd be nice." Hunt said. Before following Hem in he asked Madsen, "Who's Grace?"

"His wife, been gone a long time."

"Sorry." It was unclear whether Hunt was saying he was sorry about Madsen's grandmother, or the way he almost had to shoot it out with an old man.

Madsen saw quickly his fears for Cisco had been unfounded, Adair wasn't about to be bullied into letting anyone interview Cisco. "We will be filing a grievance with the civil liberties union, shall I add your name to it?"

"That won't be necessary." Davis said, mouthing "It's over." to his partner, leading him out of the cabin.

Hem smiled past his coffee mug to Adair, then to Madsen. "Your wife may talk funny, but she's one hell of a gal."

"Yes, she is." Madsen felt no need to correct his grandfather on any counts.

The whump of rotors announced the arrival of Deputy Chief Bette Fong. Stepping from the helicopter dressed in a light gray suit tucked into Italian hiking boots, topped by a tailored trench coat, she didn't need to say she was in charge, her style spoke for her.

Sheriff Duffy happily ceded his authority, "My men have more important work to do than cleaning up LA County's messes."

"Thank you." Fong shook his hand, almost as if he had a choice.

After being briefed by Davis, Hunt, and Booker, she took Madsen aside. "You're a boil on my ass, Niels. Sooner or later I'm going to have to lance you."

"I'd prefer later, given the choice." She didn't laugh. She turned on her phone's recording app and asked for his version of events. After he finished, she turned off the app and dropped her phone into her jacket pocket. "Is any of this connected to the David Torres murder?"

"Yes and no, parts are."

"Parts? Not good enough. I'll ask another way, did Fransisco Gutierrez murder Torres?"

"No." Madsen kept it all simple, factual. "I have a suspect. By tonight I should have a confession or at the very least enough evidence to book him."

"Would that be Officer Hill or Officer Russo?"

"Booker told you about them?"

"No. There's little I don't know. You're walking into dangerous territory. If they killed Torres, we'll charge them. If you fail to prove it, you become an enemy of the Chief. He will come after you. Paint you as a rogue detective trying to damage LAPD's reputation."

"Fire me. Really? What do I care?"

"Firing? Are you hearing me? They will discredit and destroy your reputation, private and public."

"Shouldn't be that hard to do."

"Niels they'll come after Hem, and anyone else near you." She looked worried.

"You? They'd come after you?"

"For defending you? Maybe. For sleeping with you? Absolutely."

"I'm sorry." Madsen really was. But he and Bette knew the rules, and the cost of losing. "Cisco? Will they go after him?"

"Yes. Without another credible suspect, they'll charge him."

"Bette, no shit, I'm begging here, he didn't do it."

"Then prove it. Press will be all over this mess. No comment on an ongoing investigation will buy you until tomorrow morning at best."

"I'm all over it, Bette, I'll have it all wrapped up with a nice bow by tomorrow." He tried to sound sure of himself.

"I'm an idiot for saying it, but I actually believe you will."

"Thank you."

"Don't. Fail, and I'll drop an anvil on you."

"Understood, fuck up and I get squashed. Deal." He held out his hand, she looked at the dirty mess and shook her head. "I know. I need a long bath."

"Maybe get cleared by a doctor?"

"Sure, but first, I need to get back to LA. Can you get Hunt and Davis off my back?"

"With pleasure." The thought of busting Hunt's chops made Bette smile. "I suppose you want to take Gutierrez and his conservator with you?"

Chapter 35

By the time Madsen took the last switchback and the road leveled out into Hemet, Cisco was out cold in the backseat.

"Is it over?" Adair asked. "If it's not, lie to me."

Madsen took his eyes from the road long enough to see if she meant it. "Your part of it's over."

"And your part? Cisco's part?"

"If I get it wrong you two may need to go on the run."

"You're kidding."

"Mostly."

"Are people still trying to hurt him?"

He let silence answer her. He hoped those bent on doing Cisco harm were dead, in the hospital or locked up.

It was warm and muggy in LA, but it beat the searing, smoky city everyone had endured for the last weeks. Rain and lower temperatures gave firefighters the edge needed to stomp out the forest fire burning up in the San Gabriel Mountains.

Things were quiet at the Northeast Police Station. Mauk was the only detective in the bullpen when Madsen pushed through the doors.

"You getting slow, Madsen?" They had both left the ranch at almost the same time.

"I guess I am." Madsen didn't tell her he'd had to drop Cisco and Adair off, because if he did, he'd have to lie about where he'd left them. "Hill and the rookie still waiting?"

"They are. Feels kind of weird going after our own." Mauk said.

"Make it easier knowing one of them may have set up Kazim?"

"Yes, it does." Her face went hard. She picked up the Torres file. "We'll hit Russo first. Save Hill as backup."

"How do you want to play it?"

"Loose and wild. Follow my lead." Madsen and Mauk had worked the box together before. She was one of the best. She intuitively knew when to take charge and when to lay back. When to berate and when to cajole.

Russo sat uncuffed in the interview room. He wore cut-off jeans and a sweat soaked Ram's t-shirt. He looked up like an expectant puppy when Mauk came through the door. His face froze when Madsen came in behind her.

"What, not happy to see me?"

"No I, um it's just…"

"Shut the fuck up. Your jailhouse deputy friends stomped Detective Kazim to death. My partner, fuckhead."

Russo didn't speak. He tried unsuccessfully to cover his building fear.

"What do you figure Detective Mauk?"

"I don't know." Mauk studied Russo. "I guess I thought a cop killer would look more,…what?"

"Like an evil son of a bitch?"

"Yes, evil." She looked at Russo cooly. "Would you like us to call your union rep?"

"What? Yes, um, no. Um—"

"Simple question, yay or nay?" Madsen jumped in.

"He's playing it safe." Mauk gave a casual shrug.

"That it, Russo? Damn." Madsen let out a you're fucked whistle. "Solid. You're gonna play it safe all the way to the pen. Hope you like your dates burly and tattooed."

Mauk stood up. "He's not cooperating. Time to loop in the DA and Internal Affairs."

"Wait…" Russo tried to stop her but she was gone, the door whooshing closed behind her.

"You want me to call off the hounds, give me something." Madsen looked bored, like he didn't care how this went down.

"Withers did it, he's the one who grabbed Kazim."

"I guess I need to be more specific. Give me something I don't already know. Withers is in lockup, trading your life for his. And here you sit with your thumb up your keister, waiting for the axe to fall."

"Bullshit. He's not. Withers wouldn't."

"Final answer? So be it." Madsen was up and out the door, giving Russo no time to think or respond.

Officer Hill was face-down, eyes closed. Madsen slapped his palms onto the desk, popping the man's eyes open. "Whaa, Madsen?"

"Yep. Here to salvage your day. Maybe even your life, if you play it straight."

Hill looked from Madsen to Mauk. "What are you…? Why am I here?"

"Good question." Mauk went for friendly. "More importantly, why is your trainee next door telling tales on you."

"He's not. Russo—"

"Is a macho asshole." Mauk spoke over Hill. "He's a rookie and he already has two excessive force dings. You really want to go down over a trash pile like him?"

"He's green, but a good guy."

Madsen cleared his voice to pull Hill's focus. "No, he's not. You and

I both know he's not."

"He is."

"Okay, say you're right." Madsen looked like he was thinking it over. "Then, I guess what I need—or want to understand—is, why did Officer Russo shoot David Torres?"

"It was an accident." Hill spoke without thinking. Then froze. Panic flooded his face. "No, wait, he—"

"He…what?" Madsen went cold as it all clicked into place.

"He did nothing…I mean he didn't…"

"Keep digging, Hill." Mauk let a small smile leak out. "You'll find yourself six feet down staring into Russo's beady eyes."

Russo looked calm until Madsen turned on the recorder and said, "Officer Frederick Russo, you are under arrest for the murder of David Torres. You have the right to remain silent. Anything you say can and will be used against you in a court of law. You have the right to an attorney. If you cannot afford an attorney, one will be provided for you. Do you understand the rights I have just told to you?" Russo nodded numbly. "Out loud please, for the recording."

"Yes…but I-—"

Madsen cut him off. "With these rights in mind, do you wish to speak to me?"

Russo stared mutely. Mauk gave the rookie a reassuring nod. "No one wants to jam you up here, Russo. We need to get to the bottom of this and see if we can help you find a way out from under it."

"Really?" Russo grasped at any thread that might pull him up.

"If it was a clean shoot, IA will talk to you, but no charges need to be filed." While Mauk spoke, Madsen kept his eyes down, his mouth shut and his attitude neutral.

"It was clean. Swear."

"Okay. Tell it. I'm really not looking to hang anything on you."

"Madsen said Kazim died. You gonna drop his murder on me?"

"Two things about that, one, you're in no position to bargain. And two, Madsen's full of shit." Mauk smiled. "Kazim got roughed up, that's all."

Russo relaxed incrementally. "Okay, this is the truth, honest. From our unit I saw the kid at the bus stop. He looked like he was holding a gun."

"Kid, do you mean David Torres?"

"Yes, Torres."

"He had the gun." Mauk looked at the file. "A gold and black Smith and Wesson .38?"

"Yes, like I said, he had a gun. I exited our unit. Confronting Torres, I ordered him to drop the gun, three times I said, 'Drop your weapon.' But he wouldn't obey me. His hand came up and I shot. Had to."

"He couldn't hear you." Madsen said quietly to the floor. "He'd forgotten his hearing aids." He was beyond tired—past exhausted all the way to an empty place that held no emotions.

"He, he couldn't…how could I know? How?" Tears started to run down Russo's cheeks.

Mauk reached across the table, patting Russo's hand. "It does sound like an accident. Walk me through it."

"It was. I didn't… After I shot, after the shooting… I turned to Hill. I don't know."

"Youre doing good. When did Fransisco Gutierrez arrive?"

"He was standing behind the bench the whole time, right, I turned to Hill, when I turned back Gutierrez had picked up the gun and aimed it at me. What was I supposed to do?"

"No, you're right. You did what you had to." Mauk kept her hand on his.

"Nope." Madsen shook his head slowly. "You're leaving something out." He clicked his thumb along his fingers as if he was counting. "You already knew who Cisco was. Didn't you?"

"Yes, um, no…" Russo fumbled his words, trying to catch up.

"From when you worked the jail, they showed you his picture." Madsen stated a fact.

"Right. Yes. He was on a list they had of dirt bags."

"Dirt bags, ass wipes who got away. I get that." Mauk was pure sympathy.

"Yes. Gutierrez killed a kid, a baby. He walked."

"This list." Madsen spoke quietly, facing the tabletop. "What was the plan, if you found one of these, dirtbags?"

Russo looked at Mauk, eye brow cocked. "Tell him." She said.

"We were supposed to take them out."

"Kill them." Madsen kept his head down. "Right. It was a hit list."

"Yes." Russo felt the noose, stepped back. "But that wasn't what happened. No, he picked up the gun, but I wasn't going to kill him."

"Because I showed up. A witness might make it hard to sell as self defense."

"No. I…he picked up the gun. A known killer. So, no, it wasn't premeditated, if that's what you're trying to hang on me."

"It doesn't matter." Madsen stood, looked down at the deputy. "You killed his friend, then tried to kill him. He never would have shot you. There was a killer at that bus stop, but it wasn't David or Cisco." Madsen cracked his neck. He felt old and very tired. "Come on." He motioned to Mauk and started for the door.

"I'll be out in a minute."

"Do what you need to, I'm done." Madsen left without looking at either of them. As soon as the door was closed he moved quickly into the monitor room. He watched Mauk on the screen, she slid to the other side of the desk, so that Russo faced the camera when he spoke.

"Where'd Madsen go?"

"I don't know. My bet, he's checking in on the detectives questioning Withers." She dropped her voice, conspiratorial. "He doesn't like you. He'll hang a conspiracy for the attempted murder of Gutierrez and

Detective Kazim on you, if he can. Guess it will depend on Withers. But like you said, he's a stand-up guy, you'll be fine."

Russo's eyes flicked back and forth. Finally he looked at Mauk. "I don't want to jam anyone up. But after the shooting I called Withers, told him about Gutierrez. They had been looking for him for a while."

"Really? So all you did was feed them some harmless information about the investigation. Help them find a dirt bag."

"Yes, swear, that's all."

"I believe you. You told them Gutierrez was regaining his memory?"

"I said I though he was, but Withers said he was faking it to begin with."

"Sound straight to me." Mauk said. "If anyone stepped over a line it was Withers."

"Exactly. You get it. Explain it Madsen."

"No need." Madsen stepped into the room. "We have it all on tape." Russo's face fell. "That's not fair."

"No, but it's legal. You're going to jail." Madsen told Russo.

"Detective Mauk? You said…"

"Madsen's right about jail." All sympathy was gone from Mauk's voice. "Messed up part? You probably would have skated on the shooting. But the cover-up, the selling out of Kazim and Madsen, that fucked you."

Mauk and Madsen had what they came for, a full confession. As they collected up files and prepared to leave, the pungent smell of fear-based sweat poured off Russo. He couldn't meet their eyes as they walked out. They didn't even care to meet his.

After locking the interview room door Madsen put in a call to Bette Fong and spelled out what had gone down. She wasn't any doing verbal cartwheels so he asked her why not.

"You did good, Niels, but no one is going to like this outcome. The chief explicitly told us to leave the Sheriff's Department alone. Sheriff White has many powerful friends."

"We didn't make them criminals, we just caught them."

"Act like a grown up. You know that thing about shooting the messenger?"

"I'm the messenger."

"Yes you are."

Chapter 36

The storm had passed Coachella Valley, heat evaporating all signs of rain. The sun dropped behind the San Jacinto mountains, bathing Palm Springs in a pink glow.

When Madsen called the E.R. where Kazim was taken, the only thing they could tell him was that Kazim was in the ICU. Madsen dropped the Torres/Russo case on Mauk to file with the DA.

Madsen flashed his badge to the ICU nurse and was told that Kazim had a broken jaw, wrist, four fingers and six ribs. Broken ribs had punctured both lungs. Fluid in his chest cavity collapsed his lungs, which were operating at less than thirty-percent capacity. Once chest tubes were inserted to drain the cavity, he had been put on oxygen, and they started to work on his other broken bones. He had a concussion, and they feared brain swelling. All of that, and the doctor still called him lucky. If Hertzog had waited for the paramedics, or driven down the mountain with less abandon, Kazim would surely have died choking on his own blood.

When Madsen asked to see his partner. The nurse said, "Detective, you are a walking germ colony."

"That bad?"

"No way are you going anywhere *near* my ICU." She gave him a pair of scrubs, a plastic bag for his clothes and pointed him toward the nurses' locker room. "Soap, wash, rinse, repeat. Repeat. Repeat." He did as told, and was both amazed and sickened by the amount of blood and dirt going down the drain.

Returning to the waiting room, Madsen was met by a pretty young blonde. She held out her hand, "I'm Chloe Kazim."

"Detective Madsen." He shook her hand gently, trying to hide his shock.

"You were expecting dark eyes peering from a hijab?"

"No, I…" She had nailed him.

"It's okay." She smiled. "A game Darius plays when he meets new people. We met at Berkley."

"You're Muslim?"

"Lutheran, or raised that is. Agnostic now, you?"

"I would have said Christian agnostic leaning towards atheist, but right now? You got me."

"Darius says faith is a road traveled, not a destination. Today, I've been praying my ass off to any deity who might be listening."

"How's that working?"

"He's still alive."

Kazim lay with tubes running out both sides of his chest. He was wired to monitors and had a cast on his left arm and splints on his hands. When he focused on Madsen he started moving his lips. Madsen leaned close to hear the whisper. "Did we get them?"

"Yes, you were right about Cisco, Russo, the whole deal."

"Good." Kazim closed his eyes.

"You're a hell of a cop, Detective Kazim." If the younger detective heard Madsen it was unclear. Kazim was sleeping. His wife squeezed Madsen's arm and mouthed a thank you.

"No rest for the wicked, and the righteous don't need it." Hem liked to say. Madsen wasn't sure which he was, but either way, rest wasn't likely. He still needed to get Nat's truck towed to a mechanic he knew in Idyllwild, arrange to have the horses hauled to Tujunga, and collect Hem and Nat and drive them home. They both seemed healthier and more vital for the adventure. Twice, Hem confused Madsen with his father, but he had a solid memory of facing down a horde of assassins with star badges.

A new day was dawning by the time Madsen got the old men and their horses settled. All he wanted was a pillow to lay his head on. But he still had many rivers to cross. Number one was to return a call from Bette Fong.

She picked up on the first ring, sounding almost perky. "I was right. The chief asked for your head on a platter."

"You going to give it to him?"

"Well, there is a problem, you and Kazim are heroes. Someone leaked to the press the whole damn sordid tale."

"So we get a parade instead of kicked to the curb?"

"Much as I hate to say this, yes Detective Madsen, you will both be getting commendations."

"Thanks, Bette."

"Don't thank me, Madsen. I had my way, you'd spend the rest of your career guarding a warehouse in Pacoima."

"You say so." He knew no one would ever prove that she had been the one to leak the story to the *LA Times*. Bette Fong was too good at covering her tracks.

Madsen's next call was to Holly and Edward Torres. He asked them to meet him at the Northeast Station. He wanted to speak to them before the news broke. Holly and her father sat on either end of a wide couch, not looking at each other.

Madsen told them the sad stupid truth: David died because he crossed paths with an overzealous and under-experienced rookie.

Because David forgot his hearing aids. Because David loved shiny things. Because David's grandfather didn't keep his guns safely locked up.

Hearing the last part, Edward Torres broke down. His normally stern face crumbled. Tears ran freely. He reached out to his daughter, for forgiveness or comfort it wasn't clear. He got neither.

Holly stood and looked only at Madsen. "Is that it?"

"Yes. I doubt it's any consolation, but the DA will be charging Officer Russo with manslaughter."

"You're right, it's not." She said and walked out. She shed no tears. She was cried out, for now.

It was almost noon by the time Madsen arrived at Rafael Ortiz's cul-de-sac stronghold. Casper and the others didn't step off their porches when he parked the Lincoln. Whether because Rafael warned them that Madsen was coming or that the Lincoln lowrider was his pass, he'd never know.

"You did okay, Detective." Rafael sat in his backyard under a pergola sipping iced tea with Adair.

"Did my job." Madsen said.

"More than a lot of your kind do."

"You'd be surprised." Madsen took an offered glass of tea.

"Hettrick's been filling me in on this police abuse cluster fuck. Is it true it was Sheriff's county jail dogs beat Cisco?"

Madsen thought about being noncommittal or even lying, but it would all come to light soon enough. So, he laid it out. Told Rafael that the deputies beat Cisco into his current state. Told him about Detective Wasson dumping Cisco in the alley. "Wasson's confession won't hold up, it was kind of coerced with a hammer and a hacksaw."

"Hacksaw." Rafael nodded, smiling.

Cisco came out of the garage, Chuy rolling behind him. "Tricky.

We were racing. Chuy won again."

Chuy typed furiously, "Want to win, Primo? Got to get your own ride."

"Can I do that, Adair? Can I get my own ride?"

"As long as it's 1/24 scale, I can't see why not." Adair said.

"Sweet. Hear that, Chuy? I'm getting my own ride." Cisco started to fist bump his cousin, but went in for a hug instead.

Pushing Cisco back, Chuy typed, "Get off me. Ha. Ha. See you around, Primo." Then he rolled back into the garage.

"Do we have to go?" Cisco asked Madsen.

"We do, Bud. I'm the walking dead."

"Not really?"

"No not really, I'm just very, very tired." They were almost out the door when Cisco stopped walking and looked at Rafael. "You used to scare me."

"Not no more?" Rafael hardened his face.

"No. Chuy forgives me. That means I did a bad thing, right?"

Adair started to speak but Madsen pulled her back. This was between Cisco and Rafael. Two men who needed to work this out if they were going to step past it.

"I'm the reason Chuy can't walk, right?" Cisco spoke in a whisper. Hoping if he said it quiet enough it might not be true.

"Yes, Primo, that's on you." Rafael spoke plainly.

"Then I'm a bad man. Right?"

"Maybe, I guess."

"But…can't I ever be…not that?"

"Way I see it, we do some heinous shit, we do some good. But all we are is who we are today. Who you gonna be?"

"Cisco, I guess."

"Good choice."

And there it was, Madsen couldn't have said it better. He tossed the badass Lincoln's keys to Rafael.

"You take my mother's car off-road?"

"Wouldn't dare. It's dusty, but in one piece."

"Better be." Rafael laid it down hard, but ruined the effect with his sly smile. "See you around, Detective."

"Hope not." Madsen smiled. They both knew the only time homicide detectives came to a gangster's home they were carrying either bad news or handcuffs.

Climbing into the Honda, Adair looked wistfully at the lowrider. "Someday." She muttered.

"That was not a good deal." Cisco said watching the Lincoln out the back window as they drove away.

"Your cousin loaned me his car, but he needs it back."

"Still not a good deal."

"True that. On the upside, I found out who killed David."

Cisco went ashen. "Was it me?"

"No."

"I'm glad I didn't shoot David. He was my friend."

"Do you want to know who shot him?"

Cisco thought about this for a moment before speaking, "I have enough good people to think about. I'll let you worry about the bad ones."

"Makes sense. You won't have to worry about going to jail."

"I know." Cisco said, as if he never doubted Madsen would discover the truth. Just once Madsen wished he could be that certain of anything.

Acknowledgments

This book started with a moment. A police officer shouted at my intellectually disabled son, one hand on his gun and the other pointing at his badge, "Do you know what this means?" That moment was horrifying, I wanted to forget it, and I knew one day I would need to write about it. From that moment to the completion of TRICKY I was helped by a huge gang of amazing people.

Researching I read a ton of nonfiction, some key sources were, "Ghettoside" by Jill Leovy, "Homicide Special" by Miles Corwin, "Rise of the Warrior Cop" by Radley Balko. The documentary series "Lost L.A." (a co-production of KCETLink and the USC Libraries) was a great source for LA history.

Research of a more personal nature, I am in debt to Nino Gabaldon for sharing a chunk of his life with me, and for making sure East Los was done justice. James Coomes loaned me his knowledge of LA county mental health systems and introduced me to members of the LAPD SMART team.

Early first readers, all fine writers in their own right: Thomas Pluck, Holly West and Neliza Drew read drafts that were so rough I'm amazed they still speak to me. My brother Lark Stallings and sister Shaun Anzaldua read my books as I write them, they give good notes and tons of love. Jamie Mason was blunt about what didn't work and effusive about what she loved. Lou Berney was kind enough to read and give a blurb before it was fully edited. All of their encouragement kept me going.

The editorial work fell on the shoulders of three amazing women, first as always is Erika C. Stallings, nothing leaves my office before she both de-dyslexias it and helps to make my voice its strongest. Second editor is my brilliant agent Amy Moore-Benson, who helped refine my main character into a much different and better man than I started with. I am grateful to Amy, Glenn Cockburn and all at Meridian Artists for having faith in my words. And then there is Chantelle Aimée Osman, editor at Agora Books. I was afraid we might battle over the manuscript. We didn't always agree, but we collaborated until the right solve was discovered. She loved the book enough to push me to make it even better. I am very lucky to have Chantelle and Jason Pinter and all at Agora - Polis Books in my corner and publishing TRICKY.

Jay Stringer, thanks mate for suggesting I get TRICKY to Chantelle.

And then there is my spirit sustaining crime fiction community. Tad Williams, Deborah Beale, Terry Shames, Ian Ayris, Sabrina E. Ogden, Elizabeth A. White, Tim Hallinan, Johnny Shaw, Tom Pits, Joe Clifford, Travis Richardson, Teresa Wong, Nadine Nettmann Semerau, Eric Beetner, Stephen Blackmoore, Gary Phillips, James L'Etoile, Steve W. Lauden, Stephen W. Buehler, Sarah M. Chen, Fiona Johnson, Pearce Hansen, Elizabeth Amber Love, Erin Micheal, Renee Pickup, Naomi Hirahara, Tyler Dilts, Ellen Byron, Rob Pierce, Jim Thomsen, Lisa Alber, Susanna Calkins, Jennifer Hillier, Ed Aymar, Lauren Winters, Lisa Brackmann, Victoria Helen Stone, R.D. Sullivan, Chris Holm, Katrina Niidas Holm, Mike McCrary, Daniel B. O'Shea, Jedidiah Ayres, Tony Peyser, Pamila Payne, Alex Segura, Scott Montgomery, Bobby McCue, Jen Hichcock, Brian Thornton, David Cranmer, Chelsea Cain, Sara J Henry, Tanis Mallow, Terrence McCauley, Craig Faustus Buck, Dan Malmon, Kate Hackbarth Malmon, Dru Ann Love, Hilary Davidson, J.D. Allen, Eileen Rendahl, Jay Shepherd, Kristopher Zgorski, Steve Weddle, Matt Coyle, Owen Laukkanen, Rob Brunet, Sarah RH, Charlie Huston... I know I've forgotten more than one, I also know I wouldn't make it though some of these days without all of you.

Finally I owe a huge debt to my grandfather Chief Harold Stallings. He taught me to believe that every one of us is redeemable. He went from beat cop to Chief of Corrections for the LA Sheriff's Department, where he fought an uphill battle to reform our jails. Near his death in 1990 I asked him, knowing what he knew now, what would he do with the prison system, "I'd tear it down and start over. We got the whole idea wrong."

About the Author

Josh Stallings's Moses McGuire trilogy found itself on over fourteen best of the year lists, and *Young Americans*, a standalone, was nominated for the Lefty and Anthony awards. His short fiction has appeared in *Beat To A Pulp, Protectors Anthology 1* and *2, Blood and Tacos, Crime Factory*, and *Muder-A-Go-Go*. Born in Los Angeles, and raised by counter-culture activists (and sometime Quakers) in Northern California, he grew up undiagnosed dyslexic and spent some time as a petty criminal and failed actor before becoming a movie trailer editor. He, his wife, and various four legged fiends now live in the San Jacinto mountains. *Tricky* was written in honor of his son, Dylan, who is intellectually disabled. Visit him at www.joshstallings.com or on Twitter at @Josh_Stallings

CPSIA information can be obtained
at www.ICGtesting.com
Printed in the USA
LVHW041048181220
674508LV00001B/1